CHANGING COURSE

What Reviewers Say About Brey Willows's Work

Spinning Tales

"This was a charming read! I liked the main character and the way the fairy tale realm works. I also found some of the problems and solution to be quite funny and fun to read. This is a good read for those who like fairy tales and retellings."—*Fierce Female Reads*

Fury's Bridge

"[*Fury's Bridge*] is a paranormal read that's not like any other. The premise is unique with some intriguing ideas. The main character is witty, strong and interesting."—Melina Bickard, Librarian (Waterloo Library, London)

Fury's Death

"This series has been getting steadily better as it's progressed." —*The Good, the Bad, and the Unread*

Fury's Choice

"As with the first in the series, this book is part romance, part paranormal adventure, with a lot of humor and thought-provoking words on religion, belief, and self-determination thrown in…it is real page-turning stuff."—*Rainbow Reading Room*

"*Fury's Choice* is a refreshing and creative endeavor. The story is populated with flawed and retired gods, vengeful Furies, delightful and thought-provoking characters who give our perspective of religion a little tweak. As tension builds, the story becomes an action-packed adventure.The love affair between Tis and Kera is enchanting. The bad guys are rotten to the core as one might expect. Willows uses well placed wit and humor to enhance the story and break the tension, which masterfully increases as the story progresses."—*Lambda Literary*

The Afterlife, Inc. Series

"The whole is an intriguing concept, light and playfully done but well researched and constructed, with enough ancient and mythological detail to make it work without ever becoming a theology lesson. …Brey Willows has created an amusing cast from Fates and Furies to the gods of old. The gods are extremely well done, literally personifying the characteristics we associate with them, drawn with wit and humour, they are exactly who we would expect them to be. …Thoroughly enjoyed these; romances with a difference, fantasy set in the here and now with an interesting twist."—*Lesbian Reading Room*

Chosen

"If I had a checklist with all the elements that I want to see in a book, *Chosen* could satisfy each item. The characters are so completely relatable, the action scenes are cinematic, the plot kept me on my toes, the dystopian theme is entirely relevant, and the romance is sweet and sexy."—*The Lesbian Review*

"This is an absolutely excellent example of speculative dystopian fiction. …The main characters are both excellent; sympathetic, interesting, intelligent, well rounded within the context of their situation. Their physical chemistry is great, the slow burn romance which follows behind is a wonderful read, and a great cliff-hanger to match the will they/won't they of the Chosen. Whether you like fantasy or not you should give this book a go. The romance is spot-on, the world building excellent and the whole is just speculative fiction at its best."—*Curve*

Visit us at www.boldstrokesbooks.com

By the Author

Chosen

Spinning Tales

Changing Course

Afterlife, Inc. Series

Fury's Bridge

Fury's Choice

Fury's Death

CHANGING COURSE

by
Brey Willows

2019

CHANGING COURSE
© 2019 By Brey Willows. All Rights Reserved.

ISBN 13: 978-1-63555-335-2

This Trade Paperback Original Is Published By
Bold Strokes Books, Inc.
P.O. Box 249
Valley Falls, NY 12185

First Edition: November 2019

Credits
Editor: Cindy Cresap
Production Design: Susan Ramundo
Cover Design By Jeanine Henning

Acknowledgments

Thank you always goes to Bold Strokes, a publisher I'm proud to write for. And thanks to Rad and Sandy, whose support and humor have meant the world to me over the years. To my editor, Cindy, who always makes me laugh and says things that keep me writing; thanks. And thank you to the readers, who keep picking up my quirky books and come back for more. And forever and always, thank you to my wife, without whom this journey would never have begun, and who makes every day an adventure I can't wait to take with her.

Dedication

To Robyn, for changing the course of my entire life.
I'll follow you to the next world and beyond.

CHAPTER ONE

"This is *Echo Eight Class Delta Centauri* from the outer quadrant. We are abandoning ship and request an assist from any vessel in the area." Captain Jessa Arabelle stopped to cough and pull her jacket over her face. Bruised purple smoke clogged the air and made her eyes water. "Repeat. We are abandoning ship. Twenty-two escape pods have been released and are heading toward the Andine Sector. Please send retrieval vessels."

A faint, crackled response was all she heard before the ship tilted, sending everything sliding into the opposite wall. She held onto the desk and scanned the remaining functional screens. The ship was empty except for the small crew waiting for her at the last escape pod. She squeezed her eyes shut and forced the despair away. She could deal with that later.

The ship listed again before righting itself slightly, and she ran from the control room without looking back. Walls that once displayed an array of advertisements for whatever awaited the passengers on the planet they were headed to were now filled with a flashing red beacon telling people to head to the nearest escape pod. Like anyone needed to be told when the asteroid had hit mid-ship. Sirens and warnings had gone off almost instantly, and system failure had been terrifyingly fast.

Jessa grabbed a railing as the ship listed forward this time, groaning and shuddering as it began to pull apart. She put her sleeve over her mouth and squinted against the surge in smoke. She didn't need to see, though. This was her baby, and she knew every corridor and display panel on it.

But when she turned left toward the escape pod, it was no longer her baby at all.

Exposed wires buzzed and flared, jutting out from the ceiling and sides like tentacles waiting for prey. The window panel was cracked, splitting the rainbow of toxic gasses outside the ship into beautiful, lethal shapes.

She edged past the wires, hissing when one zapped at her arm and scorched the soft white fabric of her uniform, making her life-sign reading flash on her forearm in warning. The overhead lights flickered, and there was a deep, long groan, as though the ship was giving its last breath. And then the lights went out. The sirens stopped wailing. It was silent and dark, and Jessa winced. *Ten steps forward. Then left. Then right. Nearly there.*

She felt along the wall, the flickering sparks from the wires giving her just enough light to make sure she wasn't going to walk into anything. When she heard a shout, she sighed with relief. They hadn't left her.

"'Bout time, Captain. Thought you might take that whole going down with your ship thing to heart." Teckoe Temple, chief officer and Jessa's right hand, grinned. "I'm thinking we should probably get going if we're going to do something crazy. Like, live."

Jessa clapped him on the back. She'd never hug him, that wasn't her style. But they'd known each other long enough she figured he knew how relieved she was to find them there. "I agree. All pods are on course and out of the asteroid burst." She turned to her chief engineer. "Asanka, we ready to go?"

The gills in her neck flapped open and shut as she nodded. "And just in time." She keyed in the code for the escape pod and the door slid open.

Jessa waved the five members of her crew into the pod ahead of her, and she was the last to belt in. As the door slid shut, she closed her eyes against the dark destruction of the ship she'd loved and captained for so long. She clutched the armrests on the chair as the pod jerked free, and her stomach lurched as it drifted into space before the thrusters engaged. She leaned forward as they moved toward the front of the ship, which was now almost vertical.

"Damn." Teckoe whistled softly. "I can't believe we managed to get everyone off."

Jessa didn't reply, but she agreed. The hole in the secondary cabin section looked like a giant had punched right through the metal and then pulled it apart like a tin can. Smoke floated away from the ship and soon turned into sickly green clouds of loss thanks to the gases in this part of the galaxy.

"Setting course for the Andine—"

Something crashed into the pod, slamming them all forward in their seats. The pod spun, head over tail, sirens screaming but her crew silent. Jessa fought the need to vomit her lunch and closed her eyes against the view of the pink-purple nebula flashing past.

"Asanka, what's going on?" she finally got out as the pod righted itself.

"Looks like a small asteroid hit. Probably a piece from the larger one that hit the ship." She punched buttons, her gills opening and closing rapidly. "We're not going to make it to Andine, Cap. We need to land."

"Land? There's nothing in this quadrant. Except—"

"Indemnion." Chief Analyst Benika Ployt was even paler than usual. "But if we land there, we're as good as dead anyway."

Jessa tried to remember all the things she'd heard about the remote outpost planet. It was too far off shipping routes to be important, and its reputation as a place of lawlessness and violence made it unattractive to tourist ships like Jessa's. The pinging of the alarm made her decision. "Do it." As Asanka set the new coordinates, Jessa sent out a distress signal, but it was unlikely it would make it to anyone who would help. Interference from the ship and the nebula surrounding it meant it wouldn't get very far at all.

The engine sputtered to life and the nebula slid past. Any bit of the debris passing the window could smash them to pieces, and Jessa felt the breath tremble in her chest. She wanted to scream, cry, rail at the injustice of being hit by an asteroid that had been hidden inside the nebula cloud and blocked from view by the nearby sun, meaning she hadn't seen it until it had already torn through them. But she held it together. She was captain, and she'd damn well act the part. Calm to the end, if it came to that.

"I should have gone to Pythagoran and studied math like my parents told me to." Peshta Rhoda, the ship's nutritional determiner, gave Jessa a wan smile.

"At least then you wouldn't have poisoned people with your cooking. It's amazing we're alive to escape the ship, after eating the Ordwellian bog sludge you've been feeding us." Steve, their head physic, turned one eye toward Peshta and kept the other on space passing outside. He was smiling, but the blue lines that appeared in his face only when he was stressed were clear even in the dim cabin light.

"Entering atmosphere. I don't think we're in for an easy landing." Asanka punched buttons with one hand while gripping the armrest of her seat with the other.

"Brace." Jessa bent forward, her hands behind her neck, and was glad the others did too. The pod grew uncomfortably hot and incredibly loud, the sound of them breaking the sound barrier as they entered the planet's gravity field deafening. Sweat dripped down her face and back, and Teckoe's murmured prayers to his god helped keep the total panic at bay.

The ding of the sensor to say they'd entered the atmosphere nearly made her relax, until the message, "Landing gear disabled. Please brace for impact," sounded in the pod.

Jessa's heartbeat pulsed hard and fast in her throat, in her ears, in her hands. When the pod hit the ground with a sickening crunch, foam burst from the overhead compartments, filling the pod with a thick substance that cushioned them from the metal bending and denting around them as the pod flipped end over end. When it stopped rolling, when the groaning of the metal stilled and all she could hear around her was her shipmates moving in the foam, she gave in to the sickening fear. The world faded away as she closed her eyes, blessedly unconscious.

CHAPTER TWO

Damn, damn, damn." Kylin Enderson dodged a fruit seller, tripped over a children's flyer, and went sprawling into an antiquities shop, where she narrowly missed knocking over a vase she couldn't afford to pay for in three lifetimes.

Shouts from outside told her to keep moving. The shopkeeper shook his head, looking disgruntled as usual, and pointed toward the back. She blew him a kiss and quickly navigated the piles of cloth, books, and things she couldn't name to get to the back door. The Stables in Quasi District were a maze of shops selling everything that could be gotten on Indemnion, and Kylin knew them like the back of her hand. A quick left past her favorite mechanic, a hard right next to the best bread maker in the Stables, and then she'd be home free—

A hard hit to her chest slammed the air from her lungs and she landed hard on her back. She looked up at one of the ugliest linari collectors on the planet. "Ow. That was totally unnecessary." Slowly, she got to her hands and knees and felt for the knife tucked into her boot. Of all days to leave the energy taser at home. A hard kick to her side sent her sprawling onto her back. "Come on, guys. I was just having a bit of fun. You know I'm good for my debts."

"Orlin wants to see you."

"And I imagine he wants to see me in one piece. So lay off with the heavy flirtation stuff, would you?" Kylin got up, dusted off her pants, and straightened her shirt.

Another ugly mug joined the first and Kylin sighed. For the most part, Orlin believed in handling Stables matters in the Stables, and if she'd been able to make it home she'd have bought herself some time before having to face him again. As the starfish faced linari collectors walked ahead and behind her, she mentally ran through her options and bargaining power. She had precious little of either and was no farther along when she entered Orlin's marketplace warehouse.

He sat with his long, spider-like legs propped on the desk and a bubbling glass pipe between his skeletal fingers. "Kylin Enderson. My favorite fighter and biggest pain in my thorax. I'm hurt that you didn't want to spend time with me."

Kylin flopped into the seat in front of his desk. "It wasn't that I didn't want to…well, yeah, actually, that was why. We both know spending time with you isn't good for my health."

He laughed, a grating sound that echoed around the warehouse. "That's very true, but it's been good for you in other ways. You've made some money and managed to get your precious papa the flagweed he needs, haven't you? I've been good to you, haven't I?"

"You've put me in the ring to win fights for you, and then you paid me half in money and half in flagweed, instead of letting me just buy the flagweed for way less money somewhere else." She tried to keep the venom from her voice. Orlin tolerated a lot, but outright disrespect wasn't on that list.

"You were already fighting, and we both know you enjoy it. I put you in *my* ring because you needed money and somewhere to dump all that beautiful rage that builds up inside you." He took a long puff on the pipe and blew out a cloud of sickly yellow smoke. "And you still need those fights for both of those reasons." He took his legs from the desk and sat forward, his red eyes hard. "But we both know you took a dive last night. There's no way that Skiva took you out." He tapped out the yellow crystals from the pipe and added fresh ones. "And that makes me ask where your loyalty is these days, Kylin. And you know how I feel about loyalty."

Kylin knew exactly how he felt about it. Every time a fresh body floated down the river, there was no question who sent it there. Quasi could be tough, and the Stables especially so, but Orlin was the only truly big player in it. "I didn't dive. If I had, it would have been way more dramatic and interesting. It's your fault I hit the mat." He narrowed his eyes and she hurried on. "I told you I wasn't ready to get back in the ring yet after that match with the Belfura. She did a number on me, and she messed up my collarbone. The Skiva last night got lucky and got in a hit in the same place."

Orlin sat back and stared at her for a long moment. "You made me a lot of money on that Belfura fight."

Kylin's nerves settled slightly. If he was willing to acknowledge her usefulness she wasn't about to go for an unconscious swim. "I don't dive."

"I'm adding my losses from last night's fight to the debt you owe me. Everyone expected you to take that Skiva down with no problem." He shrugged. "Show me your collarbone."

Kylin hesitated until fish face moved toward her. "Back off, sucker face. Go play with a rock." She tugged open the laces holding the top of her shirt together to show Orlin the black bruise that spread along the bottom of her throat, over her collarbone and onto her chest.

He glanced at it and then motioned for her to close her top. "You should have showed me that yesterday."

Be calm. Don't be stupid. "I told you yesterday and you said you didn't want to hear it."

"I'll delay your fights and put your debt on hold. But you get back in that ring within fourteen sets of the first sun, understand? And my collectors will be watching, so don't try to pull some stunt that means you won't be paying up." His pipe burbled and yellow gunk splashed onto his black tunic. "I own you, Kylin. Don't forget it. And if you don't turn up, I'll personally pay a visit to your dad to see if he knows where you are."

The words made the bile in the back of Kylin's throat burn, and she had to stop herself from spitting it onto his desk. She stood. "I have things to do. Women to enjoy and sand fleas to eat. And I'm sure you have butterflies to de-wing and small children to torment."

He waved and she pushed past the collectors to make her way into the Stables. Her collarbone ached and various other bits of her were bruised and tired. Fighting used to be fun, a way she could push herself, a way to always make sure she was better than the next guy. Now, it was an anchor wrapped around her waist, pulling her down and drowning her nights. She headed home, the pit in her stomach heavy with the dread that this was all life had to offer.

❖

Smoke sliced through the scarlet sky like an arrow pointing to treasure. One long, thick trail, and then plenty of smaller ones scattered through the sky beyond it. Kylin held her hand above her eyes to block out the sun's glare and tried to place the location at the end of the smoke trail. It was a good distance away, but that could work in her favor if she moved fast. She raced inside, tripping over the loose floorboard under the unraveling rug the way she always did. She grabbed her pack and shoved in rations and bottles of fluid.

"That good, huh?"

She looked over at her dad, who was propped up on an array of mismatched and ragged pillows. His cheeks had grown more gaunt over the past few months, and the yellow rings in his eyes were as faded as the pillows behind him. "Looks like we've got a crash landing, maybe out by Versach Forest. If I can make it before the other scroungers we could get a good haul. Enough to eat more than beans and river leaf next month. Auntie Blue is coming over to yell at you a lot and pump you full of drugs."

He nodded and started to speak, but a coughing fit overtook him. He held up his hand to get her to wait. When he could breathe again, he pointed to the trunk at the end of his bed. "Take the seaful gun." He waved her off when she began to protest. "Do it. The forest is dangerous this time of year, and you're not going to feed us if you're dinner for someone else."

She sighed and opened the trunk. The seaful gun was old but in perfect condition. Her dad had been an excellent hunter in his prime, and he'd always cared for his weapons, since that was what put food on the table. But the gun was large and heavy, and she'd need all her energy to get to the forest first. But he was right. The forest was overrun with predators right now. She hefted it out and adjusted the strap so it fit comfortably across her back, then she slung her pack over her shoulders. She wouldn't be able to get to the gun easily, but hopefully she wouldn't need it until she got to the forest anyway.

She leaned down and touched her forehead to her dad's, lingering for a moment. She never knew when she left the house if it would be the last time she'd get to speak to him. "Don't go pounding the pubs while I'm gone, eh?"

He squeezed her hand. "I'll try not to, but if I elope with the beauty from the Falls, I'll leave you a note."

She grinned and headed for the door. "I've already had her. She's nothing to elope with. Way too high maintenance." She could still hear his wheezy laughter as she made her way down the side of the house and into the maze of houses that made up the Quasi District. When her mother was alive they'd lived farther out, in the Fesi District, which had better air and more room between the houses. But after they'd lost her, Kylin's dad had needed to be out most of the day and didn't like leaving her in such an open, unguarded place. Quasi was tight, but it was a community and they looked after each other. And they'd taken to Kylin, who ended up with more people watching over her than she'd liked, especially as a teenager.

Now, she was grateful for the community who helped watch over her dad. She knocked on a bright red door painted with little blue dots and then walked in. "Auntie, you here?"

Vesta Blue, affectionately just known as Auntie Blue throughout Quasi, came out of a back room, her traditional long headdress covering her long, pretty blue hair as usual. "I thought I'd see you any minute. News of the crash is running through here like flames on tinder. You need me to watch your dad?"

Kylin pulled a few linari from her pocket and put them on the table. "Thank you. This should help until I get back. I'll try to be as fast as I can."

Auntie Blue nodded. "You know you don't need to pay for help, but I'll be sure to get some flagweed for his cough. And I'm going to see if he'll come here, so I can keep an eye on him but still run the inn." Her eyes narrowed slightly. "Be careful. You'll have plenty of competition on this one. And Orlin's boys are watching for you, as usual."

Kylin nodded and backed toward the door. "I'm taking a flyer to the edge of the forest, so I'm hoping to be ahead of the rest. And if I can get what I need from this scrounge, Orlin's boys won't be a problem anymore." She waved as she left, knowing her dad was in good hands. Auntie Blue had been a good friend from the moment they'd moved into Quasi, and for a while Kylin had hoped she and her dad would hit it off. But her mom had been her dad's one true love, and when he said he'd never be with another woman, he'd meant it. But she hadn't missed the gentle adoration in Auntie Blue's eyes when she looked at him.

That was what love did to you. You gave someone your whole heart, your being, and then you lost them, or they didn't love you back. It wasn't worth it, and it was a trap Kylin would never fall into again. She forced herself to focus, and when she noticed the atmosphere around her she picked up the pace. Other people were heading out with packs like hers, and in the same direction.

She turned left down a narrow alley, then another, until she had to turn sideways to fit down the last one. It let out in front of an old air stable, a place she'd loved to whittle away the time when she was a child. She pressed her thumb to the lock and it popped open after a quick scan. The door slid back on squeaky hinges to reveal her pride and joy. She flipped the heavy dust sheets off the small, lightweight flyer she'd painstakingly rebuilt herself. Flyers were hard to come by unless you lived in the wealthy districts, and the fuel core for them was even harder to find. She'd been lucky enough to come across a trader in trouble who gladly paid her in core when she'd saved his life.

Opportunities to use it were few and far between, since she didn't want it stolen, and a good way to get it on people's radar was to show off. She jumped in, flipped the switches, and hit the buttons, and the resulting shudder as it lifted from the ground sent a shot of total elation from her toes to her neck the way it always did. She angled it and pulled back. It was important to get out fast, to make it harder for someone on the ground to pinpoint where it was being stored. She pushed the wheel forward and slammed out of the space and into the air. She looked down at Quasi rushing past below her and waved to the kids running along the river below the craft. She'd done the same as a child, wishing with every breath that the pilot would slow down just enough for her to jump aboard and fly off into adventure.

She shook off the weird nostalgia and set a course for the forest. It would have taken at least three days to get there on foot, but the flyer would get her there in less than a day. Once she was there she'd have to land and hide it as best she could at the edge of the trees. Then it would be all about tracking the smoke and damage to the forest to find the haul.

Land passed beneath the flyer and she watched curiously. She rarely got far outside Quasi these days, and the districts around them were always changing. The nomad territories flexed and shifted like muscle, one day bulging with traders and merchants, the next stringy with drifters and scroungers, like her. When she saw the gathering of white that looked like a scar on the sand dunes, she frowned. *Reformers.* Just the sight of them left a bad taste in her mouth, and this was a particularly large group. It looked like they were headed toward Quasi, and Kylin was glad she got out before they descended on the district with their long, boring speeches about the afterlife and praying to their god because everyone was inherently horrible. She'd met a hell of a lot of people who were better creatures than the reformers ever seemed to be.

She closed her eyes and relaxed. The flyer was on course and didn't need direction for such a simple flight. Her shoulders slowly came down, and the deep breaths she took almost hurt, it had been so long since she'd had time to do it. The air was the only place she could truly let her guard down. The only place where she didn't have to think about the next step, the next meal, the next batch of medicine for her dad. Up here, she was alone and free.

CHAPTER THREE

Jessa had no idea how much time had passed, but her body ached and she desperately wanted to stretch it out. She shifted and the foam around her cracked and crumbled to the floor. She was glad to see the same thing happening around her as her crew, too, came back to life. She unbelted herself and brushed away the foam from her legs.

It was only then that she noticed one of the foam encrusted forms wasn't moving. She stumbled across the pod and clawed at the foam, pulling it free in chunks. "Steve? Can you hear me?"

The others joined her, pulling foam free to help get him out. When Benika made a sound of dismay, Jessa looked over. Benika shook her head and pointed.

Jessa looked around Steve's motionless body and saw what Benika was pointing to. A jagged piece of the pod had come loose and lodged in Steve's back. Blood pooled in the dark grass showing through the gash in the ship. The life-sign readout on his forearm was black.

Jessa sat back on her heels and slowed her breathing. She'd never lost a crewmate before, and all she could hope was that Steve had died quickly. She took a steadying breath. She was still responsible for the four crew who had made it. She needed to think. She turned to Asanka. "Atmosphere and geo reading, please."

Asanka moved slowly away from Steve, her gills so tightly closed they were white against her neck. She pressed buttons on the console, and the mechanical voice informed them it was a life sustaining planet and safe for those in the pod. "There are cliffs approximately forty clicks to the north. We're in an extended forest, and beyond that are deserts. I don't see any large bodies of water."

Jessa sighed. At least there was that much. She'd already known Indemnion had people living on it, but that didn't mean it was safe for people who weren't used to the particular makeup of air. She opened the overhead locker and pulled the three energy blasters from the compartment. She handed one to Teckoe and one to Asanka. Both were trained in intergalactic combat, as was she. There was no telling what they'd find when they opened the doors, and she wanted to be ready.

She nodded to Asanka, who hit the release button. The door jerked open slowly, revealing a lush green landscape with trees so tall they blocked the intense sunlight from the nearby star.

They stepped out and Jessa looked around, watching for any hostile visitors. She didn't assume there would be helpful, friendly people waiting. It wasn't that kind of planet. But there didn't appear to be anyone around. A stream burbled peacefully nearby, and long, wispy tree branches swayed in the breeze. It smelled earthy and fresh, something Jessa hadn't come across in a very long time.

They moved cautiously around the escape pod, but it was soon clear they were alone.

Jessa breathed a quick sigh of relief. "Okay. There's no doubt our entry will have been noticed, and we don't want to be with the pod when someone comes to see what they can take from the crash, even though part of me wants to stay and protect it. We can't see what's coming at us here, and I want to get to higher ground, somewhere we can see who is coming toward us. This world is known as one to avoid, and I'm assuming hostile until we know otherwise. Grab whatever supplies you can fit into the land packs. Be sure to grab fluid sheets. We don't know if the water here is compatible with our systems, and until we do, we'll use the sheets."

Teckoe groaned. "I hate the sheets. Hydrating through a patch is nothing like drinking actual liquid. I'll take my chances with the scavengers."

Jessa pointed at the craft. "Go. And pack me a bag too, would you? I'll stand watch until you're done."

"And Steve?" Asanka asked.

Jessa stilled and thought about the training manuals, the courses she'd taken, and the instructors she'd had. Surely somewhere there'd been mention of what to do about deceased people when you weren't in space. She looked around, stalling for time. The forest was dense, the carpeting of moss, branches, and leaves thick under her boots. A rustling in the trees made her jump. "If we can come back and bury him, we will. But for now we have to leave him. If we come across people who are friendly we'll ask for help with him. I think sticking around to bury him is a bad idea until we know what we're dealing with."

Though no one seemed comfortable with it, there seemed to be tacit agreement.

As always, the crew moved into action. They were close, as they'd been for the many years they'd flown together, and though they joked around and teased Jessa about her "command voice," there was no question she'd earned their respect. And she respected each of them, too. Steve was a huge loss, and one they'd grieve together later once they had the time. Emotions were never as important as duty, something Jessa's parents had drilled into her from a young age.

And right now, she was grateful for that lesson. "Don't forget to grab the domicile units."

Benika waved over her shoulder in acknowledgment as the group disappeared into the pod.

Alone and surrounded by the surprisingly beautiful landscape, Jessa felt her knees go weak. They were stranded on a planet known for its outlaw culture. One of her crew was dead, and the others were depending on her. But for what? Survival, at the very least. Was there any hope of rescue? She looked at the blue light of her life-sign in her forearm. It would act as a tracking beacon, should their distress message make it through the chaos of space. It wasn't likely, but it was hope, however slim.

Jessa planted her feet more solidly in the soft earth. She hadn't been planet bound in a very long time, and the heaviness of her body was strange, but also comforting. She was solid, and if there was a way out of here, she'd damn well figure it out.

❖

"This looks fine." Jessa pushed aside the curtain of hanging vines over the cave's entrance. The ledge they'd climbed to was wide and dry, and the cave behind it was tall and open. She couldn't see very far into it, and when she thought back to various nature programs she'd watched she wondered if it was wise to venture in. Apparently, she wasn't alone.

"Why don't we set up the domicile blocks here? If nothing comes in or goes out for a day or two, then we can head in." Benika squatted in front of the cave and looked into it warily.

"Agreed." Peshta dropped her bag and sat on it. "We're high enough here to see around us, but no one can sneak up on us, either. I can make us some dinner if we grab some branches from the forest."

Teckoe threw a rock down below, but it didn't make a sound when it hit the forest floor. "I think sending up smoke signals is a bad idea." He turned to look at Jessa. "Any thoughts as to what we do from here?"

It was a question she'd been waiting for, but not one she wanted to hear. "I think we take it step by step. Night is coming, so we get the domicile units set up as quickly as we can. We get some sleep, and see where the morning brings us." It was a weak answer, but it was all Jessa had in the moment.

They worked quietly, setting up three small domicile units. Peshta and Asanka would share one, Teckoe and Benika would share one, and Jessa had her own. It made sense to double up for safety, but the units wouldn't hold three people comfortably, so Jessa was on her own. Being alone meant she'd have time to think. And plan. And no one would see that her panic was only just below the skin, waiting to burst out.

Peshta took several packets of food supply and mixed them in a collapsible pot. The resulting soup was cold but nourishing, and it didn't take long before everyone went to bed. Jessa could feel their worry and fear, and as she slipped into her own bed unit that closed comfortably around her, she wondered if she should tell them she was scared and worried too. Or would that make her look weak? She sighed and listened to the sounds of the forest around them. High-pitched trills mixed with lower-pitched howls. Most seemed far away, and around daybreak she finally managed to drift to sleep.

Voices woke her, and when Teckoe opened the door to her tent she looked at him with her heart racing. He put his finger to his lips and pointed down, then moved away from her tent. Jessa scrambled from her sleeping unit and pulled on her boots. She tucked the energy gun into the pocket on her thigh and left the unit to find her group gathered on the edge of the ledge, lying down to look into the forest below. She lay quietly beside Benika and saw what they were looking at.

The forest below resounded with raucous laughter and shouts. The trees swayed and bent as people lumbered through, sweeping long handled tools ahead of them that beeped rhythmically. They could have been any group of passengers on Jessa's ship. Their clothing ranged from scruffy and raw to elegant and clearly expensive, though they didn't seem to be searching as a cohesive group. Jessa noted the sideways glances, the looks of contempt and cunning. Palms sweaty, she shimmied back from the ledge and the others followed. They stood at the cave entrance and Jessa tried to keep the tremor out of her voice.

"They're probably searching for things they can use or sell, not for people." Jessa wiped away a bead of sweat sliding from her forehead. She wanted to blame it on the humidity and not the fear soaking through her, but she knew the truth. "If we stay quiet, they won't know we're here."

Teckoe put his hand on her arm. "Captain, we left a trail through the forest a blind waftmonkey could follow. We just have to hope there are some decent folks down there, too."

Jessa blanched. She hadn't thought of that, and she should have. She'd just been focused on getting them to safety. A sudden shout made them all turn toward the cliff edge, and someone calling from below was clearly saying they'd found something. Jessa knew what that something was, and when she heard the word for slaves in a language she was fairly adept at, she made a decision.

She darted into her domicile, grabbed her pack, and moved to the far edge of the cliff.

"You're leaving us?" Peshta crossed her arms and glared at her.

"She's leading them away from us." Benika brought over a geo locator and tucked it in Jessa's hand. "I've marked the cliff and the escape pod. Don't stay gone after dark, okay? We can set out as a group tomorrow. Maybe find a city." She kissed Jessa's cheek softly before stepping back.

The kiss tingled on Jessa's cheek and she gave them a weak smile before beginning a swift but careful descent down the cliff side. She could hear the commotion at the base of the cliff where they'd climbed up, and when she was on the ground again she edged around to the front. Her pulse was hammering in her neck and fear was making her dizzy, but she didn't have time for that. She stepped out into the open and made a noise. She'd meant to shout, but it came out as more of a frightened mewl when she saw the group about to ascend the cliff. Almost as one, they turned toward her. Like the frightened animal she felt like, she turned and sprinted into the woods. She glanced at the geo locator. If she made a wide circle around the escape pod, she could make her way back here and hopefully lose them along the way.

She darted one direction and then another, leaping over fallen logs and ducking low hanging branches, and the sounds of her pursuers enjoying the chase was enough to make the bile rise in the back of her throat.

Suddenly, she was faced by a thick wall of trees too dense to get past. According to the geo locator, she should be able to run forward, across the river, and then double back. But this wall of trees went on for ages. Indecision tore at her. Left, and she was moving into an area she hadn't been to yet. Right, and there was no telling if it would take her to the river or cut her off. Her hands shook as she wiped her hair out of her eyes. Just as she was about to go left, she screamed as a hand closed around her upper arm.

"Do you lack the sense of a cripson? They're nearly here."

Jessa blinked at the woman standing beside her, unable to come up with words.

"Come on. Unless you want to end up in the slaver's net." She tugged on Jessa's arm again, and then let go and headed to the right.

Jessa's legs were like rubber, but she forced them forward, after the woman. If the woman was a threat she would have kept hold of her and let the others know where she was. Instead, she'd let her go and allowed her to make up her own mind. That was enough, for now. Jessa followed and realized she'd lost sight of her. When the woman reached out and grabbed Jessa from between two trees, she very nearly screamed again, but managed to keep it together as the woman pulled her into a narrow gap.

She laced her fingers together and bent low. "Up."

Jessa looked up and saw the small platform in the tree. She put her foot into the woman's hands and accepted the boost to the small metal hand and footholds in the tree. She made her way quickly to the platform and swung herself over, collapsing onto her back and breathing hard. When the woman landed gracefully beside her she started to thank her, but the woman shook her head and pressed her finger to Jessa's lips.

Jessa nodded her understanding and sat up. They waited for what felt like forever, until she could no longer hear any voices or shouts, even in the distance.

The woman sat with her back against the tree trunk and looked at Jessa curiously. "Why'd you come down off the cliff?"

"You knew we were there?" Jessa thought they'd left the pod long before anyone had come looking. Apparently not.

The woman shrugged. "I was there before you even left. I followed you to the cliffs to be sure none of the prowlers got you, and then I went back to get what I came for."

Only then did Jessa notice the pieces of metal and wire sticking out of the woman's bag. Her stomach sank. "You pulled apart the escape pod?"

The woman's gaze was searching. "It's not like it was doing you any good, and if I hadn't, everyone else would have. I'm heading out to see what else may have come down. Was yours the only escape pod to land here?"

Jessa stared at her. "I didn't *land* here. We crashed. We were heading for Andine when we were hit by an asteroid. And if you're only interested in other pods coming down so you can pull them apart, and not because you have any interest in survivors, well… you can just…just…" Mortified, Jessa felt the tears sliding down her face.

The woman looked away, her jaw clenching. "If you'd landed in the Heather District, or even Waterside, maybe it would have been different. But you crashed in open market territory, and that's the way it is. If they'd caught you, you'd have been sold at the slaver's market on the docks."

Slavery. Jessa had read about it in history books, and she'd even heard that it was still practiced in some galaxies that hadn't been properly colonized yet. Evidently, the tales of Indemnion didn't tell the full horror story. She wrapped her arms around herself and pulled her knees to her chest. "Thank you for helping me."

The woman held out her hand. "Kylin."

Jessa took it and noticed the rough skin and strength in Kylin's fingers, along with a slightly raised scar between her thumb and finger that looked like a brand of some kind. "Captain Jessa Arabelle."

Kylin gave a low whistle. "Captain, huh?"

Jessa nodded, but it was getting dark and her thoughts turned elsewhere. "Do you think we can make it back to my crew on the cliff?"

Kylin stood and stretched. "You did a good job of getting the other scroungers to follow you, so your crew is probably still safe there. But we'll have to hoof it to get back to the cliff before night hits. You don't want to be on the ground when the prowlers come out."

Just the word made Jessa's skin crawl. "Prowlers?"

"Lots of them in this forest. They breed here this time of year and then spread out next season." She slung her bag over her shoulder and climbed over the edge of the platform. "If you see one, it'll probably be the last thing you see. So let's move."

Jessa climbed after Kylin, her hands shaking on the metal pegs. Thank the heavens she'd spent so much time on the climbing deck on the ship. It had been a good way to exercise and a good release for tension. Now it might save her life.

CHAPTER FOUR

Jessa followed Kylin through the forest, awed that she seemed to know exactly where she was going without ever looking at a locator, though Jessa checked hers occasionally to make sure they were going the right direction. When they got to the cliff base Kylin motioned for her to go ahead.

"Probably best if the first head they see come up is yours. I'd hate to lose mine." She grinned.

Jessa smiled in return and quickly climbed the rock, cresting the cliff top just as the sun left the sky.

"Thank the heavens." Asanka pulled Jessa into a tight embrace. "We thought they'd got you."

"And you can't do that again. We can't lose—" Teckoe stopped and leveled his energy gun to Jessa's right. "Watch out!"

Jessa stepped in front of the gun. "Wait! She saved my life."

Kylin stepped onto the cliff ledge and stuck her hands in her pants pockets, looking for all the world like she was at a party instead of facing an energy gun. "Hey there."

Teckoe lowered the gun. "Sorry."

She shrugged. "Not the first time, won't be the last." She looked at their domicile units and her eyebrows raised. "Wow. These would get a fortune in the marketplace. Haven't seen one in years."

"Well, I don't imagine you get a lot of people who need them here." Jessa flinched inwardly at the caustic tone in her voice, but she couldn't help it. She was sweaty, scared, and she wanted to go home. But then, without a ship, where was home?

Kylin was walking around Jessa's domicile unit, poking at it and looking in the entrance. "Sleep units too. Wow, you guys really know how to rough it."

Before Jessa could respond, a terrible sound ripped through the night. High-pitched, it crackled on the air like electricity along the treetops, a kind of keening that sang of death.

Jessa turned toward Kylin, who had stopped messing with the domicile unit and was looking out into the forest. When the terrifying sound died away, she turned toward the cave and swept aside the vines. "Have you checked it?"

Jessa shook her head. "We couldn't see in far enough, but nothing has come out or gone in it since we got here."

Kylin shrugged off her bag and dug through it. She pulled a short, fat stick from it and then twisted it several times until it was much longer. She gave the end a sharp tap and blue light flared from the end. She moved forward into the cave and Jessa moved in behind her.

Kylin looked over her shoulder and laughed. "I'll move a hell of a lot faster if you're not right behind me when I turn around to run."

Jessa lifted her chin and motioned with her gun. "If you're going in, I'm behind you. You saved my life. I'm not letting you risk yours again while I sit outside like a limp queen."

Kylin didn't respond, she just moved quickly into the cave, shining the light back and forth. The cave was enormous, and they could have pitched the domicile units inside it easily. But when Kylin stopped and ran something through her fingers, Jessa could tell it wouldn't have been a good idea.

"It was a prowler den, but they haven't been here in a while. Sometimes they come back and use old dens, though. You and your friends shouldn't stay here any longer than you need to."

Jessa followed her out of the cave. "Okay. Where can we get the nearest shuttle to Andine?"

Another terrible howl filled the air, but this time it was joined by several others coming from different directions. The sound made the hair on Jessa's arms stand up, and she instinctively took a step closer to Kylin. She noticed that the others drew closer together, too.

Kylin scrubbed her hands over her face and then ran them through her hair, clearly frustrated. "If you know anything about Indemnion, you know we barely have mass transports, let alone shuttles. We send off maybe one every five years from the Heather District, if there are enough passengers to make it worth it, and there hardly ever is. I have no idea when they're planning on sending out the next one. Could be tomorrow, could be ten years from now."

Asanka knelt by her unit and put her face in her hands. Her gills were opening and closing rapidly, and Jessa knew it was a sign she was crying. Benika rubbed soothing circles on Asanka's back, but she looked just as shocked.

Jessa turned to Kylin. "Could you get us to the Heather District? At least then we'd have a chance."

Kylin sighed and shoved her hands deeper into her pockets. "Look, I'm just a scrounger from Quasi. Heather District is the only one on this planet where you have to have linari practically falling from your mouth to even enter the city. It's also on the other side of the planet. Sorry, but there's not much I can do."

Jessa felt the air go out of her. She moved to the cliff wall and slid down it. There was a slim hope of getting off this cosmos forsaken planet, but there might as well be a universe between them and that chance. She was responsible for four other people, but she had no idea how to keep them all alive long enough to get off planet.

Kylin turned toward the rest of the group. "Look, it's not my place, but I'd suggest you get inside your bubbles. Prowlers have a good sense of smell, and it's better if you're not out in the open where they can pick up your scent. They really only hunt at night, so you should be okay to make some kind of move tomorrow."

Jessa watched as the rest of her crew shuffled into their units without so much as another word. When Kylin turned toward Jessa, she finally pushed herself to her feet. "Thank you for your honesty. If you'd like to sleep in my unit tonight, you're welcome." She turned and left Kylin standing there looking surprised. Just because this planet was barbaric didn't mean Jessa was about to forget her own upbringing. She wasn't surprised when Kylin pushed into the unit and dropped her bag beside the empty sleeping unit.

"Thanks."

Jessa nodded, unable to find any words. Tomorrow, maybe, she'd find more. She'd think up a plan and they'd make a move. But right now, she wondered if Steve was better off than they were. "When you pulled the pod apart... What did you do with Steve?" she asked quietly as she slid into the chamber that encased her body.

Kylin frowned. "There was no one there." When Jessa looked at her wide-eyed, Kylin flinched. "I didn't know you had someone that didn't make it. As soon as you left, one of the forest predators probably came and took him. I'm sorry."

Jessa curled into a ball. "We should have buried him."

Kylin grunted softly as the chamber closed around her body. "It wouldn't have mattered. They'd have dug him back up, and you probably would have been captured by the scroungers that arrived later." She seemed to realize how blasé that sounded. "It's the nature of the forest. Nothing goes to waste."

Jessa let the tears fall, not caring if Kylin knew she was crying. This world was brutal and unfair. She wanted out. There simply had to be a way to get to the one launch station they had here. She'd find it no matter what it took, and if it took all the credit chips she had left, she'd use them. As the light faded she stared at Kylin's profile. She was extraordinarily tall, had short, bluish-black hair that almost touched the collar of her beat-up leather jacket, and there were thick yellow rings around the edges of her light gray eyes. In any other circumstance, Jessa would be entertaining very different thoughts about a woman like Kylin. She was ruggedly handsome, at ease in her own skin, and clearly knew her way around. Jessa liked capable, intelligent women, and she had a feeling that's just what Kylin was.

The question was, could she convince Kylin to help them? Or would Jessa have to figure this out herself? Even as she drifted into an uneasy, exhausted sleep, a plan began to form.

CHAPTER FIVE

Kylin watched the stars fade from the sky as the sun began to filter over the trees. She'd slept fitfully and had finally given up when she sensed dawn breaking. She had a load of metal and wire to trade from the single escape pod, but it wasn't the haul she'd been hoping for, and it wasn't nearly enough to get her out of debt to Orlin. And what she'd told Jessa about their dead crew member wasn't strictly true. He wasn't in the pod, that part was accurate. Rather, pieces of him were strewn around the outside of the pod, the scavengers already having dragged him out by the time Kylin arrived.

But Jessa didn't need that image in her head. Kylin knew women like her. She enjoyed women like her. Soft, gentle hearts and equally soft hands. Women who smelled nice and warmed a bed perfectly. Women who were only part of Kylin's world for a moment before she moved on, keeping them from the dirty and often cruel underbelly Kylin had to deal with for survival. The fact that Jessa had led the other scroungers away from her crew was impressive, but it didn't mean she belonged out here, either.

One thing Kylin was sure of. If she didn't help these people get to Quasi, they'd end up in a slaver's net. And she didn't care what kind of people they were, no one deserved to end up in that kind of life. But she also wanted to follow some of the other smoke trails to see what she could find. Her dad was safe with Auntie Blue, so she had time to search. Her little flyer could only take one other person, so that didn't help them much. With a sigh, she took out her comms unit and tapped the screen.

When Maana's face showed up she wanted to change her mind. The thick wedged lines down both sides of her face marked her as someone from another galaxy. The black soullessness in her small eyes marked her as someone you didn't want to mess with on any planet.

"Well, well. If it isn't my favorite playmate." Maana licked her small, pointed teeth. "To what do I owe the pleasure? Have you come to your senses and decided to play nice?"

If there was another way, she'd have taken it. The memory of those sharp teeth piercing her skin made her shudder. "I need a favor, and I'll owe you one."

Maana's smile widened, making her even more menacing. "I like the sound of that more than you know. What is it?"

"I need you to arrange a flyer pickup for five people at the edge of the Versach Forest. West entry. And then deliver them to Auntie Blue in Quasi." Cosmos be damned, this wasn't a good idea. She should have let the strangers fend for themselves. If they couldn't survive on someone else's planet, well, that was their issue. Not hers. But if the slavers got them…

Maana tapped something into the screen on her desk. "They'll be there just after mid-sun. And when can I expect you back to pay your debt?"

Kylin sighed and closed her eyes, but the memory of her last foray with Maana quickly made her open them again. "Not for another seven first sunsets, at least. I'm scrounging out in the east. I'll comm you when I get back. You know I pay my debts."

Maana's laugh was like splitting rocks in a cavern, harsh and hollow. "Oh, I remember, sweet scrounger. And tasting you again is worth transporting any number of people." She looked interested for a moment, unusual for someone who gave a damn about very little. "Who am I picking up, anyway? I can't imagine what would be worth owing me a pound of flesh."

Just then, Jessa appeared behind Kylin and touched her shoulder. Damn it.

Maana's eyes widened and her laugh was even louder. "I should have known it would be a woman. You'd think you'd learned your lesson from the last time." She leaned forward, clearly trying to get a better view of Jessa. "And a sweet piece of flesh at that. She'd be so tender—"

Kylin pulled the comm closer to block the view of Jessa. "She's not part of our deal. Me, and only me."

Maana grunted and leaned away. "You'll do." The screen went black.

Kylin put her unit back in her bag and pushed away the thought of an unpleasant future. At least she wouldn't have the lives of these people on her conscience. They could figure out how to get themselves to the Heathers from Quasi. She'd done her bit, and now they could fend for themselves.

"Friend of yours?" Jessa asked from behind her.

Kylin turned and tried to look like she wasn't fazed. "Business associate with a lot of history. But she's the only one I know with a flyer big enough to get all of you to safety. She'll take you to Quasi, to my auntie Blue. You'll be safe there, and you can figure out how to make your way to a station."

Jessa's big green eyes were lovely in the morning light, and Kylin had to look away.

"You're not going with us?"

Kylin began to reorganize her pack, more for something to do that didn't require her to look at Jessa's pretty face than because it needed to be done. "I want to see what the rest of the crash brought down, so I don't have time to go back yet. But Maana loves making deals with me, and she's never broken one. You'll be fine."

When Jessa didn't respond, Kylin finally looked up at her. She was biting her lip and looking out over the forest. When she finally looked at Kylin, she could see a layer of steel beneath the pretty surface, and in that moment she saw what had made her a captain.

"I'd like to go with you. My crew can go to Quasi."

Kylin shook her head. "Nope. I don't work with other people. I go where I need to go and I move fast. I don't need someone with no survival knowledge slowing me down."

Jessa put her hands on her hips and raised her chin. "I got us onto this ledge, didn't I? And I managed to avoid my pursuers."

Kylin grinned. "You did. But if I hadn't pulled you onto that platform, you'd be in a cage headed toward the sea right now."

Jessa flinched. "Maybe. But I want to go with you. It was my ship that came down, and I have a right to see what's left of it."

"Captain, you don't have a *right* to anything down here." Jessa's tone set Kylin on edge. She wasn't about to be ordered around by a princess who bypassed her planet on a regular basis. "I don't care what you do when you get to Quasi, but you're not coming with me." She pointed over her shoulder with her thumb. "I'll take you to the entry point where you'll get picked up, and then you're on your own."

Jessa turned away without another word, but Kylin could see the anger in her eyes. Why should she care what burned up pieces of her ship had made it down here? Surely she'd want to get to a station as quickly as possible? Kylin shook her head and rammed the wire deep into her pack. Women were a mystery.

The rest of the crew began making their way out of their domicile units and Jessa explained what was happening. Kylin stayed out of the way, eager to get going and not wanting to get attached to any of them. But when one of them touched her arm, she turned.

"Thank you for helping us."

The woman had gills, and it made Kylin smile. "You're from Gestix. I hadn't noticed."

"Asanka. You've known others from Gestix?"

"I have." Kylin noticed Jessa listening to their conversation, though she kept her distance. "Indemnion gets a lot of people who are looking for a different way of life than is allowed on their planet. When I was a kid, a family from Gestix moved in next door. I was friends with their daughter until they left about five years ago." Kylin pointed. "There's a saltwater lake just north of where you're being picked up. We can stop there so you can replenish your internal stores, if you want. We just need to leave soon."

Asanka took Kylin's hand in hers and pressed it to her forehead in the traditional Gestix greeting. "That would be greatly appreciated. The universe has seen fit to bless us with your presence."

Kylin smiled, uncomfortable with the sentiment. She wasn't anybody's blessing. "No problem. But we should get going."

They went about pulling down their domicile units, and Kylin tried not to show how impressed she was with the technology. Those huge units folded into perfect squares not much bigger than her backsack. The superlight substances of thin, expandable tubing and cloth-like materials they were made of meant that, despite all the comforts they included, they weren't all that heavy, which was incredible in and of itself. Their tech on Indemnion was always years behind other planets, since trade ships almost never stopped here, and even if families came from elsewhere, they rarely brought with them enough to build the kind of tech they were used to.

While the others were busy, another of Jessa's crew came over. Kylin recognized his type. His stance, the way he looked around. He'd been trained in combat as surely as Kylin had learned to fly. "Will they still be looking for us down there?"

Honesty was the only option. "They'll be keeping an eye out, yeah. But after the amount of prowlers we heard last night, they'll assume anyone not in a group was food."

He nodded, his expression inscrutable. "And how do we know you're not leading us into some kind of trap?"

She nearly laughed. If he had any idea who she'd had to bargain with... "You don't. And you're welcome to turn down the ride to Quasi and make your own way. I won't try to stop you, and my conscience will be clear because I tried to help."

"I don't like that you won't be there with us. At least we have an idea who we're dealing with when you're around." He looked at the rest of his little group. "Jessa feels responsible for us, but the truth is, she's not. In this situation we're all just people trying to survive. We don't have to take orders, and we don't have to stick together."

So much for loyalty. Kylin wondered if Jessa knew he felt that way, and if it came down to his own skin or theirs, she doubted he'd jump in front of a gun to save the others. "Yeah, well, that's up to you guys. Get on the flyer or don't, stay with people I trust in Quasi, or don't." When she looked into his eyes she saw the kind of fear that made people do stupid things. He was trying to hide it, but Kylin knew the signs.

"I think we're ready." Jessa came over and her officer nodded and walked away. "Everything okay?"

Kylin watched him go, uneasy in the sense he wasn't thinking properly. "I think so. They're your people, so you'd know better than I would." She looked around and saw that the ledge was clear. "Let's get going."

One by one, they climbed down the cliff side and then walked single file down the almost invisible paths. Kylin made sure to stay far away from the ruined escape pod. The last thing these people needed was to see their friend's chewed up body parts. When the path widened, she was surprised that Jessa moved up beside her.

"Can I ask you something sensitive?" she asked.

Kylin couldn't fathom what sensitive meant coming from a stranger. "Sure."

"Why does Asanka need a saltwater lake?"

Kylin looked at her incredulously. "Isn't she your crew member? Shouldn't you know that kind of thing?"

Jessa's cheeks flushed and she stared at the ground as they walked. "I rarely ask any of my crew personal questions about their state of being. It always seems too intrusive."

"But how do you get to know about people if you don't ask questions?" Surely a ship's captain wouldn't live in that kind of ignorance just because she didn't want to intrude?

"I read, and if it comes up in conversation that's fine. But it never has."

They walked in silence and Kylin wondered if she should make Jessa go back and ask the Gestixian herself. But she looked embarrassed, and it wasn't like she didn't care… "Gestix is a planet with a high saltwater content. Their people are amphibious, and while they mostly live on land, they can just as easily live in water. They tend to take saltwater baths a few times a month to keep their skin supple. Otherwise it gets dry and flaky. Not deadly or anything, but really uncomfortable. The humidity here will be making her sweat, and she'll dry out really fast."

Jessa stayed quiet, but Kylin could tell she had heard her and was thinking it over. She let her think. It wasn't any of her business.

"I need to ask more questions." Jessa's tone was decisive, like she was saying what she wanted for dinner.

Kylin wasn't sure how to respond, so she didn't. She didn't want to answer a bunch of questions, and she wasn't sure if Jessa meant she wanted to ask Kylin more questions, or if she wanted to ask more in general. Either way, questions meant getting to know someone, and Kylin didn't want to know these people. Under different circumstances, yeah, maybe she would have taken Jessa home for a few nights of no-strings sex. But Jessa was a ship's captain, someone used to being in command and getting what she wanted. She gave orders and she expected other people to jump when she wanted them to. And she had that upper-class thing going on, like she wasn't just used to the finer things in life, she *was* one of the finer things in life.

No, as soft and beautiful as she was, Jessa was way out of Kylin's league, and Kylin wasn't good with taking orders from anyone, for any reason. Staying in control meant less risk, and she was always in control of her sexual relationships, whether they lasted a night or several days. So it was just fine that the captain was out of her league. She'd get on the flyer, and there was a good chance she'd be gone from Quasi by the time Kylin got back from scrounging. She'd be nothing more than a hot fantasy on a cold night.

CHAPTER SIX

The saltwater lake was one of the most beautiful things Jessa had ever seen. She'd pictured something far smaller, but this could easily have accommodated several boats at once. Swirling greens mixed with ribbons of blue and edges of pink. Though she desperately wanted to see how Asanka did what she needed to do, Jessa turned away with the others and gave Asanka her privacy.

"Where are we going again?" Benika had been quiet for the most part, though Jessa knew she was anxious.

"Quasi." Kylin sat on the ground cross-legged, plucking at patches of moss. "We're set up in districts here. Quasi District is kind of a central ground, closest to the main trading markets and where people go when they need to find things. Or if they're looking not to be found."

"And who are we staying with? Your relative?"

Kylin shook her head. "Kind of. Auntie Blue is everyone's auntie, but she's actually really close to my family. She's looked after me for a big chunk of my life, and she'll be fine with having you stay with her. She runs an inn, so you'll have plenty of room." She shrugged. "Maybe she can help you figure out what step to take next."

"Is there anything we need to understand about where we're going? Etiquette?" Peshta asked.

Kylin seemed baffled. "Don't pick fights with people bigger than you. Try not to go out after dark. The usual, I guess."

Jessa couldn't imagine picking a fight with anyone, ever, and the likelihood of going out after dark was about as likely as her growing a horn in the middle of her head. Most planets had codes of conduct. Not this one, evidently.

"Do any of you have any linari? Or just credit chips?" Kylin asked.

"My linari went down with the ship." Teckoe looked at the others, who nodded agreement.

"No big deal. Credit chips can be used pretty much everywhere. Auntie Blue can help you get what you need." Kylin smiled up at Asanka, who'd returned from the lake. She was practically glowing, her eyes bright and her gills pink. "Okay, let's get to the pickup point. They'll be here anytime."

She hefted her pack over her shoulder and the others followed. Jessa was working out how to approach Kylin about her plan, but couldn't seem to find the right moment. They moved beyond the trees and Jessa stared at the long, low landscape of rippling green hills that went on for as far as she could see. But she didn't have much time to look at it before a medium sized flyer settled onto the hill in front of them. The lower door opened, but no one came out.

Kylin turned to the group. "That's your cue. Good luck, if I don't see you when I get back to Quasi."

Jessa watched her crew head for the flyer, but she didn't follow them. Instead, she turned to Kylin. "I'm not getting on that flyer. I'm going with you."

Kylin sighed dramatically. "I've already told you no."

"And I'm telling you I'm not getting on that flyer, so if you don't take me with you, you're leaving me to the prowlers or slavers." Jessa crossed her arms, hoping Kylin wouldn't call her bluff and leave her there.

"Why? What do you possibly hope to find?" Kylin's exasperation was clear.

The problem was, Jessa didn't know the answer. She rarely stepped foot on a planet even when they were docked for a few days, and she hadn't spent this much time on one in many, many years.

But if there was any chance another escape pod had been hit and had crashed here, if there was any chance there were other survivors, she had to know. Her ship, her responsibility. Instinct told her Kylin was trustworthy, and her small crew would be safe with Kylin's contact in Quasi, so Jessa could rest easy knowing they'd be okay until she returned. And, if she were honest, she didn't want to leave Kylin's side. The thought of going to a strange city without the only contact they'd made here was terrifying, and something about Kylin made her feel safe. But that point was secondary, of course.

"I told you. That ship was my life. It was my home. I was responsible for the crew and the passengers. If any other escape pods came down, I want to know. And if there are survivors, I can be with you to tell them they're safe." It sounded lame, but it was true. Mostly.

Kylin glared at her. "And how would you know they're safe? I'm not out to rescue the world, Captain. I probably shouldn't have rescued *you*. But I did, and I'm going to owe someone with very pointy teeth, bad breath, and a penchant for using things with spikes a favor because of it. So, no."

Jessa felt her stomach turn at the callousness of the statement. But actions were clearer, and Kylin's showed she wasn't as jaded as she sounded. "Like I said. I'm not getting on that flyer."

Kylin gave a huff of irritation and then raised her hand in a thumbs-up gesture. The door closed and the flyer took off. "And what are your crew going to think now that you haven't gotten on the flyer?"

"They'll be safe with your auntie until we get back. And if I return with anything useful, it can only help us get back to where we need to be." She was grasping at straws, and it wasn't really an answer. She should have told Teckoe, as her second in command, what she was thinking. But she didn't want anyone talking her out of it, though she knew it was foolish.

Kylin slung her pack over her shoulder. "Fine. But if you fall behind, I'm leaving you."

Jessa had no intention of getting left behind now that she'd set her course. "I can keep up."

They made their way to Kylin's flyer, which was a two-seater that looked hand built. Jessa eyed it, wondering just how air safe it was. Kylin rolled her eyes and stowed her pack.

"Feel free to head back to the ledge and set up camp. I can stop and see if you're still there on my way back."

Jessa threw her pack behind her seat and climbed in. She'd made her decision and she needed to stick with it, even if that meant falling out of the sky. Again. "No chance."

Kylin got the flyer off the ground and headed east, in the opposite direction Jessa's crew had gone. She was pleasantly surprised to find that the flight was smooth and quiet. "Where did you get this?"

Kylin glanced at her and then looked away. "I built it."

Jessa waited, but no more information was forthcoming. "What do you mean, you built it? I thought you said you were a…what was it? A scrounger?"

"I am." Kylin stroked the control panel like it was precious. "But I always wanted to be a pilot. Whenever anyone arrived who could fly or engineer, I made myself a pest. I learned everything I could, and a mechanic from Orwellian stayed here for almost two years once. She taught me everything she could, and gave me hands-on instruction in building this."

There was something about Kylin's tone, something that spoke of memories soft and painful, that made Jessa decide not to pursue that line of questioning. But if Jessa had to guess, the hands-on lessons weren't restricted to just building the flyer. She looked down and saw that the forest was gone, replaced by sand dunes with strange patterns in them.

Kylin looked down too. "The nomad lands. Beautiful, in their own stark way. The patterns are made by the caravans that move across them. Sometimes their groups can be a hundred or more."

Jessa scanned the area. "How do people survive there? It looks so desolate."

"There's water, if you know how and where to look. Not everything comes from a dispenser in a temperature controlled environment."

Jessa felt the rebuke, but Kylin's smile was gentle. And the truth was, Jessa wouldn't have any idea where to look for food or water in an environment like the one they were flying over.

"Where are you from, anyway?" Kylin asked as she adjusted their flight path, turning southwest.

Jessa had to think for a moment. Her initial answer was to say her ship, but that was gone, which meant it wasn't really where she was from. But she hadn't considered her home planet in a long time. "Othrys, originally. But I haven't been back in years."

The small lines around Kylin's eyes tightened, as did her hands on the flight stick. "Wow."

The single word was heavy, and Jessa wasn't sure what else to say. She was fully aware of her planet's reputation. Othrys was known for its beauty and refinement. There was no poverty, no illness. From afar, it was a utopian world. Trying to explain that it had its troubles like any world would sound disingenuous, but she could tell Kylin had already judged her and found her wanting.

They flew in silence until something occurred to her. "How do you know where you're going?"

Kylin tapped a sequence on the vid screen and a number of flashing blue dots appeared. "I used a geo scanner to plot the different smoke trails and where they might lead. It's not pinpoint accurate, but it will get me to each vague area. Then I'll foot search from there."

It was a good plan, and Jessa wouldn't have considered using a geo scanner that way. "That's ingenious."

Kylin tilted her head in acknowledgement. "I reprogrammed it to act as a guide rather than just scan. It works pretty well, for the most part." She gave Jessa a small smile. "Probably nothing like the tech you're used to."

It wasn't. Jessa was used to top of the line tech and had been all her life. But seeing someone build something to spec, something they needed and so figured out how to create, was impressive. Not only had Kylin saved their lives, she was also something special in her own right. A sense of deficiency crept into the back of Jessa's mind, and she pushed it away.

They were still over the nomad lands when they began approaching one of the blue dots. This one wasn't hard to find. A long, dark gash in the sand ended in a charred piece of metal bigger than the flyer they were in. It was a piece of the main ship, and it made Jessa's heart sink. It wasn't an escape pod, which was good. But it was part of something that had been special, and that hurt.

It also wasn't alone.

A small group of people with whitewashed vehicles with enormous tires were camped beside it. Children kicked up sand as they chased a glowing yellow ball that darted one way and then the next. Pots of food were cooking over wide, open fire pits. There was laughter and a type of music Jessa had never heard.

"What is it?" Kylin asked, looking at her curiously.

Jessa stared out at the camp. "They look so happy."

Kylin laughed. "Wouldn't you be if you could travel the world and not answer to anyone?" She jumped out of the flyer and headed toward the nomads, leaving Jessa to follow or not.

Jessa watched as Kylin approached the group, her hands up and open to show she wasn't aggressive. When two children launched themselves at her and she swung them into the air, one in each arm, Jessa grew even more confused. They seemed to know her, and when she was in their midst several people stopped to press their foreheads to hers. Kylin looked so relaxed, so totally at home among them, and Jessa wondered what that would feel like. Once again, she pushed away the unwelcome meandering thoughts and jumped from the flyer. Several people nodded and gave her a small sign of acknowledgement, but most avoided eye contact and turned away. So, outsiders weren't welcome. That was interesting to know. It meant Kylin wasn't one, and Jessa wondered just how she'd come to know a traveling community like this one.

She joined Kylin at the edge of the mammoth piece of twisted metal.

"Any idea what part of your ship it is? Was?" Kylin studied it but didn't reach out to touch it.

Trembling, Jessa dragged her fingertips along the side. When she felt the raised emblem and traced it, she said, "It's the cargo hold. Or, about a third of it, anyway."

Kylin stared at her. "A third of the cargo hold. *Just* the cargo hold."

Jessa shrugged. "Is that interesting?"

Kylin's laugh didn't hold much humor. "Not to you, I guess. What kind of ship did you fly? I should have asked before, but I was focused on making sure you didn't get eaten or caught."

"It was an *Echo Eight Delta Centauri* passenger vessel. The most up-to-date luxury transport in the cosmos right now." Jessa didn't try to rein in the pride she felt at her answer. She'd loved every inch of the massive ship and had worked her ass off to have one she could captain on her own.

Kylin, however, didn't look impressed. "Luxury transport. So, people traveling between planets with everything at their fingertips."

"People shouldn't feel bad for enjoying themselves just because your planet isn't interesting enough to land on." Jessa hadn't had to defend her line of work to anyone but her parents since she'd decided on her career choice, and she certainly wasn't going to do so with a woman who'd never been on anything bigger than a two-seater flyer she'd had to build herself.

Kylin's jaw clenched and the yellow rings around her eyes darkened. "Whatever you say." She used the twists of metal to climb to the top and walked along the edge. "The nomads say it sounds hollow but there's no way in. But that doesn't seem likely if it's just a piece of the bigger thing. True?"

Jessa hesitated. What was in here belonged to the people who had evacuated her ship. But it wasn't as if they were going to get it back. It would remain here, on this bypassed planet, forever. Who knew where the other two compartments that had adjoined this one were. She jumped when a couple of children raced around her legs, using her as a wall between them before they dashed off again, their laughter echoing off the dead metal. She watched them go, then looked up to see Kylin's silhouette above her, looking down, waiting. Strong and solid, she looked like some kind of superhero from the ancient stories, and it made Jessa shiver in an extremely pleasant way.

She moved back to the insignia marking it as a cargo hold. The print scanner wouldn't work anymore, but the punch code might.

She brushed away burned pieces and pried away the thick plastic covering from the key pad. She entered the code and it flashed weakly and then began to hum. The creaking and groaning as the ten-foot door struggled to open caught everyone's attention and they gathered around. They spoke a strange mixture of a language Jessa hadn't heard before along with Universal Lingua, the common tongue spoken in the colonized cosmos, so she caught a few words here and there. When the door shuddered to a halt, Kylin jumped down into the sand beside her.

"I knew you were a softie." She grinned and ducked under the partially open entrance. "Cliff suckers. There's more in here than even the people in the Heathers own!" she called out from inside.

The nomads ducked in after her, and soon there were excited shouts all around. Jessa made herself comfortable in the sand by sitting against a short outcrop of rock. Though most of her possessions had been on the ship, she still had a storage locker on Othrys and she had enough on her credit chip to live comfortably on pretty much any planet she chose without ever having to work again. She didn't need anything in the cargo hold. But to Kylin and the people carrying things out, the hold was a treasure trove, and the joy in their faces made Jessa glad she'd relented and opened the door.

Kylin came out, her arms laden with clothing and jewelry, along with some small tech items. "I don't even have a pack big enough for this. Lots of stuff is damaged from the crash, but there's plenty to keep everyone going for at least a few seasons."

Jessa watched as she carried her armful to the flyer and loaded it into a compartment toward the rear. She couldn't fathom what life would be like if she had to forage for things to sell in order to eat. The thought made her ache inside, and the knowledge that this planet got passed over because it had nothing to offer was made worse by the knowledge of the position it left the inhabitants in. She'd never considered life like this.

Kylin came back over and sat beside her in the sand. "Thanks for opening it. Taking things like this to market will make a huge difference to this clan when the cold season blows in."

"They live out here even then?" Just the thought of it sent a chill through her.

"Not here in the sands. They move on, and they take shelter in the forests or in the outskirts of cities like Quasi. But they don't like being penned in, so they never stay anywhere for long. And there's a stigma attached to being a nomad. People don't trust people who don't answer to anyone and live freely. It freaks them out." Kylin smiled as a little girl with pale purple pigtails and large, soft purple eyes ran up to her holding out a doll. Kylin took it and gave the girl a little nuzzle with it before the child laughed and bounded away, the doll clutched to her chest.

Jessa could easily be one of the people who didn't understand. Order, command, organization. She lived by standards and codes and procedures and couldn't imagine sleeping under the stars and only moving on when she needed food or shelter. Even the thought of it made a ball of panic form in her stomach.

Kylin was watching the group contemplatively. "I think I've got what I want from this. What say we move on and see what else we can find?"

Surprised, Jessa looked away from the family unit she'd been watching. "Isn't this exactly the kind of thing you need to make money in Quasi?"

Kylin stood and brushed sand from her pants before holding out her hand to help Jessa up. "It is. And I've got enough to get me the really important stuff, plus a little extra. But this group has kids to feed, and a haul like this can keep them going for months. They need it more than I do. We'll find something else."

Jessa waited while Kylin said good-bye to several people, some of whom sent knowing looks over Kylin's shoulder and were clearly teasing her. When they got back in the flyer the nomads waved from below as they took off.

"I don't understand."

Kylin looked confused. "About what?"

"You could have shared what was in there. Split it into sections so it was fair for everyone, including you. But you didn't. I know you said they have children to feed, and that's noble, but surely you've got people to take care of as well. Doesn't it feel unfair to leave it behind?" While Jessa understood the concept, she'd never come across someone truly altruistic. She didn't think that kind of person existed in any real sense.

Kylin sighed. "Are you really that jaded? Does everything have to be an equal portion so you get your fair share, even if you don't truly need it?" She tapped the screen, moved it to another blinking blue dot, and set the locator to take them there. "Haven't you ever done anything for someone just because it was the right thing to do, and not because there was anything in it for you?"

Jessa swallowed hard and stared unseeing at the passing landscape. Her mind scraped and scrabbled through memories as far back as they could go, but she couldn't come up with an answer that didn't make her sound like...well, like the kind of person Kylin probably thought she was. But it wasn't a fair comparison, was it? She hadn't been born into a difficult world. Othrys was based on everyone having an equal share. That wasn't her fault, and she shouldn't be ashamed of the person she was. It was merely circumstances.

That train of thought felt an awful lot like justification, and the silence between them like condemnation.

"You seemed to know them." A change of subject felt like a good idea.

"After my mom died I used to run off a lot. On one of my many trips I came across that group of nomads, and it was during one of their more stationary moments, so I got to know them. They didn't have much to share, but they had all the time in the world for a grieving child who didn't know what to do with herself." She cleared her throat like she was physically shoving away emotion. "I try to catch up with them whenever they're in the area. I'm glad it was them near the wreck."

For the life of her, Jessa couldn't think of anything to say. She'd never been close to anyone other than her crew, and because of the power disparity she was never truly close to any of them, either.

"It just occurred to me. Do you have family who are going to be worried about you?" Kylin asked.

That should have been a simple question to answer, but it wasn't, and Jessa hesitated. "I have family, yes. I imagine they'll be informed that my ship went down, and that I'm not among the survivors on Andine." Would her parents and sibling be saddened by the information?

She looked away from the pitying look in Kylin's eyes. There was nothing wrong with detachment. It meant you didn't have distractions.

"We don't have interplanetary communications in Quasi, but they've got facilities in the Heathers. When you get there you can send word that you're safe." She tilted her head. "If you want to."

In truth, Jessa hadn't considered her family once since she'd crashed. "Perhaps I will. That would be the responsible thing to do."

Kylin just shook her head, and she kept whatever thoughts she had about that to herself, for which Jessa was grateful. Talking about her family was never comfortable, even with her family. "Where are we headed now?"

"Twenty clicks north of Mount Zulphi. Rocky terrain, a lot like the moon, but mostly made up of ice. Have you ever seen a cryo volcano?"

Jessa's heart raced at the thought. "I've read about them, of course. Is it true they erupt ice?" Kylin's grin made Jessa's heart race that much faster.

"Ice magma. It's super hot magma that rises into the layer of ice and then the force of them coming together ejects them into the air. You don't want to get hit by one, but when the sun is just right, it's something to see."

Kylin's excitement was so open it made Jessa aware of how tightly her own shoulders were held. She tried to lower them. "Thank you for letting me come with you."

Kylin gave her a sideways glance. "It's not like you gave me any choice. I wasn't about to leave you with the prowlers or slavers. And you opening that hatch has given me a good haul. So we're even, and it turns out it was good I didn't leave you to see how you'd survive on your own."

"But you could have. You let me force your hand and I appreciate it." Jessa nearly reached out to touch her but kept her hands firmly on her legs. She never usually wanted to touch anyone. Strange.

"Banking left. Look to your right."

Jessa gasped. A towering black volcano nearly blocked out the sun, and lines of glittering white veins ran from the caldera to the base. White rocks with black veins shot from the volcano, caught the sunlight, and burst into balls of rainbows before falling to the surreal rocky landscape below.

Kylin banked again and they made a wide circle around the volcano. Jessa pressed against the window, wishing she could catch and hold one of the rocks, just so she could hold a rainbow in her hand. As they flew away from the volcano, Jessa kept it in sight as long as she could, then sat back with a sigh. For all she'd read or watched about them, nothing was like seeing the real thing.

Kylin brought the flyer in to land, expertly managing to put it down on the uneven surface. They got out and she opened a handheld locator. "It should be nearby, but I've only got a general idea. I think we're better off searching on foot for a while. Anything black will blend into the rock here and be hard to see from up high."

Jessa could follow that logic and agreed, though it was obvious Kylin wasn't asking for agreement or permission. She was just letting Jessa in on her way of thinking, which was appreciated.

"Have you considered doing a grid search? Measuring out a certain amount of steps in a radius and then moving beyond it in sections?" Jessa asked.

Kylin laughed. "When it's just you a grid search seems like an awful lot of work. Why don't we just get as close to the blue dot as possible and see what happens?"

Jessa reminded herself she wasn't in control here. "Sure. If that kind of haphazard thing works for you."

"You know, it does." Kylin smirked and set off, scanning the area and occasionally checking the locator.

Jessa followed, more interested in the landscape. "Does anything live here?"

Kylin shook her head but didn't turn around. "Too cold. Once the sun drops it could freeze the nipples off a snow cur."

How she wished Kylin hadn't mentioned it. She'd been fine since they crashed, but now, wandering the barren rocks, she felt the chill through her uniform. She rubbed at her arms and told herself to get over it and focus on something else.

Unfortunately, the thing that caught her attention was Kylin's backside. The black pants with several large pockets fit her perfectly, molding to her butt and giving her thighs some room to move. The muscles of her back were defined under the tight long-sleeved shirt, and they bunched perfectly as she moved the locator and steadied herself over loose rocks. Her short, blue-black hair reflected the sun, and Jessa wondered if it was as soft as it looked. Her thoughts wandered to the size of Kylin's hands, and how they'd feel—

"Look!" Kylin pointed to the chunk of metal ahead. "That wasn't so bad."

Saved from thoughts that couldn't lead anywhere sanity resided, Jessa looked over the piece. "It's part of the mainframe."

Kylin looked enthralled as she combed over it, moving wires and pieces aside. When she got to the circuit board she looked ecstatic. "Do you have any idea what I could do with this?"

"None, I'm afraid. I know how to use it when it's working, but I don't know a thing about how to put it together."

"I do," Kylin said softly. She took a tool from one of her many pockets and started cutting and moving things. "With enough of this kind of thing, I could build my own transport and leave this planet."

The longing in her voice made Jessa pause. "You could?"

"Damn right I could." She gently lifted the large circuit board from the bent, dented casing. "Can you hold this?"

Jessa took it and watched with interest as Kylin removed cables and wires and rolled each one carefully until she had a stack at her feet. She gathered them up and turned to Jessa. "Are you okay to carry that back to the flyer? I've marked the location so I can move it closer, but I don't want to leave this stuff here, just in case anyone else comes looking."

Jessa set off without answering. There was still something slightly sickening about watching the pieces of her beautiful ship being cannibalized, though she knew that was absurdly emotional.

When they got to the flyer, Kylin set down her armful of wires and cables and punched a code into her locator. The flyer buzzed and shook, and then the roof opened. A mechanical arm lifted a long box from the flyer and then closed again with the box along the outside. It opened and Kylin took the circuit board from Jessa. She climbed up and put it gently into the box, then got down and gathered the stuff she'd brought back and added it to the box. She slammed the box closed and looked down at Jessa.

"That's incredibly impressive. External storage is a great idea." Jessa really was impressed. Storage was something she'd never needed to consider, like so many other things.

"Thank you." Kylin bowed dramatically. "I'm brilliant and sexy. Some people are just that lucky."

Jessa laughed, surprising herself. She got into the flyer and held on as Kylin barely lifted it off the ground enough to fly to the mainframe. They spent another half hour pulling it apart for the parts Kylin thought she could use, and they seemed to be in tacit agreement to move fast, as the temperature was dropping quickly.

Jessa could barely feel her fingers when they got back in and she couldn't control her shivering. Kylin reached behind her seat and pulled out a jacket.

"Take this. We'll fly into the next district. There's a small landing space there. If you don't mind, we can set up your domicile unit next to the flyer. That way I know the flyer is safe but we don't have to sleep in it. Work for you?"

Jessa nodded, her teeth chattering as she pulled the jacket tight around her. It smelled of Kylin; spicy and earthy, a combination that was strangely sensual. She breathed it in and found herself growing warm.

They were only in the air for a quarter of an hour before the bright lights of a small runway appeared. Kylin got permission to dock at the edge of the port, and when Jessa got out to put up the domicile unit, Kylin's gentle touch stopped her.

"Let me. I'm used to this weather. I don't want to have saved you from the prowlers only to have you freeze to death." She grinned and was out of the flyer in an instant.

Jessa didn't argue. She'd never been so exhausted, and now that it was just her and Kylin under a starlit sky, she could sense the emotion of the situation knocking at her subconscious. She hugged herself and watched the domicile unit unfold and light up. When Kylin waved, she jumped down and hurried into it. Warmth hit her and she sank onto the sleeping pod.

"Sorry. I didn't think about the fact that you're used to climate control." Kylin worked off her boots and sat swinging her legs on the opposite sleeping pod.

"I should have been prepared." Jessa didn't want to admit to weakness, but denial was silly. "I can't wait to lie down."

Kylin looked like she was going to say something but changed her mind. She swung her legs up and lay back with her hands behind her head. "You know, I'm not used to having anyone with me, but this has been nice."

Jessa nodded, her eyes already closed. A small voice in the back of her mind wished Kylin would come over and share her sleeping pod. Keep her warm. Safe. She shoved it away and concentrated on falling asleep. That was a complication neither of them needed, and she wasn't even sure if she was Kylin's type, though she was fairly sure Kylin was interested in women. *Just not this woman.* Kylin's feelings about their difference in economic class was loud and clear. And maybe she was right. They were as different as a sun to a moon, with miles of space between them.

She rebuked herself for the stray thoughts. She would find her way off this planet and this whole experience would be nothing but a memory.

CHAPTER SEVEN

Kylin stretched and appreciated the soreness in her shoulders. Pulling apart the mainframe yesterday had been physically demanding, and she was glad to know she was still in good enough shape to handle that kind of thing, probably thanks to the amount of time she'd spent in the ring lately. Granted, that time in the ring also meant her collarbone was still giving her trouble, and she'd had to move carefully after a sharp reminder that it hadn't healed yet. Having someone to hand the pieces down to had been incredibly useful, and had probably saved her collarbone more irritation as well. She wondered if she should consider getting a regular helper when she went on these jaunts. One of the nomad teenagers would love the chance.

She turned on her side and looked at Jessa, who was frowning even in her sleep. She was so rigid, so buttoned up. Was she always that way? Or was it only because of the situation? She felt like there was more to her, maybe deeply buried, but there. Her reaction to the cryo volcano was so free, so childlike. It had allowed Kylin to see what she might be like without all the stress and responsibility she put on herself. Her long, silky hair covered part of her face, the red streaks dark against her perfect pale skin. Those beautiful jade eyes had lit up as the rainbows had cascaded through the air, and Kylin wondered what other experiences could bring out the simple joy she'd seen.

She wouldn't find out. People from Othrys weren't capable of real emotion, something she'd already seen when Jessa talked about her family. No matter how beautiful Jessa was, Kylin wasn't going to go there. She'd finish looking at the pieces, then they'd make their way back. If her crew hadn't already moved on, she'd help them figure out how to get to the station at the Heathers. That was it. She didn't owe her anything.

So why was she glad to have her along? Granted, having a beautiful woman around wasn't usually a hardship until things got complicated. Kylin had always been a sucker for a beautiful woman, and this one had fallen from the sky and practically into her lap. But there were plenty of women back home who didn't come with the baggage this one did. She needed to remember that.

Kylin ran her hands through her hair and got out of the pod. They should get in the air to make the most of the day. The next stop was a good distance away and she wanted to get back to Quasi. Her dad was on her mind, especially after the conversation about Jessa's family.

She went out quietly and ran checks on the flyer. Everything was in place and there was plenty of power in the core. As long as she took it steady she'd be fine.

Jessa came out tying her hair in a messy ponytail and looking perhaps more beautiful than she did when she was all put together. "Morning."

"Morning. We'll get in the air as soon as we've broken down." Kylin didn't mean to sound distant, but Jessa's beauty was distracting.

"No problem." She ducked in, came back out dressed in Kylin's jacket, which was adorably too big for her, and then hit the program to take the domicile unit down. Within minutes they were seated in the flyer and taking off.

"Where to next?" Jessa asked, covering a yawn.

Kylin pointed to a blue dot on the screen. "Thalla District. They've got a city, not unlike Quasi. But there's more bartering and way less tech. They try to live as close to the land as possible. Not big on outsiders. If things had been different, I think my dad and I would have gone there."

"And if what you're looking for is in the city? Will they let you just walk in and take it?"

Kylin had wondered the same thing. "I don't know. I mean, they don't like or use tech, really, so in theory they wouldn't want it anyway. But if they think it could be useful one day..." She shrugged. "We'll just have to see."

They flew in silence for a while, and when Kylin looked over she saw that Jessa was asleep, her head pillowed against the hood of Kylin's jacket. Kylin gently moved a piece of hair away from Jessa's eye and fought the desire to touch her cheek. Instead she concentrated on the flight and watching the land below. They weren't far from the blue dot when Jessa finally woke.

"I'm so sorry." She yawned and stretched, rolling her neck to get the kinks out. "I hadn't realized how tired I was."

Kylin smiled. "No big deal. I'm used to silence. Not someone snoring beside me, though." She laughed when Jessa looked mortified. "Kidding."

Jessa looked at the land below. "Pretty."

It was. The rock formations of red stone were painted through with minerals that caught the light and flared out in pinks, blues, and purples. It always reminded Kylin of a child's painting. "It looks like our dot is just on the outskirts rather than in the city, which is good news for us." She nodded at the sky. "But I think we'll need to move quickly on this one."

Thick green clouds were zipping along the sky, and a storm out here moving that fast would pack a punch. She didn't want to get caught in it.

She set the flyer down and they jumped out. The wind tore at their clothes, stirring up rock dust and making it hard to see, let alone speak. Kylin used her locator and it took far longer than she was comfortable with before the black shape loomed out of the growing dust storm.

Jessa cried out and ran to the escape pod, but Kylin hung back. She could tell there wasn't any hope. The charred outside was badly damaged, with holes and gashes everywhere. The strange foam stuff she'd seen in Jessa's pod filled some of the holes, and there was no question they were tinted crimson.

Jessa stood at the entry of the pod trying to punch a code into the mostly melted keypad. When it wouldn't open she banged her fists against the door. Tears ran down her face, making tracks in the red dust covering her cheeks.

"Jessa!" Kylin called over the howling wind. "Nobody could have survived that. We need to get back to the flyer!"

Jessa shook off her hand and tried the keypad again. "What if someone did? What if they're in there alive and we leave them?"

The thought was planted, and Kylin swore into the wind. She pulled a small utility laser from her pocket and went to the largest hole in the side. The laser flashed weirdly in the dusty wind, and it wasn't long before she had a hole big enough to reach into easily. Jessa moved to her side and together they pulled out all the foam they could reach, clearing the hole. Kylin shone her flashlight into to the hole and Jessa peered in.

She stumbled back, her hand over her mouth and fresh tears tracking down her cheeks. Kylin looked in and saw the carnage. The foam had kept the people's bodies intact, but hadn't protected them from the asteroids that had crashed through the metal and into the interior of the pod. It was a scene out of a nightmare and there was no longer any question of anyone being alive. Kylin didn't want to scrounge anything from this pod, that was certain.

She grabbed Jessa's arm and pulled her back to the flyer. Once inside, the wind and dust pummeled the glass, but at least they could breathe again. Jessa's shoulders shook as she cried, and Kylin wrapped her arms around her, letting her get it out. She couldn't imagine how Jessa was feeling, but she was relieved to see some emotion. Holding that kind of thing in couldn't be healthy. Not that she was one to talk, but that wasn't the point.

Jessa calmed as the storm raged around them. The flyer wasn't meant to be out in a storm like this, and Kylin prayed to the cosmos it would still fly when the storm passed. There was no point in trying to get it off the ground now.

Jessa sat back and wiped her tears away with the sleeve of Kylin's jacket. "I'm sorry. I'm not usually so affected. But those poor people…"

"Jessa, it's okay to be upset about people dying. What kind of person would you be if you didn't care?" She wiped the tears from Jessa's cheeks, managing only to smudge the red dirt further.

"Being overly emotional keeps you from thinking rationally and making good decisions." Jessa sounded defeated rather than convincing.

Kylin wasn't sure what to say without sounding hypocritical. Emotions weren't friends of hers either, but hearing it from someone who was so clearly hurting was strange. Although, given where Jessa was from, her engrained reaction made sense. So, since there weren't words, she pulled Jessa close and wrapped her in her arms, giving comfort the best way she knew how. Well, the second best way, but the first one was out of the question and would have been difficult to manage in the flyer anyway. She half expected Jessa to pull away, but after a moment of stiffness she relaxed and rested her head on Kylin's shoulder.

There was nothing to do but wait, and with Jessa in her arms, Kylin was strangely reluctant to see the storm end.

Hours later, Kylin opened her eyes and blinked against the grit in them. Jessa stirred too and sat back in her seat, wiping at her face. Kylin ignored the flash of disappointment as the cold air hit where Jessa's warm body had been. The windows were caked with red dirt that had turned to sludge when the rain began, but it was silent now.

"Let's see what the damage is." Kylin had to shove hard on the door to get it to open, and when it did it was heavy with red mud. She jumped out and groaned. The right propeller was clogged with mud, and the wing was sagging under the weight of it. "Ragweed tits." She moved slowly around the flyer checking damage and trying to work out what to do. When she rounded the tail she froze.

Jessa stood with her hands in the air, facing a group of people with energy guns pointed at her. They wore the heavy protective face cloth of the local Thalla tribes so all Kylin could see were their eyes, which were hard and suspicious. One of them turned a gun toward her and motioned with it toward Jessa.

She held up her hands and moved slowly, not wanting to give them any reason to fire. Her dad had made her bring the seaful gun, and she kept leaving the damn thing behind. "We're not looking for trouble."

"That's good, because if you were, you'd find you were out-matched." The one at the front lowered their gun. "What are you doing out here?"

Honesty seemed like the best option. Partial honesty, anyway. They didn't need to know she was a scrounger. "We came to check on a piece of wreckage from the recent ship that came down. The storm hit before we could leave."

"And did you find what you were looking for?"

Jessa lowered her hands to her sides. She looked exhausted. "Dead people. Nothing more."

The person at the front pulled their face cloth down. "That's what we found, too." The others lowered their weapons and Kylin could breathe again. "Looks like you could use a shower."

Jessa looked at Kylin, who nodded. Her flyer wasn't going anywhere, and all she could hope was that no one would take off with what she'd managed to scrounge so far. It wasn't like they were city center. Someone would have to come looking for her flyer, and that wasn't likely.

"That would be wonderful, thank you."

The group turned and moved off ahead of them, and to her surprise, Jessa reached out and took Kylin's hand. Only then did she realize Jessa was scared. Her hand trembled even though her eyes looked calm. Kylin squeezed her hand and kept hold of it. She'd assumed Jessa was soft, ill-suited to life in a harder world, but there was a bit of steel in her, a subtle strength that wasn't a facade. She was scared but tough. It was an intoxicating combination.

"Are we safe with them?" Jessa asked softly.

Kylin considered the question. "I think so. They're generally a pretty peaceful people, but watch what you say and how much you give away. People are people, and you get good and bad like in any community. Slavers would pay big money to someone willing to sell a ship's captain. Especially an attractive one. Even if you do look like a mud monster right now."

Jessa shook her head and gave Kylin's hand a squeeze. She'd tried to lighten the statement, but she needed Jessa to know that the career she took so much pride in could get her into real trouble here.

"*You* look like a mud monster," Jessa mumbled.

Kylin laughed, and one of their new friends glanced back at her. She gave them a little wave and they turned away. They'd walked for about half an hour before they finally arrived at the walled city of Thalla. Jessa stopped and looked up at the towering stone walls.

"Protective of their city, I think you said."

Kylin shaded her eyes against the sun. "You'll find out that I'm very rarely wrong. It's annoyingly charming."

Jessa gave her a quick smile as the forty-foot stone gates swung open and they followed the Thalla group into the city. The gates swung closed behind them, and Kylin's gut twisted. They couldn't just leave if they wanted to, and her flyer was out there alone. She forced herself to focus. They were in a new city with an armed guard.

They stopped at a simple white building with black timber windows. "Go on in. The innkeeper will help you out." The woman who had taken off her face cloth tilted her head. "I'll be back around dinner time to chat."

She and her group walked away, and Kylin turned to Jessa. "Shall we? Even if they decide to execute us later, I'll be glad to die clean."

Given the look on Jessa's face, the joke wasn't appreciated.

They headed into the inn and a woman stood at the foot of the stairs, waiting. Her eyes were kind but wary. "Room three is all set up. I'm afraid the other rooms are in use, so you'll have to share. Dinner is in an hour, down here to the left."

Kylin led the way up the stairs. She wasn't entirely sure where they stood. The people with the guns had walked ahead of them, not behind. That suggested some measure of trust and that they weren't necessarily prisoners. But it wasn't like they were welcome guests either, and they'd clearly comm'd ahead to say they were bringing people in. In Quasi, people came and went all the time, and suspicions were only raised if it looked like they were going to be trouble. Here, it looked like you had to prove you weren't trouble before they invited you in.

She opened the door to their room. It was clean, the furniture all looked like hand-carved wood, and the bed…there was only one. The feeling of Jessa in her arms rushed through her, and she cleared her throat. "You want first shower?" That brought with it an image of Jessa in the shower and her knees went weak.

"Thank you, yes." Jessa hesitated by the door like she was going to say something else, but then just gave a quick smile and closed the door behind her.

Kylin blew out a breath and pinched the bridge of her nose. Stupid. It was stupid to think of Jessa as anything more than a quick side note to a fruitful trip. A knock at the door interrupted her thoughts of Jessa in the shower.

The innkeeper stood there with a pile of white cloth in her hands. "I thought you might need something to wear. If you'll leave your things outside the door I'll get them cleaned up for you. Storm mud is practically impossible to get out."

Kylin accepted the white clothing, holding it at arm's length so she didn't get dirt on it. "That's incredibly kind of you, thank you. I'm Kylin, by the way."

"Sherta. I own this place, and the woman who directed you here is my mate, Liselle. I'm sure she didn't introduce herself." Her smile suggested she knew just how they'd been greeted. "Give me a shout if you need anything." She walked away, humming quietly as she went downstairs, her long skirt flowing around her.

Kylin ducked back into their room and tapped on the bathroom door. "I've got some fresh clothing here, if you want it."

Jessa opened the door and stuck her hand out. Kylin put the cloth in her hand and sighed when the door closed. Not even a glimpse… She looked out the window at the street below. Thin, flowing fabrics with patterns that varied from intricate to subtle seemed to be the fashion here. Kylin was only somewhat familiar with the Thalla people, mostly through stories told by people who had encountered them on their travels to Quasi. But the people going about their lives outside appeared to be normal folks. There wasn't an atmosphere of fear or violence. Just, life.

The bathroom door opened, and Kylin turned around to see Jessa come out towel drying her hair. Kylin leaned against the door and tried to keep her expression neutral.

Jessa's hair, loose and clean, looked even softer. It framed her beautiful face perfectly and highlighted the deep green of her eyes. The loose white robe had a deep V-neck that showed the generous sides of her breasts. Kylin swallowed hard, unable to look away.

"As much as I appreciate the look in your eyes right now, it's you who looks like a mud monster." Jessa's tone was teasing, but her voice was husky in that way Kylin loved when a woman was turned on.

Kylin moved past her, careful not to touch her for more reasons than not getting her dirty again. "Sorry. Wasn't looking, really. Right. Be out in a minute." She turned on the shower, stripped off the filthy clothes, and moaned out loud when the hot water sluiced the grime from her. As she washed she thought of Jessa doing the same, and the way her curves would feel soapy and wet. She let her imagination run and leaned against the cold shower wall as her fingers found their way to her clit. She got off in record time, making sure she didn't make a sound. She couldn't face Jessa if she had any idea that she'd driven Kylin crazy.

A little more relaxed and in control once again, she put on a loose pair of white pants and a long, loose shirt. The material was incredibly soft and felt like a lover's touch caressing her everywhere at once. It didn't help the flame that jumped to life when she came out and saw Jessa reclining on the bed.

Kylin turned away and gave herself a mental slap. She gathered her dirty clothes, along with Jessa's, and put them in a pile outside their door.

"Feel better?" Jessa asked.

Something in Jessa's tone made Kylin grin. "I do. There's nothing like getting clean after you've gotten really dirty."

Jessa blushed but didn't look away. "Do you have someone in Quasi?"

It was an innocent enough question, but it was like being doused with ice water. It was also a timely reminder to think with the right part of her body. "Not anymore, no." She looked at the timepiece. "Should we head down to dinner?"

Jessa frowned slightly. "Sure."

She felt bad for shutting the conversation down that way when it felt like something might be opening between them. The flash of hurt in Jessa's eyes made her uncomfortable, and she put her hand on Jessa's lower back as they made their way to the dining room, hoping the gesture would be taken as the small apology she meant it to be. She was both pleased and frustrated when Jessa pushed back into her touch.

The smell of cooking food was divine, and the spread on the table looked heavenly. Sherta motioned them in. "Have a seat. Liselle will be here any second." She set drinks in front of them then disappeared into the kitchen.

Kylin leaned close to Jessa, trying to think past the way she looked and smelled. "It just occurred to me that we don't have a story about who we are together." She'd told Jessa not to say she was a ship's captain, but she hadn't told her what she should say.

Before Jessa could answer, the front door opened and closed and they heard Liselle shout from the front. "Anyone home?"

Sherta came out with a huge smile on her face, and when Liselle entered the room she practically threw herself into Liselle's arms. "I missed you."

Liselle gave her a lingering kiss. Kylin knew it was polite to look away, but she couldn't. They made a striking couple.

"I missed you too. Our guests give you any trouble?" She looked over Sherta's shoulder and winked at Kylin.

"Only in the fact that they brought half the storm back in their clothes." She gave her another quick peck and then moved away. "Dinner is just about ready."

Liselle took off her coat and rested her energy gun against the wall in the corner.

"Thank you for bringing us to your home," Jessa said.

Liselle nodded. "Sorry about the welcoming committee, but we're careful about who we bring in, and when the lookouts said there were people in the storm, we had to wonder who would be crazy enough to come this way at the start of storm season. I made a judgment call that you weren't a threat." She looked between them before leaning toward Kylin. "I saw your mark." She looked toward the door and lowered her voice. "I trust we're good, scrounger?"

Kylin winced. Her mark had been with her for so long she'd forgotten about it, and no one had asked about it in years. She rubbed at the raised scar between her thumb and forefinger. "We're good. I never take anything that isn't given freely anymore. Just a youthful indiscretion." She saw Jessa glance at her hand and covered the mark with her other hand.

Liselle sat back and turned her attention to Jessa. "And just to make things clear, I don't need some convoluted backstory about who you are. I recognized your uniform. Sherta and I took a trip for our honeymoon, and we sat at the captain's table." She gave Kylin a disbelieving look. "I can't believe you let her walk around wearing it. Dangerous move."

Kylin's stomach turned. She hadn't even thought about what Jessa's uniform would tell people. She never thought about clothing much beyond its function, but that V-plunge in Jessa's robe was enough to make her start paying close attention. And like Liselle said, it was an amateur move to not suggest she change.

"*Let* me?" Jessa said, her head tilted and her cheeks pink. "I'm not sure how you do things in Thalla, or on this planet in general, but no one *lets* me do anything. I've got a fully functional mind, thank you."

Liselle put her hands up in surrender. "Bad choice of words, sweet lady. No disrespect meant. But as the person you're traveling with, for whatever reason, she should have suggested that you change into something less conspicuous, given that she knows what a slaver's squad would do to get to you."

Seemingly mollified, Jessa sighed. "I should have changed the moment she told me about that issue, but I didn't think of it. It was my responsibility and I wasn't paying attention."

Responsibility. That was a word Jessa used a lot, and Kylin wondered if there was much she didn't feel responsible for. Other than another planet's poverty, of course.

"Well, it's taken care of now." Sherta put a dish of food on the table and gave Liselle a look of mild reproach. "Let's enjoy dinner."

The food was delicious, and when Kylin asked about the city, the rest of the meal was spent hearing anecdotes about some of the city's oddball residents. She felt Jessa relaxing beside her and was glad she wasn't scared anymore.

After dessert, Liselle poured some flaxberry wine. "Now it's your turn. How does the captain of a pleasure cruiser end up in the storms of Thalla with a scrounger?"

Kylin turned to Jessa and let her start.

"We were on our way to Andine when we were hit by an unexpected asteroid strike. It was in the glare of a solar flare, so we didn't catch it in time to move above it." Jessa picked at her napkin. "It did so much damage so fast. We managed to get everyone off ship and into escape pods before the ship came apart. But then our escape pod took an asteroid hit as well, and this was the closest planet."

Sherta put her hand over Jessa's. "How terrifying. And how amazing that you lived through it."

Jessa took a deep breath and smiled at Sherta. "It was, and it is. If it weren't for Kylin, though, I'm not sure we would have lived much longer."

The look she turned on Kylin made her breath hitch, and the softness of her hand over Kylin's made other parts twitch.

"She saved us from the prowlers in the forest, from other scroungers, and ultimately from the slaver's nets."

It sounded so heroic when Jessa said it like that. But that wasn't how it felt. She'd just done what was right, and even that she'd regretted here and there. She shrugged and didn't say anything. She liked the version of herself Jessa saw.

Liselle looked at them speculatively, her fingers under her chin. "So…why were you out at the wreck?" She pointed at Kylin. "You were scrounging, weren't you? No harm in that." Then she looked at Jessa. "But why would you risk coming way out here?"

"I needed to see if there were other survivors from escape pods that crashed here. Kylin was going to check out other areas where pieces of the ship had come down, so I came with her."

That left out the blackmail bit, but Kylin didn't mention it.

Liselle nodded and accepted the drink Sherta handed her. "Makes sense. A little foolish, really, but makes sense."

Kylin wondered how trustworthy this couple was. Her instincts about people were rarely wrong, and they seemed okay. And it wasn't like they had a whole lot of options. "I was heading to the Doreen Mountains next. How bad is the storm sand when it's packed in like that?"

Liselle looked apologetic. "Sorry, friend. That storm was a bad one and you didn't have any kind of buffer. If you want, some of the others and I can go back out with you tomorrow and assess the damage. But if I had to guess, you won't be leaving in it any time soon."

That was pretty much what Kylin had expected, but it still hurt. To be grounded, to have her plans go black hole, not because of an enemy she could fight, but because of a stupid storm…she wished she was in one of Orlin's fights right now. Her shoulders ached with the need to hit something. "I'd appreciate that, thanks. It okay if I get some air?"

Liselle nodded like she understood, and Kylin looked away from the empathetic look Jessa sent her. Kylin went onto the porch and sat on the step. She rested her head in her hands and tried to calm the rage inside. What the hell was she going to do now? If she was on her own it would be bad enough, but now she had Jessa to worry about too. She'd told her she'd leave her behind if she didn't keep up, but that was bravado talking. She'd let her come with and now she was responsible for her. There was that word again. But hell, she was safer here in Thalla than anywhere on the planet with Kylin, so now she could decide how to take the next steps on her own. So why did the thought of leaving her behind make Kylin so uncomfortable?

Chapter Eight

The morning was clear and the sunlight through the curtains created pretty patterns on the walls. Jessa had crawled into bed not long after Kylin had gone outside, and she'd barely registered when Kylin had slipped into bed next to her. When a soft knock at the door had woken her, she'd been curled up against Kylin, with Kylin's arm wrapped securely around her waist. She'd never woken with anyone before, and it was both novel and extremely comforting.

She'd rolled over and watched as Kylin pulled on the borrowed clothing, quickly covering the hard body that was hard to appreciate fully in the dim light. Even in the dark she could sense the stress and worry she was feeling. When she left the room Jessa wrapped herself in the thick blanket, but it was nothing like the deep warmth of Kylin's body against hers. When she woke again what felt like hours later, it was from a nightmare of falling from the sky and into a gaping black hole that would tear her apart. Someone reached for her, and she knew if she could just stretch a little farther...

She blinked back the tears filling her eyes. A black hole would have been quick, at least. Here, she was surrounded by things she didn't understand and a hostile environment she felt dreadfully unprepared for. If only she'd spent some time on the planets where she'd docked and learned more about the cultures there, maybe she wouldn't feel so out of her depth. She got up, showered, and dressed in her borrowed clothes. Downstairs, the dining room was empty so she headed into the kitchen. Sherta stood at the table, her hands in a massive wooden bowl filled with what looked like blue goop.

"Good morning." Sherta nodded toward the counter. "Help yourself to a drink."

Jessa poured herself a steaming mug of tea and murmured in appreciation. "Can I ask what that is?"

Sherta pressed and pulled, pressed and pulled, and then lifted a piece of material from the goop. "It's a special material we make only in Thalla. You noticed how soft what you're wearing is? The material itself comes from the farms and then we weave it and dye it using different types of softening rinses, like this one. We're the only ones on the planet who make it."

The pride in her voice was clear and made Jessa smile. "It's beautiful and so incredibly soft. I've never felt anything like it in all the planets I've been to."

Sherta's smile could have lit the room. "That's possibly the best compliment ever. Thank you."

Jessa sat at the table and watched in comfortable silence as Sherta worked the material. Eventually, she asked, "How did you and Liselle meet?"

She knew right away it wasn't a good question to have asked. Sherta pulled back slightly and looked away.

"I'm sorry. That was insensitive. I never ask about people's personal lives. I know better. Please forget I asked."

Sherta shook her head. "It's just a sensitive subject, that's all. It's a sweet story, in a way." She pulled the material from the goop and placed it in a different bowl, one with white goop in it. "I was a nomad. Have you come across them yet? Then you have some understanding of what that means. Total freedom. It can be a hard life, but it's built on community and love." She smiled. "That sounds a little silly, but it's true." She pulled up a thick wooden spoon and began to swirl the material in the white goop. "And then one day we were attacked by a slaver's caravan. Nomad tribes are kind of forbidden territory for the slavers. It's an unwritten rule that we're left alone. But this caravan didn't care. Most of my tribe got away, but I wasn't so lucky."

She pressed the material into the bowl and then turned to wash her hands. Jessa couldn't imagine the pain the story still brought with it, and probably always would. "I'm so sorry."

"It's not your fault, is it?" Sherta shrugged slightly. "I was taken to the docks in the slaver's nets and put on auction with some others. Thank the universe Liselle was there selling material to merchants. She saw me on the auction block and spent every linari she'd made on the material to buy me."

Jessa wasn't sure how to process that. "But you're not a slave now? And who buys slaves here? Do the slaves get taken from a particular group?"

"No, I'm definitely not a slave now. And she never treated me like one. By the time she brought me back to Thalla, I was in love with her and didn't want to go back to my tribe. Or what was left of it, anyway. I knew I wanted to be beside her for whatever years we have left here. As for who buys slaves…" She made a disgusted sound. "The people with money. People in the Heathers often have slaves, as do some of the outlier cities and villages. It's outlawed in Thalla, and I think it's outlawed in Quasi, too, except that if people have them when they arrive they're allowed to keep them. And who gets caught in the slaver's nets? People associated with cities are usually safe. The slavers don't want anything to do with angry families or politics. But anyone outside the walled cities, in the villages or towns, are often slavers targets. People alone, outsiders, people who can't fight back. People who come here for a new life, but don't make it to one of the cities fast enough." She gave a long, deep sigh. "Anyway, I'm incredibly lucky that the worst moment of my life turned into the greatest blessing."

It was a beautiful story, and Jessa smiled at the romance of it. How rare a pairing like theirs must be.

"What about you? Have you and Kylin…" Sherta raised her eyebrows and grinned.

Jessa felt the heat flood her face. "Cosmos, no." She tilted her head as she thought. "I suppose, in a roundabout way, our story is a little like yours, except for the love part. I was in a terrible situation, and she saved me. She took me with her when she could have left me behind."

Sherta's expression was inscrutable. "And now?"

Jessa sighed and let her shoulders slump. "Now…I don't know. She's been exceedingly kind—"

"And she's as sexy as a Rohemian in a naked stage show." Sherta wiggled her eyebrows.

"Well, yes, and that." Jessa smiled. "But I'm afraid I'm a weight around her neck. In the flyer I wasn't such an inconvenience, but now it will be two of us trying to get to wherever she's going next." Jessa hated the thought of being a burden.

Sherta got up to stir the material. "And you don't want to go to Quasi without her?"

Jessa could see exactly where this was going. "Oh no, you don't. It's not that I don't want to be without her in the way you didn't want to be without Liselle. I just trust her, and she was checking out the wreckage of my ship. Nothing else."

Sherta crossed her arms and was about to say something, but before she could the front door opened and Liselle and Kylin came in.

Jessa's heart sank at the forlorn look in Kylin's eyes. She wanted to go to her, tell her it would be okay. But she couldn't cross that line.

"Bad news?" Sherta asked.

Liselle hung up her jacket and set down Kylin's pack before taking Jessa's from Kylin and setting it next to it. "The flyer is caked. It's going to take weeks to get it all cleaned out, and then there's no telling how much damage has been done to the engine."

Kylin sat at the table next to Jessa and put her head in her hands. "The thing is, we're really far away from Quasi. Without a flyer it's going to take us ages to get back, and I have an appointment I have to keep no matter what. I'm going to have to leave the flyer behind and find another way back."

How much that hurt Kylin was clear. "And all the things you put on board, to sell at the marketplace?"

Kylin sighed heavily. "I guess I have to leave them behind, too. Most of it is too heavy to carry any distance."

Liselle pulled Sherta onto her lap and wrapped her arms around her waist. "If you trust us, we'll drag your flyer into Thalla for you and start cleaning her out. We can store your things until you can come back to get them."

Kylin looked up, obviously surprised. "You'd do that for me? But I'm a stranger."

Liselle looked up at Sherta. "Sometimes strangers become the best things in your life."

Sherta smiled at her and kissed her forehead softly. Uncomfortable with the display of affection, Jessa looked away, but she saw Kylin smile at the scene.

"That would be truly incredible, thank you. I'll owe you."

Liselle laughed. "Spoken like a scrounger from Quasi. Here, you don't have to owe someone who does something just to help you out." She looked between them. "In fact, there's plenty of room in Thalla. We could really use someone with your talent for building, and, Captain, I'm sure we could find something you'd enjoy doing here, too."

Kylin reached across the table and squeezed Liselle's arm. "I can't tell you how much I appreciate the offer, and if things in my life were different I'd take you up on that in a heartbeat. But I have obligations back home. Maybe one day though." She turned to Jessa. "That's not to say you shouldn't stay here. It's a good place, a safe one. They'll get news if a transport is planned from the Heathers and they'll help you get there."

Jessa wasn't tempted for a second. "If you go, I go." She didn't miss the look Liselle and Sherta shared, but she dismissed it. She didn't need to analyze the reasons for her desire to stay beside Kylin. She just knew it was where she needed to be. And, of course, she wanted to get back to her crew and figure out the next step.

The fact that it was a side note in her thinking was disturbing, but not something to be dealt with at the moment. For now, she'd concentrate on what Kylin wanted to do next and on helping her do whatever that was. If she hadn't been determined to check for survivors in the pod, they might have been able to fly ahead of the storm and get out of there. It was going to take longer to get back, and thinking of the extended time with Kylin sent a thrilling, if somewhat confusing, chill through her. Perhaps it was time to start looking at this as a difficult adventure rather than a trial to get through.

CHAPTER NINE

Kylin stared at the map, desperately trying to figure out the fastest, but safest route. The problem was that those two things didn't seem to fit together. One route was fast, but certain to get Jessa caught in slaver's nets. One route was safe, but would take them too long. She told Orlin she'd be back, and she wasn't about to risk her dad's safety by being late.

She heard footsteps overhead and rolled the tension from her shoulders. Sleeping beside Jessa had been torture. She'd been fast asleep when Kylin had come in, and she'd been careful not to make too much noise. But once she was under the covers next to her, the scent of her, the way her hair spread across the pillow, and the cute little sounds she made while dreaming all served to make Kylin think thoughts she really shouldn't be thinking. Like of rolling over and making it so Jessa made entirely different types of noises. When she'd woken later and found Jessa's thigh pressed against her own, she'd shot out of bed so fast she'd nearly fallen off it, and her thigh felt branded by Jessa's touch.

Since then she'd been in the kitchen, staring at the map and trying to figure out if it would be possible to leave Jessa behind. Surely she could just refuse to take her with? If she categorically said no, then what choice would Jessa have but to stay behind? After all, Kylin had to come back for the flyer, so she could just pick Jessa up after she'd done what she had to do in Quasi. It was the best idea, but she had a feeling Jessa wouldn't go for it, though she wasn't sure why.

Liselle came in, yawning, her hair tussled. She patted Kylin on the shoulder as she passed. "Morning brew?"

"Please." Kylin waited until Liselle set the steaming mug in front of her and sat down. "Sherta still asleep?"

"I wish. She went out on patrol last night. She won't be back for another hour or so."

Kylin looked at her in surprise over her mug. "Wow. Don't you worry? I wouldn't have thought you'd be okay with that."

Liselle shrugged and sipped from her own mug. "Of course I worry. Just the same way she worries about me when I'm on patrol. She may look soft, but let me tell you, under all that gorgeous hair and those perfect curves is a soul of rock. She survived the slavers because she's stronger than I'll ever be. I could no more keep her from going on patrol than I could stop the second sun from rising next month." She tilted her head. "And I wouldn't want to. I'd never do anything to take away her spirit or independence. She may not be a fighter like you and I, but she's a fighter nonetheless."

Kylin sipped her drink and thought that over. She had a feeling Jessa and Sherta were a lot alike. If she forced Jessa to stay behind, if she simply left without her, would that be taking away her choice, her independence? Or would it be protecting her?

Liselle laughed. "I can see the wheels turning in your head, and I have a feeling I know what's going on in there. If you don't mind some advice, stop overthinking it. She's strong and can make her own decisions. Trying to control the situation, or her, will make things very bad for you, my friend." She winked knowingly.

"I don't want her blood on my hands if we get caught up in something and she gets hurt." That was simplistic, but Kylin knew Liselle would read between the lines.

"I get that. But like I said, these soft looking women are stronger than Nyxian steel. Leave her behind, and it will hurt her a lot more." Liselle turned her attention to the map. "Which way you headed?"

Kylin ran her hands through her hair. "I can't find a decent route."

Liselle studied the parchment, tracing lines in one direction and then another. "What about the water?"

Kylin frowned. "Going down to the docks seems like a bad idea."

"Normally, I'd agree." She tapped the map. "But if you can get on a ship headed for the Falls, you could get off at the edge of the nomads' lands when they stop to trade. From there it would hardly be a walk at all, if you can't catch a ride with the nomads in the area." She leaned forward. "Is whatever you're running back to so important you can't stay here and clean up the flyer?"

"Yeah. No other option." Kylin met Liselle's serious gaze, and she knew Liselle understood. She nodded once and looked back down at the map.

Kylin searched the map, looking at all the places of potential pitfalls. But of the options, Liselle was right. It was the best one. If, that is, they could avoid the slavers and manage to get on a fairly respectable ship. "Getting past the slavers isn't going to be easy."

Liselle rocked back in her chair and grinned. "Unless you blend in."

"Are you insane?" Jessa crossed her arms, her eyes blazing. "Because that sounds like insanity."

Kylin held up her hands. "I know how it sounds. But if you'll stop and think about it—"

"Only on this planet would disguising me as a slave seem like a good way to travel."

"Jessa, listen to me." Kylin waited until Jessa huffed and sat on the edge of the bed. "Thank you." She sat down beside her. "Liselle is right. The fastest way back is by water, and once we're on a ship bound for the Falls, we'll also be fairly safe. But in order to get onto a ship without hassle we'll have to blend in, and the best way to do that is if it looks like I've bought and am transporting a slave. I can't look like I'm selling because then we'll garner too much attention. But if it looks like you've already been bought, people will be less likely to stop us."

Jessa stared at her. "It's ludicrous. And I don't like it."

Kylin sighed and flopped backward onto the bed. "If you can come up with another way, I'm listening." She waited, but there was only silence until Jessa got up and moved to the window. She wasn't crazy about the idea either, but she was less enthralled with the idea of Orlin showing up at her dad's place. She needed to get back.

"And there's no way you can stay here and repair the flyer?" Jessa turned away from the window to look at her. "What's so important you have to get back quickly?"

Cosmos be damned. Kylin had hoped she wouldn't ask. The thought of Jessa knowing what kind of life she really led made her feel ill, and she wasn't about to share information about her dad. Information meant power, and she knew firsthand what someone having that power over you looked like. "I have business. I told someone I'd be back, and I always keep my word."

"The woman with the sharp teeth. The one you made a deal with to get my crew to Quasi."

It wasn't a question, so Kylin didn't respond, even though that hadn't been the person she was worried about. Thanks to Jessa, though, Kylin remembered she had Maana to connect with when they got back too. How much more out of control could her life get? It probably wasn't good to speculate.

Jessa sighed and sat back down next to Kylin. "Okay. I can see the logic. You've done nothing but steer me right so far. If you really think this is the best way, I'll go with it."

Kylin stared at the ceiling. "The best way is for me to go alone, and for you to stay here in Thalla with these really nice people in this really safe city." She sat up and looked at Jessa. "If I promised to come back for you as soon as I could, would you stay?"

Jessa stared down at her hands for a few minutes before responding. "You saved my life. You could have let me run past, but you didn't. And you've made a deal you've already suggested isn't beneficial to you with that woman, a deal you made to help us." When she looked up, tears were running down her face. "I feel safe with you, and if you're willing to keep me around, then I'd rather be mostly safe with you than completely safe without you."

The unexpected and clearly heartfelt response left Kylin speechless. Being someone's safety blanket was a hell of a responsibility, but she'd live, at least until she delivered Jessa to the Heathers. She gently wiped away Jessa's tears. "Then I think we need to borrow some clothing."

Together they went downstairs. Liselle was in the living room looking at a vid screen, and Sherta lay on the couch beside her, her head pillowed on Liselle's lap as she slept.

"Agreed?" Liselle asked.

"Agreed." Jessa still didn't look happy about it.

"Clothes are in boxes in the kitchen." Sherta spoke with her eyes still closed. "Try some stuff on and we can help you make sure it's right before you leave."

They headed to the kitchen and dug into the boxes without speaking. It was extremely clear which boxes were meant for which role.

Jessa held up a short, sheer dress that left little to the imagination. "Tell me why I can't be the owner and you the slave?"

Kylin smirked and nodded at the material in Jessa's hands. "I think I'm a little too tall and muscular to pull that off. And, frankly, no one on the planet would believe you could overpower me. Not to mention you're clearly an outsider, and outsiders here are always considered weaker."

Jessa put her hands on her hips and glared at her. "I'll have you know I'm trained in level three combat."

Kylin grinned and moved around the table toward her. "And have you ever had to put that combat into practice?" She moved closer and looked into Jessa's eyes. "If I grabbed you right now, like this," she grabbed Jessa's wrists and twisted them around so that Jessa's back was pressed against her, "what would you do?" she whispered in Jessa's ear.

Jessa tried to yank her arms away, and then went to stomp on Kylin's foot, but Kylin knew it was coming and moved. Her height and weight advantage were enough to make it so Jessa couldn't get any leverage. When she finally stopped struggling and slumped against Kylin's chest, she let her go and squeezed her shoulders. "And that's why we'll be playing the roles we'll be playing."

She turned away, and then the world went sideways as Jessa kicked at the back of her knees and got her right arm twisted behind her, turning her so she hit the floor facedown. Jessa's knee pressed into her back. "Never underestimate a woman used to commanding a ship through space."

Kylin laughed, more than a little turned on. "Yes, ma'am."

Jessa got up and sighed. "But I take your point." She turned back to the boxes. "And I'm wearing the least offensive thing I can find."

It took them a little while longer to find what they were willing to wear, and when they went back into the living room, Sherta and Liselle were talking softly.

Sherta stood and went to Jessa. "I'll help you dress. It's important you get it right." She led Jessa away into a different part of the house.

Liselle cocked her head. "I've got something you need to see." She held up a folded piece of paper. "We had a feeling you might want to see it alone first."

Kylin frowned and took the paper. When she saw what was on it her knees went weak and she sank onto the couch. "Cosmic shit."

"Yeah." Liselle nodded at it. "Want to tell me what it is?"

Kylin reread the words printed in bold under an old picture of her.

Reward: 20,000 linari to bring fugitive back to Quasi alive and relatively unharmed.

The contact was listed as Orlin. "I don't get it. He didn't want me back until sometime next week. Why would he put a reward out for me?"

"Sherta did some quiet asking around. It seems you owe this person a debt, but someone saw you leaving Quasi in a flyer, so there's an assumption you were running."

Kylin's stomach churned with anger and frustration. "I hadn't even considered that that's how it would look. I just planned on checking the wreckage and then heading back."

"Twenty thousand linari is a hell of a reward." Liselle spun a small wooden ball on the table, not looking at Kylin. "That could get someone into a new life."

The saliva dried in Kylin's mouth and every muscle tensed. "Tempted?" Is that why Sherta had taken Jessa into another room? So Kylin couldn't grab her and run?

"Dumb prowler." Liselle grinned. "If we were tempted we wouldn't have told you about it. I just wanted to mess with you." Her expression turned serious. "That said, there were others who were with me when we brought you in. They're good people, but that's a lot of money. So we'd better get you on the road fast. Are you going to tell Jessa?"

Kylin closed her eyes and pinched the bridge of her nose. "Would you?"

"Doesn't matter what I would do." She shrugged. "Sherta says you're not even together, right?"

"Right." Kylin wasn't about to say she'd been thinking about that subject herself. "And that means I don't owe her any explanations."

Liselle looked like she didn't agree. "But she's in this with you, and she should know that you have to watch your backs, and not just from slavers."

The fact that she was right was as bitter as lickweed. "She knows we're watching our backs. Maybe that's enough."

Liselle stared at her for a long moment before she shrugged. "It's not my place to give advice. We don't know you well enough. But an extra set of eyes making sure no one grabs you when she thinks you're safely on ship wouldn't be a bad thing." She held up the jacket Kylin had picked out. "Want some help getting ready, lover scruff?"

Kylin felt her face flush and rolled her eyes. "I think I've got it, domesticated lap safira."

"Ha! I love safiras. Their fur is the best, and they have sex just because they want to, unlike other animals." She raised her eyebrows. "And I'm happily domesticated, believe me. One day, I bet you will be too."

Kylin shook her head as she headed to the bedroom. "Not likely, buddy. Not likely." As she laid out the clothes on the bed she wondered where they'd gotten them. She knew the slave clothing had probably belonged to Sherta from her time in the slaver's nets; Liselle had told her a bit about it when they'd gone to check on the flyer. But the outfit in front of her spoke of wealth. The insignia wasn't one she was familiar with. The set of overlapping triangles surrounded by six dots wasn't from the Heathers, or any of the other wealthier zones she knew. Maybe it was something from off planet. The colors weren't the usual ones found here, either. They were richer, deeper. She took off the borrowed white clothing and put it aside. The loose black pants were simple but incredibly comfortable and a reasonable fit. The loose black shirt was equally soft and buttoned down the front. The tunic that went over it was a deep purple with a flowing black pattern woven into it. Her own black boots worked just fine, since she could barely see them under the loose cuffs of the pants. When she looked in the mirror she stood a little taller. The deep purple offset her light eyes and the black made her skin glow. She looked like she might belong in the Heathers. She turned sideways and straightened the collar of her shirt, and the mark on her hand caught her eye, bringing her back down to earth. Clothing might make a difference on the outside, but nothing would ever take away the life she'd lived to this point. And maybe that's all she'd ever be, a scrounger from Quasi playing dress up. And now they were on the run, too. If anyone captured her, Orlin would add that debt to her tab, and he'd no doubt have some of his crew teach her a lesson. But worse than that, she wouldn't be able to protect Jessa, and that wasn't acceptable.

She turned away from the mirror, the pit in her stomach an old friend. It was time to find Jessa and start their trip back.

CHAPTER TEN

Jessa turned sideways and then backward, looking over her shoulder. The outfit showed the least amount of skin of any of the clothing available in the box, but she felt nearly naked. This was something the women in the fantasy vids they had in the dark rooms on ship wore. Not real people walking around in daylight.

The long, loose skirt was a fine, thin material that changed from pale cream to see-through depending on the way the light hit it. The matching top was cut in a low V in both the front and the back so that she had to move carefully lest the material shift and expose her. It, too, was see-through depending on the light.

Sherta's eyes were wide. "That uniform you had on definitely didn't show..." she waved her hands up and down Jessa's body, "this."

Jessa tucked a loose piece of hair behind her ear. At least the length of her hair helped cover the open back, and if she pulled it forward it could cover most of her breasts, too. "I'll take my uniform over something like this any day."

Sherta laughed. "I can't wait to see Kylin's expression."

In truth, neither could Jessa. There was no doubt it was sexy, and though it wasn't at all Jessa's thing, she could see how someone might find it attractive. And she wanted Kylin to find her attractive, even if that was pointless.

Sherta held up a thick band with a silver ring on it. "This is the worst part, but if you're supposed to be an owned slave, you're going to have to wear it."

Jessa took it from her and examined it. Silver threads ran from both sides of the silver ring to silver blocks at the ends that were clearly meant to fit together. An insignia with a set of overlapping triangles surrounded by six dots was engraved in the metal. "Tell me about it?"

Sherta looked haunted, her gaze staying on the piece in Jessa's hands. "It's electrified. The owner has a remote that controls it, and if the slave acts out or tries to run, they simply activate it, sending jolts of electricity through the slave's body. It keeps people very compliant. The insignia is specific to the person who owns you, and is also a tracking device should the slave run."

Jessa dropped it to the bed. "And I'm expected to wear it?" She didn't want it anywhere near her.

"Yes." Sherta picked it up and held it out again. "But yours isn't electrified. Kylin will have a dummy remote just for show. You'll never feel that kind of pain..." She drifted off, and it was easy to see she was lost in memories.

Jessa took the band and rested her hand awkwardly on Sherta's shoulder. She'd never been good at emotional communication. "I'm so sorry." When Sherta gave her a small smile she turned away and went to the mirror. She put the band around her neck and the two ends slid into one another easily. She didn't like the constriction, but at least it wasn't too tight. She'd take it off the moment they were out of danger. She pulled on the soft leather boots that went up to her knees and was glad for at least a little bit of coverage.

She turned to Sherta. "Thank you for helping us. Indemnion's reputation seems merited in many ways, but then there are people like you living in cities like this. If people knew—"

"Then they'd bother us and we would have no peace at all." Sherta got up and held the door open. "Let's go see how your scrounger is getting on."

They made their way downstairs and Jessa wondered if what Sherta said was true. Was there some element of good that came from Indemnion's reputation? Did it mean the planet remained free from the constraints the other planets faced from severe and sometimes uncaring governments? But wouldn't it be worth giving up some of those freedoms in order to abolish things like slavery and poverty? The questions were too big to contemplate just now.

They entered the living room. When Liselle and Kylin saw them come in, Jessa was gratified to see Kylin's eyes go wide as she slowly stood. Even Liselle looked a little shocked and then quickly looked away abashed when Sherta elbowed her in the side.

"Wow. That's...wow." Kylin crossed her arms and then let them drop again, only to then run her hands through her hair.

"I take it the farce will be seem viable, then?" Jessa asked, turning in a circle so Kylin could get the full effect. When she'd turned all the way around, she saw that Kylin had sat back down, her eyes still wide.

"Sorry, what?"

A feeling she'd never had stole over her. It was raw and sexual and made her want to straddle Kylin's lap. And this time when Kylin stood up again, Jessa took in what she was wearing and it was her turn to need to sit down, though she didn't.

Kylin was the handsomest thing Jessa had ever set eyes on. The clothing she wore was clearly expensive, but that wasn't what did it. Rather, it was the way she wore it. Confidence radiated from her, and she looked like she could own any room she was in. She'd put in something that lightened her hair, and glasses hid the gray of her eyes. Jessa had never believed in the romantic ideals the vids promoted, but in this moment she was ready to fall to her knees and beg the woman in front of her to never let her go. The insignia on Jessa's collar matched the one on Kylin's lapel, and there was something strangely comforting about the visual connection between them.

Liselle cleared her throat. "Now that we've got that out of the way."

Sherta's hand was over her mouth to cover her obvious smile. "You'd better get on your way before you burn our house down." She tilted her head as she looked them over. "You both look the part."

"There's one thing, though, and we hope you don't mind that we took care of it." Liselle pulled aside the curtain and nodded toward a young man sitting on the porch. "That's Nef. He's my nephew, and he's going to be your assistant. A rich person wouldn't carry their own bags, and they're too big for your slave to carry on her own." She let the curtain go. "I'd trust him with our lives, and I trust him to get you to the docks. You'll have to find another servant to replace him once you're on board."

Jessa hadn't given much thought to what would happen after they stepped outside the house, and the fact that they had was both a relief and daunting. She could run a ship. Surely she was capable of helping plan their way back. She needed to get herself under control, even if there wasn't much she could do about her situation. "When do we set out?"

Liselle pulled over a map and handed Kylin a linari card. "You've got enough daylight left to go now, and that linari chip will get you passage. I hate to say it, but you should leave the seaful gun here. Rich people don't travel with weapons." She glanced at Kylin. "And given what we talked about earlier, it's best if you don't linger."

Jessa didn't miss the quick glance Kylin gave her before nodding at Liselle and holding out her arm. "Thank you. For everything. I'll return, and I'll pay you back in full."

"Believe me, I know you will. And I'll want to hear all about it." She grasped Kylin's arm with her own. "Send word if you can to let us know you made it back."

Jessa gave Sherta a tight hug. "I hope I see you again."

There were tears in Sherta's eyes. "And I you."

With that, there didn't seem to be much else to say. They went outside and Nef stood, his hands in his pockets. He nodded at them but didn't say anything.

"Nef isn't a talker." Liselle gave him a soft smile. "It'll take you about two hours to get to the docks, and Nef will take you to the ship heading to the Falls. We've put some food and drinks in this bag." She handed a coarse sack to Jessa. "We've also put your old clothing in your bags. Nef already has them. Good luck."

Kylin led the way down the stairs, followed by Jessa and Nef. "See you soon."

Jessa turned back once before they turned the corner and saw Liselle and Sherta watching them go. She waved and they both waved back. The three of them continued to walk in silence, and as they passed beneath the enormous gate leading out of the city, Jessa wondered at her sense of loss. She'd known those people for all of two days, but she felt like she was leaving true friends behind. For someone who'd never had a genuine friend in her life, it made no sense, and that added to the sense of unreality about this entire situation. Who would she have been if she hadn't been a captain? Would she have been a sentimental, emotional leaf lover? She didn't think so, but as she brushed away the few tears that fell, she couldn't help but wonder.

CHAPTER ELEVEN

K ylin's mind raced with possibilities. She was an imposter, and if she couldn't pull it off, it could get both of them captured. And if anything happened to Nef, she'd never forgive herself. He carried their bags like they were simple bags of grass, not everything they could carry with them from the ship. He seemed like a quiet, gentle boy, and Kylin wasn't sure Liselle should have sent him on the trip.

The ground was dry and the sky was clear, with the distant multi-hued nebula a beacon leading them in the right direction. Jessa walked silently beside her, obviously lost in her own thoughts too. This was the least dangerous option, but it felt like they were walking straight into a prowler's mouth. She ran every scenario she could think of and tried to come up with solutions, but the truth was, there was no way to know what they'd face.

"You look completely different." Jessa's voice was soft.

"Is that a bad thing?"

Jessa glanced at her and then back to the red dirt road in front of them. "Not good or bad. Just different. Do you feel different?"

Kylin hadn't even thought about it, other than the need to make it believable. "Maybe." She tugged at the expensive material. "I've never worn anything this fine. I like the way it fits, and I can see why people walk around like they're invincible when they're dressed like this." She shrugged. "But it doesn't change who and what I am."

"And who would you say that is?"

"A scrounger from Quasi. If you knew more about this planet, you'd understand that says just about everything." The words were hollow and left a bitter taste in her mouth.

They walked quietly for a while before Jessa shook her head.

"No. I don't think so."

Kylin raised her eyebrow. "You don't think what?"

"That that's all there is to you. I mean, I've only known you a little while, but I've seen how you are with people. And how they are with you. They care, and you obviously care about them too. You've let a stranger come with you rather than leave her to fend for herself, and you could have left me behind yet again, but you've acknowledged my request and let me come." She touched Kylin's hand briefly. "I think you're more than you may know. And those clothes look like they belong to you."

Kylin wasn't sure what to say. It was too intimate, too…close. She nearly thanked the cosmos out loud when Nef stopped and turned to them.

"We're going to start seeing people. You should walk behind her three steps, and keep your eyes down. And make sure to keep your life-sign covered. It's high tech and will draw attention," Nef said to Jessa. He looked at Kylin. "And you should walk with your head high, like no one here is worth your attention."

"Thank you, Nef." Kylin squeezed Jessa's hand. "If things go ass-end-up, run. Make your way back to Liselle and Sherta's."

Jessa bit her lip and nodded. She was pale and Kylin felt her hand tremble in her own. It was actually good that she looked frightened. It played into her being a captured slave, so Kylin didn't offer any more reassurances. She adjusted the light, lacy coverings over her forearm to make sure the deep blue of her life-sign was covered, then nodded to Nef, who turned and set off ahead of them. He was right. Within ten minutes, they began seeing others on roads merging with theirs. A cargo vehicle rumbled by, the cages full of shocked looking people in the back swaying precariously. Other slave owners were being carried or wheeled toward the docks, and a few nodded imperiously at her as they went past. She gave an aloof nod in return, but her stomach roiled. She tuned in to the sound of Jessa's boots in the dirt so she knew she was there.

As they got nearer to the docks, the crowds grew thicker and Kylin pulled Jessa closer and held on to her arm. She'd seen other slave owners do it, so she knew it wasn't unusual. Nef stopped and started in front of them, scanning the boats and electric readouts above them that stated where they were headed. Toward the end, he stopped in front of a smaller boat that was clean and neatly laid out. Several young people Nef's age sat to the side. Nef looked them over and then approached one. Kylin couldn't hear what was said, but Nef returned with the person in tow.

"This is Asol. She'll take my place aboard ship, if it suits you." Nef bowed his head respectfully.

Kylin looked the girl over. Her hair was shorter than Nef's and her body was all lean muscle. Her eyes were intense and intelligent, and Kylin wondered if she should chance it. A dumb one with little curiosity would be better.

"We went to school together," Nef said quietly.

So he trusted her. Kylin went to hold out her hand but Nef's quick, subtle shake of his head reminded her of her place. She looked down her nose at the girl. "She'll do."

Nef handed over the bags and the girl swung them easily over her back. Kylin saw a man standing at the top of the gangplank and walked straight toward him as though she had every right to board his ship.

"I'd like passage for myself, my slave, and my errand girl to the Falls." She waited to see what price he named. Did rich people haggle? Surely they wanted to hold on to the money they had?

"We've only got the one cabin left. Your girls will have to sleep on the floor of your room or in the hold with the other slaves being transported." He looked over Kylin's shoulder and leered at Jessa. "Or she could sleep in your bed. I know that's where I'd want her."

Kylin kept her fists at her side and reminded herself their lives depended on her staying in control. "Why would I get a slave like this one and not keep her in my bed? Or at my feet. Or wherever else I want her." She tried for a smile but knew it fell flat. It didn't seem to faze the captain.

He nodded and rocked back on his heels. "It will be twelve hundred linari."

Kylin swallowed the disbelief and rolled her eyes. "For a cabin with one bed?" She looked over her shoulder. "We'll find another transport."

He held up his hand. "You can't blame a man for trying."

She stared at him, waiting. She wasn't about to counter offer. That only got you in trouble.

He sighed dramatically. "Eight hundred linari. And I'll have your breakfast served to you each day."

"I have a servant to get my breakfast. Five hundred linari and new sheets. I don't want your crusty dead bed bugs anywhere near her perfect skin. She cost me more than your boat and lives are worth."

He looked Jessa over again, and Kylin prayed she was keeping her eyes down. She knew full well the fire that would be raging in them.

"Six hundred and new sheets." He held out his arm.

Kylin looked at it askance and barely touched it with her own. She handed him the linari card. "Where is my room?"

He swiped the card through a reader that flashed green and then handed it back to her. He called out to a young man mopping the deck in lazy circles. "Take these three to cabin two." He gave them a mocking half-bow. "Welcome aboard."

Asol followed the deckhand with their bags, and Kylin fought the desire to give Nef a parting glance as she pulled Jessa along behind her toward their cabin. The ship was well taken care of. At least the trip wouldn't be made in a leaking barrel. The deckhand opened the thick wooden door to their cabin and walked away without a word, though Kylin didn't miss the quick side-glance at Jessa.

The cabin was nicer than her apartment. The bed could easily fit all three of them, but there was a hammock hanging from a beam and pile of blankets on the floor clearly meant for servants. A decanter and glasses sat on a heavy wood table with a bowl of fruit in the middle. When the door closed behind them Kylin let her shoulder's drop and took a deep breath. She nodded at Asol. "You can leave the bags against the wall."

The girl placed the bags gently against the wall before she turned to Kylin. She looked at her for a moment before stepping close. "If you don't mind my saying, you should allow me to get you gloves. Your mark will set you apart if anyone notices. It's not unheard of for a scrounger to become wealthy enough to own a slave, but it will draw attention just the same." Her voice was soft, the expression in her eyes far older than her years.

Kylin froze, uncertain whether to acknowledge the farce or forge forward. She studied the girl and saw a kind of hunger she recognized. "That would be much appreciated. Do you have time before we set sail?"

Asol held out her hand and Kylin handed her the linari card. "There's a stall two boats down. I'll only be a moment."

Kylin watched her go and then turned to Jessa, who was pale and silent. She led her to the bed. "Hey, sit down. You okay?"

Jessa let out a shaky breath. "There's something incredibly disconcerting about being nearly naked and pretending to be vulnerable. Because it's not pretending, not when people look at you like they've been looking at me. I can't imagine what Sherta went through. This is..." She trailed off, her gaze on the floor.

Kylin understood people looking at her that way; Jessa was stunning. But there was no need to go into that now. She rubbed Jessa's hands between her own. "We're a few days from my home. We'll stay in the cabin as much as possible, and once we're back in Quasi we'll get you something to wear that you're comfortable in. Just hold on." In truth, she didn't want Jessa to take that outfit off, and if she could bed her right now she'd gladly do it. The idea would make for sweet, if frustrating, dreams.

Jessa looked around the room, seeming to come back to herself. "It's not exactly luxury, is it?"

And there it was. The reminder of the vastly different lives they led. She let go of Jessa's hands and stepped away. If Jessa thought this was bad, what would she make of Kylin's actual living quarters? Nothing good, certainly. She went to put her hands in her pockets but was met with smooth material. Apparently, rich people didn't need pockets.

"Will the girl come back?" Jessa asked.

Kylin shrugged. "Hopefully. Nef seemed to trust her, and all we have to go on is people's recommendations." Faced with the girl's assertion about her mark, she'd given over the linari card without thought. But when she thought about it, and the look in the girl's eyes, she knew she'd be back. Kylin moved to the porthole and looked out at the busy ship next to them. Slaves in heavy silver collars were being shoved aboard and into cages lining the deck. Her stomach turned and she sat next to Jessa on the bed.

"What did she mean, about your mark?" Jessa asked, her finger tracing the raised flesh between Kylin's thumb and forefinger. "Liselle mentioned it too, but I haven't seen anyone else with one."

Before Kylin could think of an answer she was willing to voice, the door opened and Asol slipped in. She handed Kylin a pair of thin black gloves and the linari card. She also held up a small bag.

"I took the liberty of getting some food. The captain runs a tight ship, but he won't pay for a decent cook. And I'm guessing you don't want to be out there," she motioned to the door behind her, "any more than necessary."

Kylin slipped on the gloves, which fit perfectly, and tucked the linari card into the pocket inside her jacket. "That was good thinking, thank you."

Jessa smiled at Asol. "Nef was right to pick you."

Asol's laugh was full and low. "We got into some scrapes over the years. Don't let his quiet act fool you. He listens and he learns. He taught me to do the same." She pulled at the hammock and expertly slid into it, swinging from the thick rafter. "If it weren't for the fact that you were traveling with him, I would have thought you were exactly what you appeared to be." She grinned. "Until I saw your mark, anyway."

Kylin sighed. It was a stupid oversight, and one that could have cost them greatly if anyone had noticed. The girl had possibly saved their lives. "And you just like to serve and sail?"

She turned toward them in her hammock. "I did. But if you're going to Quasi, then I'm in. I've always wanted to go there, but I didn't want to try it alone."

Kylin frowned. "Why would you want to go to Quasi? Why not go to Thalla?"

"Are you cracking wise?" Asol sighed and tucked her arms behind her head as she looked at the ceiling. "Quasi has freedom. You can be what you want, with no one telling you what to do. And there's no slave trade." She glanced at Jessa. "There I have the chance to be whatever I can make myself. Thalla is too rigid, too boring."

Kylin didn't have the heart to burst her bubble, but at some point she should really have a talk with the kid. She had no idea there was some romanticized version of Quasi, and the truth of it being a place where you could become anything you wanted was a far cry from what Asol wanted to believe. But for now, she'd let it go.

There was a knock at the door, and Asol was out of the hammock in a flash. She motioned for Kylin to sit and for Jessa to move away. Instead, Jessa knelt in the pile of blankets beside the bed, staying close to Kylin.

Asol opened the door, her eyes down, and the captain's big form filled the doorway.

"To your liking?" he asked, leaning against the doorframe, his eyes on Jessa.

"It will do." Kylin steeled herself. "When are we setting off?"

"About five minutes." He finally looked away from Jessa. "Let me know if there's anything you need." He turned away, whistling, and Asol shut the door behind him.

Kylin had a bad feeling about him, and as she helped Jessa up from the floor she considered grabbing their stuff and getting off the ship as fast as they could. But she heard the shouts and the sound of the anchor being pulled up and their chance was gone.

Asol went to climb back into the hammock but stopped. "Sorry. I should have asked. Would you like to use this?"

Jessa looked from Asol to Kylin, her eyes wide.

Kylin shook her head. "Go ahead." She smiled at Jessa, hoping to put her at ease. She still looked like prowler prey hiding in a bush. "We can share the bed, if that's okay with you? It's big enough we won't crowd each other. And that way neither of us has to sleep on the floor."

Jessa's look of relief made Kylin wonder if Jessa really thought she'd have to sleep on the floor. Or was the reaction due to something else? Kylin pushed the thought away. Life-and-death situations weren't great places for romance.

Night fell as they pulled away from the dock and the lights of the shore receded. Soon the lapping of the waves and the sound of swooping night tishes looking for fish was all they could hear. As if by agreement, there was no conversation, and Jessa huddled with her knees against her chest, her arms wrapped tightly around them.

The bell rang for dinner, and Asol slid from the hammock with a yawn. "Want me to bring it back here?"

Kylin nodded and she left the cabin. When she was gone, Kylin took Jessa's hands in her own and gently pried them from their grip around her knees. "What's going through your mind? Talk to me."

Jessa's eyes were glassy. "It's not pretending to be a slave, though that's pretty awful. It's watching all the people being sold off. It's bad enough when it happens to animals. But the people…" Her breath came out in a shudder. "They looked haunted. And resigned. None of them looked like they had a single ounce of fight left in them."

Kylin understood. "I've seen that look myself. I'm really sorry this was the easiest way. But I don't think they had any clothing that would have suited a rich lady."

Jessa nodded and wiped away her tears. "I know. I do." She covered her face with her hands. "You wouldn't believe how much I just want to be back on my ship right now, heading for some stupid planet with no slavery and no animals who eat people and no red mud storms…"

If there had been a way to get Jessa to exactly where she wanted to be, Kylin would have done it in an instant, just to stop her tears.

"And…" Jessa took a deep breath. "I feel so stupidly weak and out of place. I'm always in control. I run ships through light speed. I've spent years moving thousands of people from one planet to another. I can do anything." The tears began to fall again. "But here, I have no idea what I'm doing. I'm like a newborn that has to be carried and watched. And I hate it. My parents would be so disappointed in my emotional state."

Now, that one Kylin couldn't relate to. She might not always like what she had to do, but she always knew what she was doing and why. Well, except when it came to women. That was something she messed up a lot. "I can't imagine how weird and hard this is for you. But I promise I'll keep you safe and do everything I can to help you get back to where you want to be."

Asol came in with a tray of food. She was right. It looked like something the cheapest stall in Quasi would sell, and it was anything but appetizing. Asol dug through the bag she'd brought on board and held up a loaf of kell. "This should help."

Jessa tilted her head. "What is it?"

Kylin accepted the chunk Asol ripped off and handed her. "It's made from a plant we use in most everything on this planet. Spiced right, it can be excellent." She sniffed hers and took a bite. "And this one is perfect." She held a piece to Jessa, who looked at the thick green slab with suspicion.

She took a bite and her expression turned to surprise. "Better than it looks."

They ate in companionable silence, and Kylin felt some of the tension leave her shoulders. They were at sea, so they were safe for a little while. She could sleep beside Jessa tonight and have uninterrupted thoughts of her beautiful body and perfect smile. She could deal with reality when they were back on land.

CHAPTER TWELVE

Jessa stirred, slowly coming awake. It was still pitch-black outside the porthole window, and she looked around, trying to figure out what had woken her. Her heart began to race when she saw Asol standing beside the door, a knife in her hand. She held her finger to her lips and Jessa nodded.

She reached behind her and shook Kylin's leg, but she didn't take her eyes off Asol.

"What is it?" Kylin asked softly.

Asol shook her head and Kylin moved around Jessa to get off the bed. She slipped on her pants and shoved her feet in her boots. What Jessa wouldn't give for something more to cover herself with. She settled for wrapping the blanket around her.

Kylin moved quietly next to Asol and listened at the door. Jessa could hear the whispers but couldn't make out any words. But whatever they were, it put Kylin and Asol on edge. The voices faded away and Kylin and Asol came back to where Jessa waited.

"What's going on?" Jessa asked.

Kylin sighed and pinched the bridge of her nose. "I was hoping I wouldn't have to say anything because I didn't want to worry you. But there's a bounty on my head—"

"What?" Jessa stared at her. "And you didn't think to mention that little nugget?"

Kylin held up her hands in surrender. "Like I said, I was hoping it wouldn't be an issue. Someone back in Quasi thinks I took off without paying a debt and they want me brought back. It seems some of the ship's crew saw the poster."

Jessa wasn't sure how to respond. The situation couldn't have been any further from her experience, and she couldn't fathom what it meant for someone to put a price on your capture.

Asol turned away and grabbed their bags. She handed one to Kylin. "By morning we'll be heading to shore so they can chain you and claim the bounty. If you'll trust me, I think I can get us to safety. We need to go."

Kylin stared at her for a long moment, then nodded. She turned to Jessa. "The outfit you're wearing is redundant now. If you have something in your bag to wear instead you should probably change. You can wear my jacket if it's a uniform."

Asol rummaged in her own sack. "If it's not beneath you, you could borrow some clothes from me. A uniform would be a bad idea."

A jet stream of thoughts ran through Jessa's head, but she couldn't focus on a single one. Silently, she took the proffered clothes from Asol and turned away to slip them on. All she had in her bag was extra uniforms. She didn't even own any civilian clothing; she'd never needed any. On ship she slept naked, and each day she put on a fresh uniform. Some were more formal than others, which was her only concession to dressing down.

Even though the clothes Asol gave her were clearly meant for the underclass they were still the same softness as the ones she'd been given in Thalla. She had to roll the cuffs of the loose pants so they didn't drag, the sleeves went well past her fingertips, and the deep V-cut showed a little too much cleavage, but it was warmer and far more comfortable. She sighed in relief and tugged her boots back on.

She turned around to find them waiting. Kylin tucked the sheer slave outfit into a bag, and then turned to Asol. "We're all yours."

Asol grinned. "If only that were true." She winked, then moved to the back of the room. She reached under a low shelf, and the sound of a latch clicking echoed in the room.

A chill wind blew in and Jessa could see the waves outside. "We're at sea. How can we possibly escape?"

Asol crawled through the hatch and disappeared beyond it. "Throw me your bags," she whispered loudly enough for them to hear over the water.

Kylin pushed their bags through and then crawled through the hatch herself.

Jessa closed her eyes. She'd abandoned ship as it tore apart in space. She could certainly do it now. Kylin's hand was there for her as she crawled out of the hatch and into the night air. They were standing on a small deck on the back of the boat. Beside them, a rowboat bobbed in the black water. Their bags were already inside, and Asol held out her hand.

Kylin jumped in and together they helped Jessa into the boat. It rocked and bucked and Jessa steeled herself. Survive now. Panic later.

Asol untethered the rowboat and shoved away from the main ship. She grabbed the oars and started back-rowing, and it wasn't long before the ship was far beyond them. Once they were clearly safe, she turned to Kylin.

"So, fugitive and captain. Where to?"

Kylin shrugged and looked at the sky. "I'm not a sailor. I have no idea where we are."

Asol looked up, and Jessa did as well. She gasped and leaned back to get a better look. Stars lit the entirety of the black night sky. The distant moons sat low on the horizon, like they were floating on the edge of the sea. It was breathtaking, and a view she'd never considered while flying through the stars themselves.

"I'd say we're about a day's row from the Falls, that way." Asol pointed. "I think they'd already gone off course, which is actually better for us as far as getting to land."

Kylin continued to stare at the sky, and slowly, she began to smile. "You know, I think I have a better idea." She pointed toward a particularly bright blue star. "Head that way."

Asol frowned. "I didn't save you just to get lost at sea. There's nothing out there."

Kylin shook her head. "Oh, but there is. Volare."

Asol's laugh was forced, her eyes wide. "That's a myth, an old sailor's tale. Nothing more. We should head for the Falls."

"What is Volare?" Jessa could tell from Kylin's expression she wasn't going to give in on this. "What myth?"

Asol slapped the water with an oar. "There have been stories about the Volare for centuries. Practically since the first ship touched down here. It's an island of people who can fly, fierce warriors and families who raise their young in trees." She cocked her head at Kylin. "It's a myth."

Kylin pointed. "I've been there. It's not a myth. And I spent a lot of time looking at the stars when I was there. If you follow the waves to that star, we'll get there, and probably before morning. They'll look for us at the Falls, but they'll never find us on Volare."

Asol's eyes were wide. She began to row. "You've been there. To Volare. To the flying people. I hadn't taken you for crazy."

Kylin shifted to straddle the seat and she pulled Jessa against her. She wrapped her coat around her, and Jessa pushed into the warmth with a murmur of thanks. She'd been so caught up in the conversation she hadn't noticed how cold she was, but now she could barely keep her teeth from chattering. Kylin's body heat soon helped, though.

"It was when I was a teenager. I was messing around a lot, always in trouble. I fell in with a bad crowd, and I stole a boat from the harbor one night. We were all drunk on brackenwine, and it seemed like harmless fun when they dared me to do it. But I got caught in the stem tide and was pulled out to sea."

Asol whistled. "That's a death sentence if no other ship comes along."

Jessa could picture a young, wild Kylin realizing she was in trouble, and it made her pulse race.

"And no ship came." Kylin wrapped the jacket tighter around Jessa. "I spent three days spinning and turning in the tide, and I had no idea where I was or which way was home. I was sure I was going to die, and that I'd never get to tell my father thanks for all the things he'd done for me."

The sadness in her voice was so clear, so deep, Jessa ached for her. She pressed against her and Kylin smiled down at her.

"I was lying on my back when a shadow passed over me. I thought I was just blacking out at first, but then it happened again. Right before I passed out I felt someone lift me out of the boat." She laughed. "When I woke up, I thought I'd died for sure. I was in the softest bed I'd ever been in, and it was high in a tree. When I looked down, I saw people going about life down on the ground, but then I saw that they were also flying from tree to tree. It was...incredible."

"How were they flying? What do you mean?" Jessa had flown throughout the universe, but she'd never heard of beings who could fly without a ship of some kind.

"Their kind were here before other races came along and spread out. They used to be all over the planet, but when the settlers came, they brought disease and violence. Many of the Volare were killed. They're peaceful and kind, not really warriors at all. So they retreated to the island they live on today, and they developed a way to keep a permanent fog around it, so it's never seen by passing ships, though not many go that far off the shipping routes anyway."

"But how do they fly?" Stories of colonization and native species being inundated by settlers were common conversation pieces on board her ship, particularly among the more educated classes. Jessa hadn't given much thought to them, other than the fact that it seemed to be the way life worked. Someone always took what someone else had.

Kylin laughed. "They have large pieces of skin that run from the tops of their thighs to their wrists. It's foldable, so you don't necessarily notice it until they lift their arms to fly. I guess it's more like dropping and riding the wind currents. They can't just lift off from the ground the way a bird can."

Although they were in a tiny boat in the middle of the ocean on a black night, and although they were running from people who were determined to capture them, Jessa was absurdly glad for this detour. She wanted to see these people, and given that Kylin had been there before, it meant they'd be welcome.

"So, how do we know we won't pass it by like all the other ships do?" Asol asked, not even a little out of breath at the rowing she was doing.

"Because I know where to look." Kylin held her hands up in front of Jessa in a pyramid shape. "We'll see a rock that looks like this. We get close to it, and the fog should be thick beyond it. We'll stay at the rock, and they'll find us."

"And if they don't?" Jessa asked.

"They will." Kylin looked up at the stars. "They will."

Kylin kept her eyes on the stars and took over rowing when Asol finally looked done in. The stillness of the sea was broken only by the sound of the oars parting the water and caressing the sides of the little boat.

Jessa sat in the bottom, Kylin's jacket pulled tight around her. She frowned even in her sleep and Kylin wondered what kinds of things filled her dreams. She looked all kinds of cute in Asol's clothing, which was far too large for her, and something about the V-neck that showed her cleavage was almost sexier than the sheer slave costume she'd had to wear. Asol, too, slept, and Kylin bet her dreams were full of adventure. Though Asol had been glad to accompany them, Kylin felt responsible for her now. Joining them when Kylin was being hunted hadn't been part of her plan, but now she was stuck with them, which meant her life would be in danger too.

Kylin closed her eyes and sighed. Life had already been complicated enough. Now it was totally upside down. When they got to Quasi... No. She couldn't think that far ahead. They had to find the Volare first. And she hadn't been quite truthful about the welcome she expected from them. She'd left in a hurry last time. Before she could ponder those old details, the pyramid shaped rock seemed to come out of nowhere, and she swore as she corrected the boat just in time to keep it from crashing into the old weathered stone. Instead they scraped along it, waking Asol and Jessa with a jolt.

"Sorry." Kylin looked up at the rock and saw the small caves and ledges the Volare used to teach their young to fly. At the top, she saw the shadow she expected as the lookout left from the rock to fly to the island. She raised her voice and called to the sky.

"I'm Kylin Enderson from Quasi. I'm seeking assistance from the Volare."

They waited, but there was no immediate answer. Kylin hooked an oar on the rock, effectively anchoring them.

"Now what?" Asol asked, looking at the rock anxiously.

"We wait." Kylin laid the other oar in the boat. "We won't find the island unless they come for us. But they will." Once again, Kylin didn't mention the possibility they might not want her company again.

Time crawled by and Kylin watched the stars slide across the sky. The first breath of dawn lit the horizon when a shadow made her look up. A tall, thin figure was backlit so she couldn't make out their features, but there was no question they weren't built like ordinary people as their wings blocked out the light.

Asol and Jessa moved closer together.

"Take this." The figure threw the end of a rope to Kylin, who tied it to the boat without being told.

The figure turned away and climbed higher on the rock, then leapt from it, the other end of the rope in their hand.

Kylin heard Jessa gasp and Asol swear softly. She remembered just how awestruck she'd been the first time she'd seen it happen. These creatures were myths and to see them in person was astounding.

The boat moved slowly into the mist and Jessa's leg pressed against hers. She pressed back, strangely glad to be sharing this moment with her. The fog lifted like a curtain, and once again, she heard her companions react.

"Welcome to Volare," she said, smiling as she remembered the first time she'd seen it.

"It's like something out of a children's story," Jessa said, her eyes wide.

"Or a pirate's." Asol leaned forward, clearly trying to take it all in.

Kylin thought it could be both. Brightly colored birds of all shapes and sizes filled the air. Rose, purple, sky blue, and onyx crystals lined the shore and distant hills, causing the sun to scatter into rainbows across the sky and land.

"So, did you say we'd be welcome?"

Asol's tone made Kylin focus, and it definitely wasn't rainbows she saw.

Instead, a group of Volare waited at the dock, and one in particular looked less than welcoming. Kylin remembered him well. As she did the woman beside him.

The boat bumped into the dock and the rope was quickly tied off. She got out and helped Jessa and Asol out of the boat before she took a deep breath and faced their welcoming group.

"Tulvia te Suow, it's good to see you again. Thank you—"

"You've got the udders of a prowler to show up here again." He crossed his arms and glared at her. "I told you not to come back."

Kylin winced. "You did. I'm sorry, we had no choice."

He grunted when the woman beside him pushed past him and held out her arms. "Personally, I'd say you're very welcome, Kylin Enderson."

Kylin breathed a sigh of relief and stepped into her embrace, resting her forehead against hers for a moment before she turned to Jessa and Asol.

"This is Fina te Suow and her father, the leader of the Volare, Tulvia te Suow." She felt Fina's arm slide around her waist and saw the flicker of annoyance in Jessa's eyes that nearly made her laugh out loud. No matter what was or wasn't between them, reading a woman's emotions when it came to other women was something Kylin was exceptionally good at. "And this is Captain Jessa Arabelle and our..." She hesitated, unsure how to refer to the young woman who had thrown her lot in with them now that the charade was over. "Asol. She's traveling with us to Quasi."

Asol's eyebrow lifted and she grinned. "Nice to meet you."

Fina tilted her head and looked at Jessa. "Not a captain from our world, I don't think, no matter how you're dressed." She turned to Kylin. "It sounds like you have much to tell us. Let's get you settled in the main hall and you can have roosting hour." She motioned toward two others waiting nearby. "Please take their things to the hall."

She turned and walked away, and her father simply huffed and walked away beside her. Kylin smiled as the group passed through rainbow after rainbow. She dropped back to walk beside Jessa. "You okay?"

Jessa glanced at her before turning back to the landscape. "I realize I'm not entitled in any way to information about your past…"

"But you'd like to know what that was about." Kylin was surprised she'd asked so soon, given her feelings about not intruding on people's personal lives.

Asol came up beside them. "I definitely want to know, entitled to it or not."

Asol's grin suggested she'd already figured a little out, but Jessa looked puzzled.

Kylin kept her voice low. "Remember the story of how I ended up here?" They both nodded. "Well, I was a wild kid. I was also insanely curious and a big fan of pretty women. Fina was my age, and we hit it off right away. Her dad wasn't crazy about her having a mainlander friend, but he went with it. The princess doesn't have a lot of friends here. It's very rigidly structured." She felt that old flush of excitement and desire when she thought of the many ways they'd found to explore who they were. "Until the day he walked in and found us going at it on his throne."

Jessa and Asol laughed and Fina looked over her shoulder and winked like she knew the story Kylin was telling.

"He got me on a boat headed home within about two hours. There was lots of stuff about ruining the princess and disrespecting the throne." Kylin shrugged and grinned. "Totally worth it." She sobered, remembering the long, quiet boat ride home. "But it meant knowing I'd never see her again." She shook off the old memories like sand from Thalla. "Funny how life works."

"Funny." Jessa's frown line was back and her tone was pensive.

Kylin wasn't sure how to read the deeper parts of Jessa yet, but when Asol shook her head and gave her a good-natured smile, she figured it had something to do with the way women often dealt with her. But then, why would Jessa be jealous of a lover from so long ago? Why would she be jealous at all?

CHAPTER THIRTEEN

Jessa couldn't take it all in fast enough, and her thoughts whirled and spun away before she could shake any sense from them.

The people were tall and lithe, their faces long and their eyes round with varying shades of iris. As they made their way deeper into the island, through thriving woodland and over lush grass, she concentrated on the sounds she was hearing. Although there were plenty of words she understood, there were also clicks and trills, a range she couldn't comprehend.

Children ran alongside them, jumping from high rocks and spreading their arms in little bursts of flight. Thanks to the loose, thin shifts they wore Jessa couldn't see the wings Kylin had spoken of, nor did she want to stare and seem intrusive. But when they got to a more crowded area she stopped walking, making Asol bump into her from behind.

The trees were full of massive nest type structures. They were round and made of what looked like branches and twigs, but instead of being open to the sky they were enclosed except for open windows. Wooden walkways connected some of the structures, and as Jessa watched someone flew from one tree to another, landing gracefully in front of the door.

"It's really something, isn't it?" Asol said softly. "Wonder what the crystals are for."

Jessa hadn't given them any thought, other than for their beauty, but now she saw that each house had at least one large crystal poking from the side. For the first time in her life, she wanted to ask questions, to understand people and their way of living. On the ship, other cultures, other lives, were simply conceptual. Sure, she had to deal with passengers and their needs, and she'd picked up information here and there from those interactions, but she was coming to realize that there was only so much words or infograms could convey. Being in a place and breathing it in made it altogether something else.

They followed the leaders of the Volare through what looked like a door built into a tree easily the size of her ship, and once again she was stunned by the beauty around her. Platforms and rooms went up the branches as far as she could see, all arranged around a middle area with nest type seats on a raised stage. Plenty of Volare were already on the platforms or in the little rooms, and there was an expectant hush as they entered, which was quickly replaced by loud conversation when they left the open space and entered a series of larger rooms off to the side.

Tulvia turned to face them, still scowling at Kylin. "Your room is there. I'm putting all three of you in the same room so we can keep an eye on you. I won't have the same…disruption in my home again. Though Fina is married now, as she should be."

Jessa wondered what the brief flash of emotion in Kylin's eyes meant, and she nearly smiled at the way she blushed and ducked her head in acknowledgement, but she figured it would be bad form to laugh at his indignation.

Fina shook her head and gave Kylin's arm a squeeze. "I'm looking forward to catching up. You can refresh yourselves, and we'll see you in an hour for roosting time." Her expression was gentle, her smile kind. "I'm glad you've come back."

If emotions were physical things, Jessa could have grabbed hers and stomped on them to deal with them. But they weren't, and so the jealousy that flared through her and made her want to grab Kylin and press against her, claiming her, was something out of her control. She wouldn't analyze it right now, though. It could wait, and when Fina left, she found she could breathe a little easier.

Kylin sat on the bed and motioned at the other two. "You'll be amazed at how soft they are. We don't have anything like this on land. They're stuffed with the petals of a plant that grows only here."

Asol flopped backward and moaned. "Can we take a mattress with us when we go?"

Kylin laughed. "It's not something I had time to ask before. Maybe this time we can."

Jessa wandered around the room, touching the branches and small green shoots in the walls. At another door, she found what she guessed was a bathroom. She looked over her shoulder at Kylin, who nodded.

"The tree absorbs whatever you put in and takes it directly back into the soil. The shower is stored rainwater."

It was ingenious as well as beautiful. Asol jumped up and moved to Jessa's side. She whistled. "Think it would be okay if I washed the sea off?"

Kylin nodded. "Go for it."

Asol was already tugging off her shirt, and Jessa turned away but not before she saw the long, angry scars on Asol's back.

"No complaints here." She closed the door behind her.

Jessa sat on her own bed, confused. "Her back…" She wasn't sure what else to say.

Kylin sighed. "She's free, but she's also an orphan. It's amazing she didn't end up in a slaver's net, but she must have come across a bad master or two."

The thought was nauseating. "But why would anyone do that to a child?"

Kylin's expression was hard to read. "Not everything is perfect like it is on Othrys. Most planets have injustice, and the weak and young are easy pickings. The rest of us get by as best we can, and most of us don't make it through without a few scars."

She was rubbing at the mark on her hand, and Jessa wondered if she even knew she was doing it. "Can I ask what yours means?" This world was making it so she asked questions she'd never dream of asking if she was aboard ship, but then, it was imperative she understand her surroundings. At least, that was an acceptable excuse, though she knew deep down it wasn't entirely accurate.

Kylin looked down at it, seemingly surprised that she was rubbing it. "I was scrounging in a part of the city I shouldn't have been in. People don't like you going through their trash, even if they don't want it. I found a piece of jewelry, something that didn't look like it should have been thrown out. I figured it had to be a mistake. So I took it up to the house." Her eyes were hard and far away as she retold the story. "When the lady answered, I showed it to her, said I found it in the trash. She dragged me inside and called the police. Told them I'd stolen it and was trying to get a reward for something I took."

"That's barbaric." Jessa could picture young Kylin, trying to do the right thing, trapped in a situation of her own making.

"Yeah, well, when the police came I explained and even though I think one of them believed me, the lady insisted something be done. So they agreed to brand me." She closed her eyes, her voice soft. "It shows people that I'm a scrounger who isn't above theft. It means they keep a closer eye on me and anyone with a good reputation won't trade with me."

Unable to keep her distance, Jessa knelt in front of Kylin and stroked the mark that looked like a tool with a cross through it. When Kylin shivered, she looked up into her eyes and saw the pain of the memory had been replaced with something else…something that made her close her eyes and lean up—

"That shower is the best thing since Thrallish silk." Asol came out wiping water from her face with a green towel but stopped when she saw them. "Sorry. Always bad timing."

Kylin smiled down at Jessa and gently pulled her hand from Jessa's. "Or the right timing, depending on what direction you're looking from."

Jessa flushed, stung at the thought of being something to avoid, and moved past Asol. "I'll shower now as well."

She closed the door behind her and leaned against it. What was she thinking? Was it just the outlaw persona that attracted her? Or was it the vulnerability? Whatever it was, the situation was already difficult enough without adding something personal into the mix.

And then there was Fina, and Jessa knew enough to know that whatever Kylin felt for the flying princess wasn't gone, at least not completely. Why did that make her feel so insecure? She'd be leaving this planet as soon as possible, and to be jealous of a woman like Fina was illogical. She was Kylin's past, and even if she were Kylin's future, too, Jessa had no say in it.

She let the shower run over her. There wasn't a temperature control, but the water was perfectly warm. She let it wash the salt from her skin and hair, and by the time she got out she felt like herself again. Asol's clothes still felt clean and warm, and she was grateful not to have to give them back just yet. She'd never thought of her uniform as restrictive, but spending time in clothing here had made her wonder if she could make some changes to her uniform once she was back on a ship.

Kylin was lying on her back, staring at the ceiling, and Asol was snoring softly. Jessa sat on the edge of Kylin's bed. "Thank you for sharing your story with me."

Kylin's expression was searching. "You asked."

"I did. And I'm glad I did." She picked at a loose thread on the blanket. "I can't pretend to understand this world, and I won't say that I don't find some of its customs abhorrent. But I will say that I'm learning things in a way I never thought I needed to, and that's a very good thing." She looked up from the thread. "Thank you for showing me new things."

Kylin nodded, still watching Jessa carefully. "My pleasure."

There was something beneath her words, something that spoke of more interesting things to learn, and despite telling herself repeatedly it would be a bad idea, she wanted to know what those things were.

A knock on the door interrupted them, and a young Volare stepped inside. "If you're willing, roosting hour will begin soon and the princess requests your company."

Jessa moved away and Kylin got off her bed and gave Asol's shoulder a little shake. "Time to perform."

Asol looked completely awake as she jumped from her bed and stretched. "Let's do it."

As Jessa followed Kylin and Asol out of the room and into the main hall, she tried to push away thoughts of Kylin's presence being requested by the princess again later, and in far different circumstances. For now, she had another experience to pay attention to. She could think of Kylin's physical attention when she was in her own bed tonight.

There was a hush when the three of them joined the princess and her father on the stage. Soft trills and chirps echoed, but they too fell silent.

Tulvia stood, his hands clasped in front of him, and looked at the people around them. The silence grew uncomfortably long before he began to speak. "As you've all heard the whispers on the wind, you know we have guests tonight, and that is a rarity. We know one of them, and so we know their intentions are...harmless." He glanced at Kylin, who tilted her head and gave him a wry smile. He motioned at the empty chairs. "Please join us for roosting hour, where we tell the tales of our heritage, but tonight will hear yours instead."

Jessa sat beside Kylin and Asol sat on her other side. She wondered if she looked as overwhelmed as Asol did. It was the first time she'd looked nervous, and that didn't help Jessa's nerves in the slightest.

"Kylin Enderson, you know our ways. Tell us what brought you here." Tulvia's command was simple but clear. This wasn't just about storytelling. It was about reassuring the people they were there under peaceful terms.

She stood, her hands clasped behind her. "Thank you for taking us in, Prince Tulvia." She smiled at Fina and then continued. "We were traveling, searching for things to bring back to Quasi, when a massive storm hit. It disabled my flying ship, forcing us to take passage over the water." She paused somewhat dramatically. "And then we found that the men crewing the ship were bad, and were planning terrible things for us. This brave sailor," she motioned to Asol, who sat a little straighter, "rescued us. She got us off the ship in time, and rowed us almost all the way to your sanctuary." She held out her hands, palms up. "And though we must return home, we are thankful to you for opening your home to us."

She sat down, and Jessa puzzled over what she said. She'd left out an awful lot of details, but then, she must have had a reason. Still, it bothered Jessa's sense of propriety to leave so much information out.

Fina stood and put her hand on Kylin's shoulder. "There are many of us who remember your first time here, Kylin, and the adventure you brought with you." There was a titter of laughter and calls from the people, and Fina's father tapped his foot loudly.

"But I think this is not just your story to tell, is it?" She looked at Jessa. "I believe you have a story to tell as well."

Panicked, Jessa looked at Kylin, who looked just as surprised. She leaned closer. "It's safe to tell the truth here."

Jessa's pulse raced and she put her hands over her stomach to keep the butterflies from escaping. "My name is Jessa Arabelle. I'm the captain of the *Delta Centauri* interplanetary cruise ship, and we were hit by an asteroid that destroyed the ship. Myself and several of my crew were able to get away in an escape pod, but it too was sent off course and we landed here." She swallowed hard, remembering the noise, the heat, and the impact. "We crashed here, actually. And when the slavers were after us, Kylin found us." Tears welled in her eyes at the memory and she brushed them away. "She saved us, even though she didn't have to. And she's kept me safe since. I owe her my life."

She sat back down and took a long, shaky breath. There was silence, and then the crowd erupted into a clamor of applause and cheers. Kylin's smile was soft, her expression unreadable.

Fina squeezed Kylin's shoulder and then turned to Asol, but Jessa saw an emotion even she could recognize in Fina's eyes: jealousy.

"And you, sailor who saved our friend? What story would you share with us tonight?"

Asol grinned and not only did she stand, but she hopped up on the chair and raised her arms. "I wasn't always a sailor. I was born to poor parents who sold me to a slaver when they thought it would be better for me to live as a slave than starve to death as a peasant." There were hisses and boos from the audience. "But as I got older and more charming," she winked and flexed her muscles, "another master saw that I was more than a slave, and she bought me and set me free."

Jessa was as enthralled by Asol's story as the rest of the audience, and she admired Asol's ability to capture their attention. She was a natural, and as she continued with the tale of her young life, Jessa knew that she, too, had left things out. Things not conducive to keeping an audience happy.

"And then these two showed up at the docks, and they needed a young strapping thing to show them the way, and here we are!"

She finished with a flourish and a bow, and when her shirt rode up ever so slightly at her back, Jessa saw Fina's eagle sharp eyes catch sight of the tail end of one of the scars. Their gazes met, and she saw in Fina's eyes the same confusion and horror she'd felt when she saw them.

But Fina recovered well and turned back to the audience, clapping along with them. "I think we know who wins the night here, don't we?" A cheer resounded around them. She sat back down, and the hall went quiet. "And now we'll allow questions."

The rest of the hour was spent answering questions from the audience. Some were about the state of the outside world, some were about the kind of ship Jessa flew, and whether she'd ever stopped at Indemnion before. Many questions were for Asol, who was quick and funny. When someone asked Kylin if she'd missed Fina, she'd blushed and said, "Who wouldn't miss a princess like yours?"

When it was over, Jessa was exhausted and more than ready to fall onto the incredibly soft bed. People stopped and touched their foreheads to Kylin's, welcoming her back, and a group of giggling young people stopped and asked if Asol would join them at a nearby nest party. She looked at Kylin, who shrugged and smiled, before she let herself be led away.

Tulvia and Fina turned to Jessa and Kylin. "Thank you for that. We know it can be tiring, but it's good for the people to know what is out there, and not to be afraid, even though we know very well that the world beyond our island is not for us." Tulvia raised his chin and looked at Kylin contemplatively. "You've flown well since you left us, Kylin. I'm sure your father is proud."

Only because their arms were touching did Jessa feel Kylin tense at the statement. Her expression and body language didn't change at all. "Thank you, Tulvia. We have to grow up eventually, don't we?"

He inclined his head. "We do. If you'll excuse me, I don't fly as late as I used to. We can discuss how we can help you tomorrow."

Once he was gone, Fina turned to Kylin. "If you have a moment, I'd very much like to speak with you and have you meet my family." She placed her hand in Kylin's. "And it would be so good to catch up."

Kylin smiled. "Of course."

Before she could say anything, Jessa backed up, breaking their tenuous connection. "Enjoy your evening. I'm going to get some sleep."

"Jess, wait—"

She very nearly fell down the steps leading onto the stage but managed to catch her balance before she turned and fled back to her room. She sat on the edge of her bed and pressed her shaking hands together. Alone. She was alone in the room and, she realized, alone in life. Why should she care that people wanted to talk to Asol, and people wanted Kylin's attention, but she wasn't of interest? She was a ship's captain, damn it. She didn't need anyone's attention. Or... she hadn't. But something about this planet, this whole situation, was changing her. She didn't want to be alone anymore. She lay down on the ultra-soft bed, pulled the pillow against her, and let the tears come. There was no one to see them, no one to hold her, and no one to tell her it was going to be okay. That's how it had always been, so why did it hurt so much now?

CHAPTER FOURTEEN

Kylin laughed until her cheeks ached. Fina's kids were very much like their mother. They were fearless, throwing themselves off high pieces of furniture and expecting Kylin to catch them. Fina's husband was a kind, quiet man who clearly adored his family, and his welcome was genuine.

When the kids, complainingly loudly, went to bed, Fina's husband gave her a quick kiss and said he'd head to bed as well.

Left alone with Fina, Kylin curled her leg under her and smiled. "Family looks good on you." She looked around the neat, lived in home. "Are you happy?"

Fina picked up her drink and led them out to the porch, where they settled in comfortable round chairs. "I am." She took a sip of her drink and kept Kylin's gaze. "But I would have been happy with you, too."

Kylin sighed and looked up at the stars. "Maybe. It was an amazing time. I felt like everything was right when I was here." She tilted her head to look at Fina. "But your father would never have accepted it. And you wouldn't have those gorgeous kids."

They sat in silence, only the deep trills of night birds filling the air. It was peaceful, just like Kylin remembered. It was a place out of time, away from the insanity and politics and scrapping of the mainland. And as much as she'd wanted it, it would never have been home. Not without her father.

"Do you miss it? Not having someone, I mean?" Fina asked.

"Who says I don't?" She poked Fina with her toe. "I could have a wife and four kids at home, waiting to welcome me back with open arms."

Instead of laughing, Fina looked sad. "But you don't. And you have so much to offer someone. Why have you cut yourself off?"

This was a safe place, with a safe person. Still, Kylin couldn't bring herself to go into detail. "There was someone. I thought I wasn't good enough, but she convinced me otherwise. Then she proved me right when she left me for someone better." The memory had lost most of its poison, but there was still a bite, an itch that reminded her never to go there again.

Fina reached out and put her hand over Kylin's. "I'm sorry you've been hurt. But it happens to all of us sometime. It doesn't mean you stop living. That you stop searching for the one who understands you, who accepts all you are." She laughed. "And all you are is *a lot*. When you do find the right woman, she'll be something special."

Kylin grinned and pushed away the image of Jessa's pretty eyes. That was definitely someone she wasn't good enough for. "I still enjoy my life. I have plenty of company, and I'm not looking for more."

Fina tapped her finger on her glass, a sure sign she was trying to figure out how to say something. Finally, she let out a sharp breath. "And that's why there's a bounty on your head? Because life is so good?"

Kylin looked up, surprised. "How did you know about that?"

"We hear things on the wind. Things ship captains speak of, when we're flying high overhead. That's why it took so long for us to get you from the training rock. Father was adamant that we not bring a sought after criminal onto the island. He didn't want to put us in danger."

"What changed his mind?" Sought after criminal. Some moniker.

"I told him it was ridiculous. No one can find us unless we want them to. And even though he was pretty treed off about us being together last time, he really did like you."

Kylin remembered times where she'd sat and spoken to Tulvia, and he'd held her as she cried about the loss of her mom and the way life felt so empty. "He's a good man."

"And what about your captain?" Fina grinned. "Have you introduced her to your nest yet?"

Her place in Quasi was far from a comfortable nest. "No. And I wouldn't go there even if I could."

Fina flicked some liquid from her glass at her. "Why not? She's attractive, she's clearly intelligent, and she looks at you like you're a star guiding her home."

Kylin laughed. "She does not. That's an absolute fabrication. I'm just the person she knows here, so she looks to me for help here and there. That's all."

"And?"

"And yeah, she's attractive and intelligent and kind and sweet and funny…" Kylin flicked some of her own drink at Fina. "And she's going to leave at the first opportunity. This isn't her home, and she's not a big fan of this planet and our ways."

"And what makes that different from the women you bed in Quasi? Do they stick around? It sounds like you don't want them to. Why should you care if you bed the captain and she leaves?"

Kylin hated when Fina got philosophical. She never had a response, and this time was no different. She was right. Why would enjoying Jessa in her bed be any different from any other woman? The truth was that Jessa was different. "I can't take advantage of someone in a vulnerable position."

Fina snorted. "That's bird poop, and you know it. You're afraid of getting hurt, and you really like her."

"So? Maybe, yeah. But that's a damn good reason, and I'm sticking to it. No matter how beautiful she is. I'll get her back to Quasi, help her get to the station in the Heathers, and then she'll be gone. Life will go back to normal." Kylin knew she was being obstinate, and when Fina clicked softly but didn't respond, she relaxed back into her seat.

"Well done, telling everyone about Asol's heroism. She'll have her pick of nest mates tonight," Fina said, changing the subject.

"Yeah, well, she truly saved our lives. She wants to go to Quasi so she can be free to be who she is, but I thought she should experience the kind of attention you can only get from the Volare." Kylin winked at Fina, who blushed.

"Perhaps that attention will be enough to make her want to stay. We could use some fresh blood."

The tone of Fina's voice told Kylin all wasn't well. "What's going on?"

Fina motioned to the trees around them. "It's a closed system, and closed systems die out. We can't keep living here, closed off from the world, without it affecting our numbers. Our breeding needs new people. But father thinks the world is too unsafe, too violent. I worry that he's condemned us to extinction."

The thought of these beautiful, unusual people dying out made Kylin's heart ache. "Can I help?"

Fina shook her head. "I don't think so. Unless you can change his mind. But you know he's as stubborn as a tree owl hunting a hopper."

That was true, but there had to be a way to reach him. "I'll think about it, okay?"

Fina smiled and stood. "I believe that you were sent here to help us. You taught me how to love and how to be brave. It makes me a better leader to my people. Now, I think you'll help us again."

She leaned her forehead against Kylin's. "Don't close yourself off to possibility, my love. One day your time will come, and you have to be ready to leap. If you don't leap, you'll never fly." She let go, gave Kylin a last, small smile, and slipped inside the house.

Kylin sat staring at the stars as she finished her drink in silence. All she'd ever wanted was to leap, to fly, to…to run. And run was the only thing she'd managed to do, and it felt like she was never going to stop. She was tired to her bones of looking over her shoulder, waiting for the prowlers of every species to come after her. Fina's life was enviable, and she wondered if she'd have been happy here. She plucked at a loose branch in her seat. It didn't do any good to wonder. She'd lived a life entirely different from Fina's, and Fina was happy now. Kylin wasn't sure what that kind of happiness felt like and was pretty sure she'd never know.

She set her empty glass on the table and stood. She leaned over the banister and looked at the ground far below. One step would be all she'd have to take, and no one would be hunting for her anymore. Jessa and Asol would be safe because they wouldn't be found with her…

She stumbled backward, shaking. That dark place hadn't called to her in a very long time, and she wouldn't give in to it now. They needed her to get back to Quasi. And Jessa…was Fina right? Should Kylin be willing to go there, even if it didn't last? She'd seen the look in Jessa's eyes when she'd been dressed in the borrowed clothes. She knew when a woman was attracted to her, and there wasn't really any question of that being the case. And she'd managed to keep her heart from getting involved with any other woman; surely she could keep it safe from Jessa too, and still manage to enjoy her on a more intimate level.

She made her way down the long, winding staircase to the ground and back to the main hall. There was something deeply satisfying about being able to find her way back by memory. This place had been so special, such a perfect break from the chaos of her life. Now, in the midst of yet more chaos, it was again a sanctuary.

When she entered the room she found Jessa curled on her side, fast asleep. Her face was blotchy like she'd been crying and Kylin closed her eyes. She shouldn't have left Jessa all alone in a place where she didn't know anyone. It had been careless, and she'd have to make it up to her. She turned to her bed.

"Kylin?"

She turned around to see Jessa leaning on one elbow, her eyes puffy.

"Will you…I mean, I don't want to sound presumptuous, but…"

She trailed off, and Kylin waited. But instead of finishing her sentence, Jessa just moved to the edge of her bed and placed her hand in the space she'd created.

Kylin's heart raced. It was strange how used to having Jessa beside her in the night she had become. She sat on the edge of Jessa's bed, took off her shoes and jacket, and lay back beside Jessa, who curled up against her with her head on her chest. Kylin wrapped her arm around Jessa and held her tight. They didn't say another word, and she felt Jessa drift off to sleep quickly. Fina's words ran through her head on a loop. But try as she might, she couldn't think of a time that would be right. They were on the run, dependent on people to help them, and Kylin's life back in Quasi was the most unstable it had ever been. Getting Jessa mixed up in any of that seemed wrong.

No. For now, she needed to be happy with the growing friendship they had. Whatever lay beneath the surface had to be left buried.

❖

Morning bird song woke Kylin, and she winced at the pins and needles in her arm. Jessa hadn't moved from her position all night, and though Kylin's arm was still wrapped around her, she could no longer feel it. Jessa looked so serene, but there were dark shadows under her eyes that spoke to the harrowing journey she'd been on since her ship had been torn apart in space. Kylin didn't want to wake her.

The choice was taken away from her when the door opened and Asol came in singing. When she saw them in bed together she stopped abruptly and laughed. "I'm gone for one night and you two make it official. You could have waited so I could watch that kind of hotness explode."

Kylin rolled her eyes and Jessa raised her head as she blinked against the light. Kylin gently moved her arm and grunted as the blood began to flow back into it. Jessa gave her a small smile before disappearing into the bathroom without a word.

Asol raised her eyebrows. "Fully clothed too, huh? Not my style, but whatever works."

Kylin moved to the edge of the bed and stretched, her muscles popping and creaking. "It wasn't like that. She just wanted some comfort."

Asol flopped onto her bed with her hands behind her head. "Yeah, I got comfort too." She flipped onto her side and grinned at

Kylin. "They really like outsiders here. You did me a favor with that lifesaving bit."

"You did yourself a favor with the way you told your story. It's an oral history culture, and a good storyteller is in demand."

"As is someone with rough hands and a lot of stamina." Asol's smile suggested she'd had her fill of attention. "And wow, are they desperate for news about the outside world."

The bathroom door opened and Jessa came out looking refreshed. "It must be so strange to know there's a world out there and you're not part of it." Jessa sat beside Kylin. "Like my life, in a way. I've been all over the universe, but I've never really been part of any world."

Kylin heard the sadness in the words and put her arm around her. "Now that you know what you've been missing, you can fix that though, right? You've got a chance to dig deeper whenever you go to new planets from here on out."

She hated the thought of watching Jessa leave to explore new places, to have new adventures, while Kylin continued on with life on Indemnion.

Jessa nodded slowly. "That's true. I've been so caught up in thinking about the time I've wasted that I haven't thought about what it means to my future." She took Kylin's hand and squeezed it with both of hers. "You keep making me see things in a new way."

Kylin was saved from having to respond both to Jessa's words and whatever quip Asol was about to make by a knock on the door. A guard pushed it open, and Tulvia stepped inside.

"I would like to take a walk along the cliffs today, and I thought we could discuss things together if you'd like to come with me." He didn't make eye contact, but that wasn't unusual for the Volare.

"We'd love to. Can you give me a few minutes to clean up?" Kylin asked.

He bowed his head slightly. "Five minutes."

When he'd left the room Asol let out a whoosh of air. "Wow. He's really intense. I can't believe he didn't take your head off or peck out your eyes or something when he found you boffing his daughter."

Kylin threw a pillow at her as she crossed the room to use the bathroom. "I didn't boff her. And I don't suggest you bring that up on our stroll, or he'll throw you off the cliff and feed you to the sea prowlers." She splashed water on her face and rinsed out her mouth, both of which made her feel better, although she'd kill for a shower when they got back. The cliffs had been part of her dreams for years, and she was looking forward to seeing them again, as well as to hearing whatever advice or plan Tulvia might have in mind.

Asol washed quickly when Kylin was done, and they met Tulvia by the front door of the hall. He walked ahead of them down the forest path that opened onto the high scraggy cliffs. The ocean crashed in a foamy roar below, sending spray into the air. Through the mist, she could see a ship sailing by in the far distance.

Tulvia stood looking out at the sea. "This will be the second time I've put you on a boat and sent you away." He shook his head when she started to speak. "I'm not sure sending you away the first time was the right thing to do. Fina was lonely when you left. I don't think she's ever recovered the spark you brought out in her." He turned to her and his eyes flicked to Jessa and Asol. "And so this time I'll give you a choice. I cared for you, Kylin, and I still do. If you'd like to stay among us, and this includes your friends, you are welcome."

Stunned, Kylin wasn't sure what to say. But the thing with Tulvia, with all the Volare, was that he was patient. She stared out at the water and considered his words. If it weren't for her father, she might very well take him up on the offer. But he needed her, and she wouldn't let him down. Even if that meant giving up this world.

"Thank you, Tulvia. I can't speak for my friends. But as much as I wish I could stay, I still have someone in Quasi who needs me, and I won't let them down. Maybe one day I can come back and ask you to invite me to stay again." She felt the tears threaten at the back of her eyes and blinked them away. Tulvia knew about her father, though he didn't know about his failing health. But he'd understand what she left unspoken.

He looked at Jessa and Asol.

Jessa took Kylin's hand in her own. "Thank you for the offer. I go where Kylin goes, and if she's leaving, then I'll follow. And I think I've got people waiting for me in Quasi, too."

Her hand was warm and soft in Kylin's, and the words struck deep within her. They were the words she'd wanted to hear from someone else long ago, and now they were being said by someone else who was going to leave. Still, she was going to stay at Kylin's side for a while, and she could cherish whatever moments were left.

Asol looked perplexed. "I didn't even know you existed, and now that I do, I'm in awe. Can I think about it?"

It wasn't a smooth answer, but it was a clear one, and Tulvia had always liked clarity. He smiled at her. "So, it seems we must help you get back to your home without the slavers or bounty hunters finding you. Is that right?"

Kylin stared at the ground, embarrassed.

"Obviously, you'll go by boat, but it's storm season and the waters are treacherous. I suggest you skirt the Ellidies on your way so that you're always close to a shoreline should a storm catch you at sea. There's no one on any of the islands, but at least you'll have a place to stop if things get rough." He pointed to the left. "I'm going to send two flyers to watch over you, and they're under instructions to get involved if a ship should interfere with you."

There were no words to express her gratitude. Telling flyers to get involved meant outing their kind to the wider population. "Why would you take that risk?"

He sighed. "Fina thinks I don't listen to her, but I do. In my heart I know she's right, that we need to open our island to outsiders or we'll fade into the mists of time and become the myths people already believe us to be. But I won't have my people captured by slavers and sold like animals. So we have to be cautious. Fina believes you were sent here to help us." He shook his head, still looking out at the water. "Perhaps that's true. And if it is, then we need to be sure you arrive back in your sector in one piece. After that, it's up to you." He turned away from the cliff and looked at the three of them. "You can stay as long as you like, and, Asol, you can give me your decision when you know in your heart what it is you want."

He walked away to the edge of a farther cliff, spread his arms, and leapt from the cliff. A wind current caught him and he soared away, around the bend of the island and out of sight.

Jessa knocked rocks down the edge of the cliff in her attempt to keep watching him. "That's truly something spectacular."

Kylin never tired of it either. "Are you sure you want to go with me, Jess? If they're opening the island to outsiders, I could get you information when a ship is going to be available to take you out of here. You'd be safe."

"I feel like we had this exact conversation in Thalla." Her smile was gentle but firm. "I'm going with you."

They looked at Asol.

"Wow. I mean, wow. I can't believe he'd let me stay. I have to think about it, though. I mean, I wanted to go to Quasi. I had it all planned out, you know?" Asol ran her hand through her shaggy hair. "When do you want to leave?"

Before they left, she needed to have an honest conversation with Asol about what Quasi was like. But she wanted to do it privately. She wasn't ready for Jessa to know what her world really looked like. Kylin counted up the hours. "I hadn't planned on going past the Ellidies, but Tulvia makes sense. That puts another day on the journey, and I can't run out of time. So I need to leave as soon as we can."

Asol bent to pick up a shard of crystal and showed it to Jessa. "I found out what they're for. They take in energy from the sun, and the people use that energy to heat their nests and water. The ones along the shore and around the island create the fog that keeps them safe. It's like some kind of living energy network."

Jessa took the small rose crystal from Asol and studied it. "Truly ingenious."

Asol was stalling, and Kylin didn't blame her. It was a big decision. Kylin led the way back down the forest path toward the hall. One of the girls who had taken Asol away the night before stopped them, and once again Asol was laughingly led to a nest. Kylin and Jessa walked quietly together.

"Are you still in love with her?" Jessa blurted out.

Kylin kicked at a stone. She didn't need to ask who Jessa was referring to. "Would it bother you if I was?"

Jessa shrugged. "I don't want it to bother me. But yes, I think it would. It's illogical and emotional, but still, I can't seem to help it."

Kylin brought Jessa's hand to her lips and kissed it. "She'll always be special to me. But that life seems like a dream from another world. Our worlds are too different. She's happy now, and I'm happy for her."

She could feel Jessa relax, and it made her grin.

"I'm sorry for asking something so intrusive." Jessa held tightly to Kylin's hand. "But I couldn't breathe, and I needed to know. Thank you for answering without chiding me. I'm not used to feeling…things. I don't understand myself right now."

Kylin pulled Jessa to a stop and gently moved a piece of her hair from her eyes. "Jessa, you have to know I'm attracted to you. That I think you're an amazing woman and you've got the body of a cosmic goddess."

Jessa blushed and stared up into Kylin's eyes.

"But just like I'm from a different world than Fina's, our worlds are too different too. You're going to leave, and I'll be left behind wondering if you ever think about me, if I meant anything to you. And I can't take that." She cupped Jessa's face in her hand, and her stomach fluttered when Jessa pushed her cheek into her palm. "You're something special. Don't ever think that I don't think so."

Jessa remained silent, and Kylin dropped her hand from Jessa's face and took her hand once more. They walked back to the hall without saying another word, and Kylin wondered what Jessa was thinking, but she seemed so deep in thought she didn't want to intrude and ask. Which felt more like a Jessa thing to do, really. The thought made her smile. It was good to have her feelings out in the open. Maybe it would make things easier between them, ease the tension a little. Or, maybe it would make it harder. Either way, she'd been honest, and that felt like the right thing to do.

Too bad there were still so many other secrets she couldn't, wouldn't, share.

CHAPTER FIFTEEN

Jessa sat on a cliff edge staring out over the water. Kylin had gone to see about getting their boat ready, and Asol was still being entertained by the locals. Unwilling to lie in bed crying again, she'd decided to explore and spend some time in the sun. Children had run alongside her for a while before they'd disappeared into the forest, chasing a pretty glowing ball.

The island was so serene, a true haven in a world of chaos and injustice. She thought of Kylin's assertion that she could stay there on Volare and wait for information about a ship. Kylin's admission that she had feelings for Jessa had been both welcome and distressing. While it was good to know she wasn't alone in her growing feelings for Kylin, it hurt unexpectedly deeply when she said there couldn't be anything between them. She understood, of course. Emotional entanglement during this enterprise would only end in anguish for them both. It was sensible. Staying here and letting Kylin go on her way would make resisting her feelings far easier.

But she couldn't stomach the idea of being away from her. Not when she was still stuck on this planet, and not when she thought her crew might still be waiting for her in Quasi. Once she was on a ship back to Othrys, she'd have to deal with all that had happened here. She didn't have to yet, though. She would enjoy the rest of the time they had together, even if it meant they had to look over their shoulders until they were back in Kylin's home territory.

She threw a pebble and watched it arc down to the water, where it sank without disturbing the water. Did anyone miss her? Were they searching? Or, like the pebble, had she sunk without a trace, not to be missed?

"Those seem like heavy thoughts on such a beautiful day."

She looked up and saw Fina smiling down at her. Not exactly the person she wanted to see. Granted, Kylin said she wasn't in love with her anymore, but next to her, Jessa felt like dull moss on an old stone.

"May I join you?" Fina settled in next to her, also dangling her legs over the cliff.

"Of course." It wasn't like she could tell the princess to find somewhere else to be.

They sat in awkward silence, but Jessa had no idea what to say to her. The image of her having sex with Kylin anywhere and everywhere was never far away.

"She's quite special, you know." Fina rolled a pebble between her fingers. "I don't think there's another like her in all the universe."

And there it was. Kylin might not be in love with Fina anymore, but the love and longing in Fina's voice was clear. She wanted to have this conversation about as much as she wanted to lick the seaweed below. "Yes, I think you're probably right."

"We weren't meant to be. We had a moment in time, but that's all we were given. It's a gift to be able to see her again at all." She glanced at Jessa and then looked back out at the water. "Anybody could see how much she cares for you."

"Yes. She said as much earlier." Jessa figured she may as well be direct, if Fina wanted to talk about it.

"She did?" Fina gave her a small smile. "I'm happy for you both."

It galled her to say the words out loud, but she couldn't let there be confusion. It would feel too much like a lie, and she hated liars. "Perhaps under different circumstances your happiness would be warranted. But she feels, and I agree, that we're simply from worlds that don't mix. And getting involved…" Now that the words were out, they tasted metallic and bitter.

Fina sighed. "The problem is, Kylin is always from a different world from the people she loves. She chooses women she feels she can't have. It keeps her from getting close to anyone, from really giving her heart."

"She gave it to you," Jessa said softly.

Fina laughed. "We gave our hearts to each other, but deep down, I think she knew she'd leave. In me, she again chose someone she wouldn't be staying with, no matter how much she cared for me."

Jessa thought about that. She didn't know enough about Kylin's other romantic partners to know if there was a pattern, but it sounded like Fina knew full well. And if that was true, then it was incredibly sad. But then, who was Jessa to say anything? She hadn't allowed anyone close either, but mostly because she wouldn't let anyone get in the way of her career ambitions.

"Where I come from, my people believe that emotions overall are a hindrance. We live in an ordered, egalitarian society where knowledge is sought above all else, and we're expected to achieve great things." It felt so strange to be speaking so openly like this, but once she'd started, Jessa didn't want to stop. "We marry for convenience or strategic alliances. Love is considered a waste of time, although it's good if you can like and respect the person you're with. Obviously."

"Obviously." Fina closed her eyes and tilted her face to the sun. "Here in Volare, we believe that love is what makes life worth living. That kindness, and laughter, and family, and desire are what create beautiful communities. We search for a mate who can bring out the best in us. There's no ambition, no inequality. We live for the beauty of every day and love as best we can." She opened one eye and looked sideways at Jessa. "Which would you choose if you hadn't been brought up in one or the other?"

Jessa frowned. "That's an illogical question. I was born into that, so that's what I believe."

"Kylin was born into a place where life is valued by what a person has to sell and what they can deliver. A ruthless society, one that would brand a child for trying to return something they hadn't taken in the first place." Fina held up a blue crystal and the light hit it and sent rainbows across Jessa's lap. "And yet, her respect and desire to help people has never diminished. Like a crystal that is basically just glass, she's so much more, and she shapes the world around her as best as she can, bending the light to create something beautiful in the dark." She handed Jessa the crystal and closed it in her palm. "She was born into chaos, and yet she believes in love. You're not required to be the person others raise you to be."

She stood, squeezed Jessa's shoulder, and walked away quietly.

Jessa opened her palm and studied the crystal. Was that true? Could she let go of the ways of her people and learn to be... something else? And, really, did it matter? Because when it all came down to it, she was going to leave. She'd find another ship and go back to the career she loved and had worked so hard for. It wasn't simply that they were very different people. It was that their paths were going to be separate, and getting involved before she left was folly.

Wasn't it?

Kylin handed Asol another bag of food, and Asol tucked it away under the seat. The boat rocked gently, but Asol didn't seem to notice. She looked so relaxed, so in her element. And so young.

She picked up another sack and passed it over. "I need to talk to you about something."

Asol motioned for another bag. "I'm listening."

Where to start? "Look, I know you said you wanted to go to Quasi, where you could be anything you want."

"Yeah? Don't you think I can be something other than a dock rat?"

Kylin stopped mid-handover. "Hey, wait a second. Hear me out before you get crazy on me, okay?"

Asol reached for the bag. "Sore spot. Sorry. Go on."

"I just want to make sure you know what you're getting into, that's all." Kylin wiped away the sweat on her forehead with her sleeve. "Quasi isn't some kind of paradise. It's not like the streets are paved with linari and credit chips are growing on trees. It's a good community, yeah. And we look after each other. But it's a tough place, you know? You have to fight for your space, and you have to find a way to make a living. Jobs can be hard to come by. It can turn you into someone you don't want to be."

Asol stopped and crossed her arms, and she looked far older than her age as she looked at Kylin seriously. "You think I don't know that? Cosmos shit, Kylin, you're running from bounty hunters because of some debt you owe some very bad man. And I've seen the way you change the subject when Jessa asks about Quasi. I'd bet a slaver's shipload that you've got a whole heap of other secrets we don't know." She shrugged. "Anything has to be better than working the slaver's docks. Anything. Shoveling prowler shit during breeding season wrapped in bloody meat would be better, and if that's what I have to do in Quasi, it's a step up. But at least I'm the one who gets to decide, not someone who puts a collar around my neck and zaps me because they want to make their friends laugh. On the docks, I'm just waiting to get snapped up by some other slaver who rips my life from under me. And watching all those people being loaded on ships…"

The naked pain in her eyes made Kylin shudder. Of all the paths she'd had to take, of all the issues she faced, thank the universe that had never been one of them. "But you don't have to shovel prowler shit naked in the streets. You could stay here. Find a mate, live in peace."

Asol reached down and splashed water at Kylin's face. "I didn't say anything about being naked, you dirty old swooper."

Kylin laughed and tossed a water bag to her.

Asol returned to being serious. "You know what it's like. When you're from somewhere hard, somewhere that gives you edges that can't be sanded down. I love it here, and yeah, the girls like a bit of the rough side right now. But I'd always feel out of place, and eventually, they'd see me as the outsider I am. The novelty would fade. And I'd be right back where I am now, except that I wouldn't have you and Jessa to travel with."

The truth in her words was hard to hear, but she was right. And Kylin understood perfectly. When she'd sailed away from Volare so long ago, she'd been devastated, but a part of her knew she couldn't stay there. They were special, unique. Nothing like her.

"So you're coming with us, then."

Asol rolled her eyes. "You're a smart one, too."

"Hey, I can still leave you here with the beautiful people, dock rat." Kylin grinned and gave Asol a hand out of the boat and back onto land.

"You wouldn't last a day without me on the sea."

Laughing, they walked back to the main hall together, where the Volare were gathering for the evening roosting hour.

Jessa was sitting on her bed with her back against the wall, and she smiled at them when they came in, but Kylin could tell something was on her mind.

"Everything okay?"

Jessa nodded. "I had dinner with Fina and Tulvia, and they've left food for you." She nodded toward a covered tray. "They said we're leaving in the morning?"

Asol went to the tray and dug in. Kylin sat on Jessa's bed. "We just finished loading the boat, and we're ready to go. We can sail at first light. Is that okay?"

Jessa nodded and took Kylin's hand. "Can we take a walk after roosting hour? I'd very much like to see the special places you liked here before we leave."

Surprised, Kylin smiled and squeezed her hand. "Sure. I'd love to."

"You should try this," Asol said, her mouth full. "I may change my mind just so I can eat this food for the rest of my life."

Kylin laughed and joined her at the table. They ate quickly, and soon it was time to join the others for roosting hour. A storyteller told the tale of the days they'd roamed the planet, when there were different tribes of Volare. It was beautifully told, and she saw Jessa wiping away tears. Tulvia also told the people that their guests would be leaving the next day, so to make sure to say their good-byes tonight.

When roosting hour was over, she took Jessa's hand, and they made their way back outside amidst people stopping to wish them safe travels. This time, Kylin had an open invitation to return, and that felt like a caress to her soul.

She led Jessa through the trees and up a hill that was far from the community. Soon, the only sounds were from the crashing of the waves and the calls of the night birds. When they stopped in front of a grouping of standing stones arranged in a circle, Kylin let go of Jessa's hand and caressed one of the stones.

"What is this place?" Jessa asked quietly.

"The Volare believe in an energy that surrounds our planet. Not a god, but an entity of sorts that looks out for us. Or for them, anyway. They come here on certain days of the year to reconnect with that entity." She traced the swirl cut into the stone. "Among other things, they believe that the entity sends them someone to help them in times of true crisis." She shrugged and sat in the middle of the circle, where Jessa joined her. "I can't understand it, and I don't get how they can still have that kind of faith when so many of them were wiped out."

"Hope." Jessa hugged her knees to her chest. "I've read about it and even talked to passengers about it. Belief isn't about evidence. It's about the need for hope that things can change." She looked up at the night sky. "You used to come here, before?"

Those days seemed so long ago. "Particularly on nights when Fina had duties or her father wouldn't let her out. I'd sit here and wonder if someone was looking out for me, and I'd ask whoever it was for help."

"And did you get any?"

Kylin sighed deeply. "No. And I learned to depend on myself."

They sat quietly for some time before Jessa spoke again.

"What is your life in Quasi like, Kylin?"

It was like she already had an inkling of the answer, but Kylin knew full well she couldn't imagine the truth of it. How much to tell her? She'd see some of it herself soon anyway. "It's not life on a passenger ship." She smiled to show she was teasing, but Jessa's expression was serious. "It's hard. Frenetic. I'm like fresh meat in a cage surrounded by predators. But I hold my own, and I do what I have to do to survive."

It wasn't much of an answer, not really. She didn't talk about Orlin and the fact that she often fought for her dinner. She didn't talk about her father and his failing health. She didn't mention Maana and the debt she had to honor when she got back, which very well might mean a painful repayment.

Jessa didn't need to know all that. She needed to know that life was hard and not pretty. Because she wasn't going to have to deal with it for long, so there was no reason to make her see Kylin as even less than she was.

"I'm sorry that life here is so hard. This planet has such beauty among the brutality. It seems to me that if we were to bring it into the trade routes, things might be easier." Jessa's head was tilted, catching the light from the first moon and making her skin glow. "If you had an Indemnion ambassador who could speak for the planet and show them that there's more here than people know…"

Kylin was interested in Jessa's line of thinking, but plenty of people had come and gone from Indemnion, and no one had ever come back saying they were interested in trade. "It's a nice thought. Who knows? Maybe one day." She stood and brushed off her pants before holding her hand out to Jessa to help her up. "We've got a big day tomorrow. We should probably get some sleep."

Jessa took her hand, and Kylin knew her well enough now to know she was deep in thought. On their way back to the hall Kylin pointed out places she'd liked to go and told an anecdote or two about the mischief she'd gotten up to. Still, it felt like Jessa was only half listening.

When they got back to their room, Asol wasn't there, and Kylin waited, hoping.

"Would you…" Jessa motioned at her bed.

She had an adorable way of drifting off when she wasn't sure how to phrase what she wanted, and Kylin bet that was a new experience for the ship's captain too. "Let me take a quick shower. I'll be right back."

The water felt heavenly, and Kylin let it wash away the pervasive feeling of melancholy running through her as she thought of leaving tomorrow. She'd get back, take Jessa to her crew, get Asol settled at Auntie Blue's, help get Jessa and her crew a ride to the Heathers, and then she'd deal with Orlin, Maana, and her dad.

No problem.

She tried to shake off the weight of her life as she crawled into bed beside Jessa and pulled her close. They had this, at least. This intimacy that ran deeper than any simple sexual encounter she'd had over the years.

She'd miss it.

CHAPTER SIXTEEN

Jessa hugged Fina and said good-bye. Much like it had when she'd said good-bye to Sherta, her heart ached at the possibility of a friend left behind. How had she become this emotional, attached person in such a short time?

Kylin gave Fina a long hug, and they put their foreheads together. Tears slipped down Fina's cheeks, and Jessa turned away from the touching display. It wasn't hers to watch. Tulvia seemed to understand when he moved next to her.

"Perhaps it wasn't just Kylin who was sent to us." He glanced at her, then away. "Perhaps the two of you will help us."

She wasn't sure what he meant by help them, but at least she understood the concept in his statement thanks to Kylin taking her to the standing stones. "If there's anything I can do, please tell me."

He shook his head. "If we knew what to ask, where the clouds lay, we would. But the way ahead is unclear."

It felt like a riddle, one with important connotations, but before she could ask him to explain, Asol called out from the boat.

"We'd better get moving. The wind is perfect."

Jessa took Asol's hand and climbed clumsily into the boat. Truly, being planet bound was something she still didn't fully appreciate. Kylin climbed in after her and they released the little sail, which immediately began tugging the boat toward the open water.

Many of the Volare had come to see them off, and there were waves and calls for a good journey as the rope was untied and thrown to them and the boat shot off into the water. There wouldn't be any rowing for a while. Jessa waved back until they were out of sight, and then looked up. Far, far above, so that they were just black specks in the sky, the Volare sent to watch over them flew. Had she not known who they were, she'd have assumed they were simply high-flying birds. Could they get to them in time, if they needed help? She pushed the thought aside. There was no point in worrying over something that was so out of her control.

Instead, she turned to Kylin. "What are the Ellidies?"

Kylin pulled a map from the bag at her feet and unfolded it so Jessa could see. "They're a string of uninhabited islands that run from the Volare toward the mainland. Some are little more than shards of rock, some are fairly large, but none are big enough for anyone to actually live on." She traced the little dots on the map. "We'll stay by them as long as we can, and then here, before we get to the last two, we'll turn off and head toward the nomad lands. There are docks there, and we might get lucky and find a caravan headed toward Quasi."

Jessa had always loved maps, and she studied this one carefully. It took on new meaning now that she'd been to a few of the places listed and could picture them for the interesting places they were.

They sailed in companionable silence, and Kylin handed food around after a few hours. They passed, as Kylin had said, some large rocks and some that looked more like islands. The boat flew along the water under the power of what seemed like an increasing wind, and she didn't miss the look shared by Kylin and Asol when a particularly strong gust slammed into the boat sideways.

"Can I ask you a personal question, Kylin?" Jessa asked.

Kylin raised her eyebrow in that sexy way that made Jessa shiver.

"As long as I can answer it in front of the innocent young one here."

Asol laughed. "The Volare didn't find me all that innocent."

Jessa smiled, but her mind was on her thoughts. "The bounty on you—is there a way to comm with someone and explain that there's been a mix-up?"

Kylin frowned. "I've been so focused on avoiding the hunters I hadn't considered that. But once a bounty is out, it's practically impossible to revoke it until the person is caught. And the person upset with me isn't exactly reasonable." She pulled open her bag and dug out the comms unit. She flipped it open and shaded the screen so she could see. "But you're right. If I let the person who put out the bounty know I'm on my way back, we might have an easier time making our way through Quasi. It's worth a try." She moved the comms unit around and then flipped it shut with a sigh. "We're out of range. But as soon as we get to land, I'll give it a try. Great idea, Jess."

She'd sailed ships through the universe. She'd seen nebulas, had dinner with kings. But Kylin's praise warmed her inside like nothing else ever had.

Asol yelped, and the sail snapped in the wind. Kylin jumped up, and she took the wheel as Asol steadied the sail. The boat was moving frighteningly fast and Jessa hung on to the side, the water lashing at her hands and spray making her eyes water. Clouds whirled and spun across the sky, turning from white to an oily gray.

"Tsuna gale!" Asol yelled over the howling wind. "We need to land!"

Jessa didn't know how they could see with the wind whipping at their faces, and images of her own ship coming apart in space flashed through her mind. Was she going to die in the ocean after all she'd survived? Surely not. She closed her eyes against the wind and water and held on.

The boat slipped sideways, water sloshing in, before it righted again.

"Two clicks ahead, to your left!" Asol yelled, and the boat turned ahead of the wind.

Jessa squinted and saw land rushing up ahead of them.

"Hold on! We're going straight onto the beach!" Kylin's arms strained as she held the wheel.

The little boat headed straight for the sandy shore, and the wind shoved them forward so hard that even when the boat's bottom hit shallow water it kept going, right into the shallowest part of the water. Kylin and Asol jumped out and together pulled the boat onto land, then Jessa got out and pushed from behind. Between the three of them they were able to pull it far from the water.

The wind made it hard to stand upright, and the sky was darkening fast. A crack of light lit the sky and sent a spray of ocean into the air, making Jessa jump.

Kylin and Asol grabbed gear from the boat, and Kylin threw Jessa her bag. They ran into the cover of the trees, but the wind was making the branches thrash and sweep in a frenetic dance of danger.

"Your domicile unit?" Kylin yelled.

"It won't stand up to this kind of wind. We need to find somewhere the wind is buffered, and then it will hold!" Jessa grabbed on to a branch to steady herself.

Asol turned and led the way, and she kept darting out to touch trees, but Jessa couldn't see what she was doing through the tears streaming down her face.

And then suddenly the screaming wind dampened to a high whistle, and Jessa nearly fell over from not having to push against it to stay standing anymore. She wiped the water from her eyes and looked around. It was a shallow cave entrance in a tall cliff surrounded by high, wide trees. That was all they needed.

Jessa dropped her bag and pulled the domicile unit from it. She'd forgotten she even had it, as they hadn't needed it since before Thalla, which felt like it had been years, not days, ago. She punched in the code and stepped back so it could unfold.

"Damn. I heard about these, but I've never seen one." Asol looked confounded as it whirred and clicked and air pumped into the frame. Once it was up, she jumped forward and pushed open the door.

Jessa and Kylin smiled at each other and picked up the bags. They followed Asol inside and Jessa put her bag down beside one of the sleeping pods. Kylin set her bag down just inside the door and put Asol's beside the other pod. Trust Kylin to be the one to offer to sleep on the floor. Sadly, there wouldn't be any offering to share, as the pods were only made to fit one body each.

"Hairy prowler balls," Asol said, running her hand over the pods and walls. "Wouldn't it be something to have this kind of tech on Indemnion?"

Kylin nodded but didn't say anything. She took off her wet shirt and draped it over the end of a pod. When she caught Jessa staring she grinned and winked.

Two could play at that game. Jessa took off the top she'd borrowed from Asol, which left her in only her compression tank, which she'd pulled from her uniform to give her some support. She wasn't big breasted, but big enough to feel self-conscious without something tight around her. She'd always loved the way the uniform hugged her and felt like a suit of armor from the dark ages. Though theirs appeared to be more bulky.

The yellow rings in Kylin's eyes darkened the way they had when she'd first seen Jessa in the slave outfit, and she felt her nipples tighten under Kylin's gaze.

Asol cleared her throat. "I'll sleep in the cave. That way if you burn down this lovely contraption with your unbridled lust, I won't be in it."

Kylin laughed, the spell broken, kicked off her boots, and threw a wet sock at Asol, who batted it away. "I think you're safe, prowler monkey."

Jessa could breathe again, and she dug through her bag to find warm, dry clothes. Surprised, she pulled out the soft white outfit Sherta had let her borrow in Thalla. She looked up at Kylin.

"She wanted you to have something to remind you of them. I didn't mention it on the ship, because it's not really the kind of thing you wear when you're trying to avoid capture. I slipped it into your bag before we left Volare." She grinned. "And you looked adorable in Asol's clothes."

Adorable wasn't exactly the description she was looking for, but it managed to dampen her desire. "That was incredibly kind of her. I think the material is safe in here, and we can dry our clothes while we wait for the storm to pass."

Kylin, too, took out the outfit she'd worn in Thalla, and Asol changed into another set of comfortable looking dock clothes. Jessa took all the wet items and opened the drying unit. She tucked them in, set it going, and turned around to find them both watching her. "What?"

Kylin shook her head and Asol laughed. "You're so used to these things you don't realize what life is without them. We don't have drying units here."

Jessa flushed. The reminders of the way she'd lived as opposed to the way the people here lived were constant, and increasingly unwelcome. She didn't want to be an outsider. She didn't want to be seen as…as…prosperous. Or whatever the right word was. For the first time in her life, she wanted to be like the very grounded, very real people around her. It was disturbing, and she had no idea what to do with it. So she ignored it and turned to the bags. "If we have any food, I can heat it in the food receptacle. It's not as nice as cooking it regularly, but I can't imagine we'd get a fire going in this wind."

Thankfully, they let the issue drop. Asol dug in one of the bags and handed her a heavy leather pouch. "We had to leave most of the stuff in the boat, but I managed to grab one bag. I can go back for water later." She looked around the unit. "If I have to?"

"The unit has an aquafier. If there's water in the atmosphere, it will take it in, cleanse it, and make it drinkable. It comes out there." She pointed to a small rubber tap on the far wall, over a small, functional sink. It was hardly opulence, but she knew just thinking that was what made Kylin say their worlds were too different.

She turned on the aquafier and the others chose food. The air was tense, and she missed the easy camaraderie they'd been sharing. The wind whistled across the cave opening, the sound of trees cracking and rain slashing against the cliff echoing outside the unit, muffled but still audible. They ate in silence, and Jessa wondered what the other two were thinking. She didn't ask, of course. She had some boundaries left.

"I'll take the floor," Kylin said. "You've got to experience what it's like to sleep on a cloud." She spread a blanket on the floor and used her bag as a pillow.

"No arguments here." Asol hoisted herself onto the bed and lay back, but when the capsule began to close over her, she sat up and banged her head on the cover. It stopped automatically. "It closes you in?" Her eyes were wide, her breathing fast.

Jessa got out of her own capsule and put her hand on Asol's shoulder. "It does, but that's just to keep out noise. It regulates your air so you're breathing well. It's particularly good for beings who need different levels of gases."

Asol slowly lay back, though she still looked suspicious.

"It doesn't lock. All you have to do is say open and it will. Or just push it, and it will swing up automatically. You're not locked in. Just protected."

She kept her eyes on Asol's as the cover closed over her. "Try it. Tell it to open."

Asol's voice was higher pitched than usual when she said, "Open." When it did, she seemed to breathe easier.

"Okay?" Jessa smiled but knew deep down that Asol's fear of being closed in came from a place far less comfortable than a sleeping pod.

"Okay."

She returned to her pod and returned Kylin's gentle smile before lying down herself. She didn't know whether it was the salty air, the fright from the storm, or the exhausting emotions running through her that she didn't know what to do with, but she was utterly spent. Still, even after she'd closed her eyes and hit the button to turn out the dome light, sleeping without Kylin by her side felt strange and lonely.

❖

Jessa woke disoriented and breathing hard. Running. She'd been running from someone, something. And she knew if she could just reach the end of the road, get to that house, she'd be safe. She squinted against the dark and saw that the small exit light had been triggered by the door. Kylin's dark silhouette wasn't there. Jessa pushed up the cover, slipped on her boots, and dragged the blanket off the bed to wrap it around her. She slipped from the unit and found Kylin sitting outside the cave on a fallen tree.

"Everything okay?" she asked softly, not wanting to startle her. Kylin turned toward her, and the look in her eyes made her catch her breath. Kylin stood, dropping the blanket she'd wrapped around her, and moved to Jessa. Slowly, so very slowly, she slid the blanket from Jessa's shoulders and then leaned down to kiss the exposed flesh between her neck and shoulder.

"I want you." Kylin's voice was husky. "I shouldn't, and cosmos be dammed, you should walk away." She kissed her way up Jessa's neck. "But lying there thinking about you, about the way you feel in my arms, how sexy you are..." She tugged Jessa's hair back to expose her throat. "I need to feel you under me, and when you go, I'll have that memory to keep me going."

Jessa moaned and pushed her body against Kylin's, and it was all the response Kylin needed.

She pulled Jessa to the log she'd been sitting on, quickly spread the blanket over it, and pulled Jessa down beside her. The kiss made Jessa think she'd never been kissed before, never by someone who wanted her with a ferocity she could taste, that she could feel burning her skin, that made her ache for more.

Kylin's hands were warm, rough, and gentle, even as they tugged Jessa's white robe off.

Lying there, naked to the sky, Jessa trembled under Kylin's intensity. She stroked Jessa's skin from her shoulder to her calf, making her shiver in the cool night air.

"You're so painfully beautiful. It makes me want to take you, possess you." She lowered her head and took one of Jessa's nipples in her mouth, sucking on it while she pinched and pulled at the other.

Jessa arched, cried out. She pushed her breasts to Kylin, wanting to be possessed the way Kylin wanted to possess her. She wanted to be taken by someone who couldn't get enough. Whatever the emotional fallout, she wouldn't ask her to stop. It would be worth it.

Kylin switched nipples, and Jessa felt herself grow wetter. She pressed her throbbing clit to Kylin's leg and cried out when Kylin pushed back. "Please. God, Kylin, please. I need you."

Kylin's hand left her breast and moved down her stomach until she reached between her legs and cupped her firmly, making Jessa buck. "Tell me you want me, Jess." She bit at Jessa's neck, at her shoulder. "Tell me you want me inside you, to take you."

She couldn't breathe. She couldn't think. All she could do was feel. The hard length of Kylin's solid body against hers, the way Kylin's hand held her, cupped her, made her want to beg. The way the air felt against her skin, the way the soft blanket kept her from the hard log beneath her. Like Kylin. Soft, hard. Perfect.

"Please." She gasped when Kylin sucked on her nipple again. "Please take me. Please make me yours."

Kylin's intake of breath was quickly covered by Jessa's cry of pleasure as Kylin pushed her fingers into her, filling her. She took her deep and hard, twisting her fingers just right, her thumb stroking Jessa's clit until she was at the brink, only to pull away as she took her deep and hard again. She kissed her with fury, her tongue plunging into Jessa's mouth, claiming her as she finally let her fall over the edge, her orgasm crashing through her like the waves pounding the shore of the island.

And then, before Jessa could begin thinking about what it meant, about how it would affect them, Kylin took her again. Still deep, but slower. Kylin pressed her forehead to Jessa's as she kept the steady rhythm that made Jessa want to beg her not to stop, to take her this way forever. Her hand was wrapped in Jessa's hair, and her mouth trailed sweet, hot kisses over Jessa's skin, always returning to her mouth. She murmured how beautiful Jessa was, how she'd needed to feel her here, under her. Be inside her.

She pushed deeper. "Come for me, Jess," she whispered. She pressed the heel of her palm against Jessa's clit.

Jessa dug her fingers into Kylin's back as her body pushed into the orgasm that was no less powerful than the last. She bit down on Kylin's shoulder, and the way she groaned made Jessa push against the fingers inside her, and they started all over again.

When she reached between them and slipped her own fingers over Kylin's clit, she moaned at the wetness she found. Kylin pressed down, trapping her hand between their bodies and ground against Jessa's fingers until she came with a gasping cry, her head thrown back, the shadows of the moving trees sliding over her face, making her look ethereal, ghostly. Stunning.

She collapsed on top of Jessa and wrapped her arms around her. Slowly she became aware of the discomfort of the hard tree beneath her, made more so by Kylin's weight on top of her. "Can we move to the ground?" she murmured.

Kylin gingerly moved off her and grabbed the blanket Jessa had come out in. She laid it on the grass and held out her hand.

Jessa, extremely aware of her nakedness when Kylin was still dressed, moved quickly to the blanket. Kylin took the one from the log and covered her with it, then crawled under it and lay down beside her. She rested on one elbow and stroked Jessa's stomach. "You okay?"

Jessa shook her head. "Okay isn't the word." She pressed her face into Kylin's caress. "Euphoric, perhaps."

Kylin grinned. "Me too."

"Can I ask what changed your mind?" Jessa turned onto her side and pillowed her head on her arm. In the darkness she couldn't fully see Kylin's expression, but she had a feeling it was okay to ask.

"Like I said, I was lying there thinking about you. It's crazy, but it's become hard to sleep without you by my side. And then I started thinking about your body, and the way you look at me like you could eat me alive." She laughed when Jessa giggled. "And then I thought about how you see life here, and how chaotic it seems to you."

Jessa started to protest, to explain, but Kylin stopped her.

"I can see why you'd see it that way. There's a lot of truth to it. And my life is unstable and out of control, but that's really nothing new. And then I thought of how long it might be until you're able to get a transport from the Heathers, and how it would be stupid to waste any second I have with you thinking about how much it will hurt when you go, when I could be enjoying the sounds you make when I'm inside you." She kissed Jessa's palm, lightly scraping her teeth over it and making Jessa shiver. "And it's honest. We both know what's going on, and because of that, I can handle it."

Jessa closed her eyes, enjoying the feel of Kylin's caress on her naked skin, and she thought about her words. "May I ask something else? Something you don't have to answer?"

Kylin's hand stopped moving. "My father always said never ask a question you're not certain you want the answer to. Because once you have an answer you have to deal with it. Whatever it is, are you sure you want to know?"

That was an interesting question, and it made her wonder just how much there still was about Kylin she didn't know. "Where I'm from, direct answers are part of day-to-day life. Emotions aren't part of things. So, yes, I'd like to know." When she felt Kylin begin to pull away, she grabbed her hand. "Not because I'm not being emotional. But because I want to know all I can about you."

Kylin sighed and shifted so she could lie back and pull Jessa to her. Jessa laid her head on Kylin's chest. "Go ahead."

"You've mentioned someone who hurt you. And when I mentioned where I was from, I thought you might leave me behind. Will you tell me about it?"

Kylin was silent for so long Jessa wondered if she had fallen asleep. When she was about to raise her head to check, Kylin gently pressed her head back down.

"It wasn't long after I got back from Volare. My father had been gone, scrounging, for as long as I'd been away, so he didn't even know I was gone. Being with Fina had taught me that I could love, and she'd softened me a little. I started fixing things, helping people rebuild houses, stuff like that. I became a go-to person when people needed things done. One day someone knocked on the door, and that was when I met her. A beautiful woman from Orwellian had just come to Quasi. She was there doing research for some educational thing, and she'd heard I was one of the few people in Quasi who had traveled some of the world. We got to talking and spending a lot of time together."

Jessa could hear the pain in Kylin's voice, the memories like ghosts rising with the dawn.

"We became lovers, and I thought she really loved me. We made plans, and we were even going to buy a place out in the Fesi District. She didn't seem to mind that I often came home dirty and tired. She was usually wrapped up in her writing, but when I had time off, we would go out to the Grasslands or to the sea."

She went silent again, and Jessa snuggled closer to her, glad when Kylin pulled her close.

"And then one day a transport arrived at the Heathers. It's always big news, and she wanted to go see it, so I arranged for a flyer to take us to the Heathers. It cost a chunk of my savings, but it was worth it if it made her happy. She brought her books and things, but she often did when we went anywhere, so I didn't think anything of it. When we got there, it was crowded and crazy, the way it always was. When she saw how nice the Heathers is compared to Quasi, I think she felt...I don't know. Betrayed, maybe? Like she'd gotten the prowler crap end of the stick."

"But surely she arrived at the Heathers, right?" Jessa asked. "If she came here in the usual way?"

"That's what I thought. But it turned out she'd come in at night and some unscrupulous guide waiting at the docking station said he'd take her to the main city. She never saw it in the light of day."

Orwellians weren't known for their forgiving natures. The ones Jessa had come across were usually distant and always looking toward the future.

"Anyway, we met a group of people who were vacationing at the Heathers, and one of them knew her from some educational place. They started talking, and they invited her to their place at the Heathers." Kylin's laugh lacked any humor. "When I started to walk with them, it was like I was something to scrape off their shoes. They explained that it was an exclusive place, and people like me weren't allowed in."

Jessa raised her head and looked at Kylin in horror. "That's horrendous. And she let them talk to you that way?"

Kylin brushed hair away from Jessa's eyes. "Not only that, she went with them, and then the following week she comm'd me to say she was leaving, because the woman from Othrys was the kind of woman she should be with. Apparently, the woman from Othrys had explained that she needed someone intellectually stimulating, someone who could answer her every question and give her the future she deserved. She believed it, and I never saw her again. The transport left the following week."

Jessa was at a loss for words. "Her ship should have been swallowed by a black hole."

Kylin sighed. "But that's how Othrys people think, isn't it? That beauty begets beauty, and beauty mixed with ugly is then forever tainted?"

Jessa winced. It was a well-known saying in her world, but hearing it here, in Kylin's voice, made her hear just how awful it was. "Yes. Our world is pretentious and shallow, and I can assure you that not a single person on all the planet has ever had the kind of sex we've just had, because we're taught never to let emotions get in our way." She kissed Kylin softly, letting her lips linger. "And you can take solace in the fact that if your Orwellian stayed with the woman from Othrys, they never had a night of truly passionate sex."

There was a moment of silence before Kylin started laughing. "I never thought of it that way, but you know, it really does make me feel better."

Jessa laid her head back on Kylin's chest. "Fina told me we don't have to be the people we're raised to be. Hearing what you've just said makes me think she's right. I'm far more emotional than most people in my world." She pinched Kylin's side when she scoffed. "And I think that's because I was around so many other cultures. I might not have asked questions or been intrusive, but I think they might have rubbed off on me just the same." She moved her hand lower and slid it under Kylin's pants. "And now, because of you and my time here, I think I'm becoming someone I like far better. Someone who wants to feel what you've just made me feel, over and over again."

She slipped her fingers over Kylin's mound and then gently pushed inside her. Kylin moaned and drew her into a kiss.

"Show me how emotional you can be, Jess."

CHAPTER SEVENTEEN

Warm sunlight made Kylin smile before she opened her eyes, and waking with Jessa in her arms under an open sky was magical. The wind had died down completely, and the call of seabirds overhead was like a song welcoming her back to life.

Jessa stirred and smiled at her sleepily. "Morning."

"Morning."

"Did you want to get dressed before Asol—"

"Wow. Seriously, you guys are crazy for sleeping out here when you've got those pod things in there. But then, I guess you wouldn't both fit in one." Asol's voice came from the entrance of the cave.

"Good morning, Asol," Jessa called sweetly.

"Morning, Captain," Asol called back, laughing.

"Too late." Kylin looked into Jessa's beautiful eyes. "I have no idea where your clothing is."

Jessa turned carefully, keeping the blanket over her, and looked around. "It's about five feet away."

Kylin grinned. "Well, here's the thing. If you get up and wrap the blanket around you to get it, you leave me here butt naked for all the world to see. But if you keep my modesty intact, then you have to go naked as a baby to get your clothes. What a dilemma."

Jessa tilted her head like she was thinking about it. "Indeed."

She was surprisingly fast, and Kylin didn't have time to catch her before she was up, the blanket wrapped around her, and walking over to her Thalla robe. She looked over her shoulder with a mischievous grin. "Your poor modesty, all out for the world to see."

Kylin lay back and laughed, relishing the sun on her skin. "Better me than you. If Asol saw what I saw last night, we'd be fighting like mangy mutts for a sniff."

Jessa laughed and walked past Asol into the domicile unit. "And you're not worried she'll be running after you?"

Asol's laugh filled the air. "Kylin and I aren't each other's type, Captain. We're more likely to build shit together than bed wrestle."

Kylin rolled over and raised an eyebrow at Asol.

"Sorry, but I'm right." She grinned and stretched. "Let's get this show on the road, lover scruff."

It was the second time in a week that someone had called Kylin that, and it made her laugh. Not only that, but she felt almost giddy. When she'd come outside in the night, it had been to escape the thoughts of Jessa that were making her insane. And what she'd told her was true. They could have real time together, and even if it hurt like hell when she left, at least she'd have had something with her, something special that had been honest, something to replace the vile memories of her last love.

And exploding cosmos dust, had it been amazing. Being inside Jessa, on top of her, feeling her body writhe and hearing her moan… Kylin rested her head on her arms. If there was a god anywhere in any universe, surely they'd made Jessa. Her heart had felt like it was going to explode every time Jessa kissed her, and she couldn't get close enough, deep enough. She'd taken her over and over again until they'd fallen asleep, and when Jessa had touched her, she'd very nearly pulled away. But she wouldn't deny herself Jessa's touch, either, and when she'd let go and tumbled over the cliff, she knew every ounce of pain in the future would be worth it, if only for what they'd had last night.

She stood and stretched and felt like a new person. She picked up the blanket and her clothes but didn't bother to wrap them around her as she walked back to the unit.

Asol crossed her arms and looked her over. "But then, maybe I'm missing out."

Kylin shoved her slightly as she walked by. "As if. We'd both fight to be on top and neither of us would get off."

Asol touched her arm before she went inside. "Hey. All seriousness, you sure about this?"

"Why do you ask?" Kylin draped the blanket around her in case Jessa came out of the shower cubicle. Seeing the scars in the morning light might change her mind.

"She's one of the shiny people, right?" Asol shrugged. "Like I said on Volare. We're never one of them."

Kylin sighed, the lightness of the morning gone. "I know. And she'll leave, back to her shiny place. But it's worth it. Better to feel it and lose it than never to feel it at all. Right?"

Asol nodded and punched her shoulder. "I want to be you when I grow up."

Kylin laughed, but the comment was like a bucket of cold water. "You can be way, way better than me when you grow up."

She gave Jessa a slow kiss before scooting past her into the shower cubicle. She didn't want real life to intrude today. She wanted to hold on to the beauty of what they'd shared just a little longer. She concentrated on Jessa's moans, on her cries and the way she'd held on to Kylin like she was going to drown every time she came. It helped wash away the doubts, and she got out of the shower ready to get underway.

"Asol has already taken our bags down to the boat." Jessa smiled at her shyly.

"That's great. With the way the wind slammed us forward yesterday, I think we'll be at the nomad lands by lunchtime." She tucked her nice clothes back into the bag and put on her normal daily clothes that looked pretty dingy next to the Thalla whites. She'd have to invest in some new ones soon.

"I have to admit to being nervous about the next stage of our journey." Jessa stepped outside the domicile unit with Kylin and hit the button for it to begin folding itself up.

"Anything in particular?" Kylin asked, relieved when Jessa took her hand. So it wasn't about them.

"The bounty on you still concerns me. And you said the nomad tribes don't always like outsiders. What if my crew has had trouble in Quasi?" She looked at Kylin seriously. "I'm incredibly glad

I made the impetuous decision to come with you, but I admit to feeling a little guilty about leaving them to fend for themselves."

Kylin let go of Jessa's hand just long enough for Jessa to pick up the blocked domicile unit, then took it again as they walked to the shore. "That's understandable. But I'm sure the person who picked them up for me delivered them to Auntie Blue. If anything, they're overfed and in love with her."

Jessa smiled, and her shoulders dropped a little. "I'm glad you think so."

They seemed to leave it at that by mutual agreement. "And as far as the bounty, I'll make that call when we get to the mainland, and hopefully that will help."

Jessa glanced at her and then back at the path. "Do you want to tell me what that's about yet?"

Kylin owed it to her, and she knew it. And yet, the truth of it just wouldn't come. "I owe someone a debt. He's a pretty bad guy, but I was desperate. He thinks I ran, so he sent people to find me. Once I pay my debt, it will all be over." That wasn't the whole truth, but it sounded bad enough. And the likelihood of her paying off that debt was like the cosmos shrinking to the size of a prowler egg. And prowlers didn't have eggs.

Jessa stayed quiet until they neared the shore. "Thank you for telling me, though I think there's far more to it. I won't ask again, because it feels too intrusive. But I'd like it if you were able to tell me the whole story." She leaned up and kissed Kylin softly before turning and accepting Asol's hand into the boat.

Asol raised her eyebrows but didn't say anything, for which Kylin was grateful. Things would get complicated again when they reached land. For now, she wanted to enjoy the sunshine and the sea, Jessa's hand in hers, and Asol's free laughter. For now, that was enough.

❖

Kylin tossed the rope to Asol, who tied it off expertly at the dock. They'd sailed along the shoreline until they found one with few people at it. That way there were fewer people to deal with in case someone was waiting to pounce on Kylin. They grabbed their main bags from the boat and looked around.

Kylin was nearly knocked over when someone crashed into her from behind, and she saw Jessa and Asol spin, ready to fight. But when she looked down at the person hugging her legs, she laughed and scooped the little girl into the air, swinging her around before lowering her to press her forehead to the girl's.

"Are your mama and papa here?" Kylin asked, and the girl nodded, chattering away in her native language as she tugged on Kylin's hand to get her to follow them.

"Friend of yours?" Asol asked, shouldering her bag.

"She's with the nomad tribe we helped on our way out," she said to Jessa.

Jessa smiled at the little girl, who smiled back and took her hand, linking her and Kylin together.

"I think she likes you." Kylin looked over her shoulder at Asol. "They took me in when I was a kid. We couldn't have asked for a better group to find us." She frowned, thinking. "But it's unusual for them to be this close to the sea this time of year. They're usually looking for shelter by now."

The girl led them around the bend in the road and through a cluster of trees, and the encampment came into sight. The little girl shouted, let go of their hands, and ran to her family. Her parents looked up and waved to Kylin.

"Well met," Kylin said, pressing her forehead to theirs in greeting.

"It's good you've come back this way instead of straight into Quasi. Bad things are happening." The little girl's father, Bakta, looked grave.

"Wait." Her mother, Creta, smiled. "Clean up and drink with us. Then we'll trade stories."

"Thank you." Kylin followed them to their main group area where chairs were set up around a campfire. They set their bags down and took seats. The children flocked to Asol, who was immediately dragged off to play with them.

Kylin accepted a mug of special spiced nomad tea that she'd always loved. "What's happening?"

Bakta sipped his own tea and tousled the hair of a child running past. "The slavers. They're out of control. They never bothered us." Creta huffed and he tilted his head in acknowledgement. "Mostly, never bothered us. There were boundaries, rules. But they've done away with the rules, and they're attacking anyone not behind walls. Our tribes are getting hit hard, and so are the villages that don't have guards."

Kylin sat back, stunned, her tea forgotten. "The cities will have to fight back."

Creta snorted. "Why? They're safe. They're not going to go help the people who are vulnerable. They won't help us."

It was true, and Kylin didn't deny it. Helplessness always made her rage, and she felt it building now. She turned to Jessa when she put her hand on her shoulder.

"Maybe it's time to get help from the outside."

"They won't trade with us. What makes you think they'd help us? Won't it be just another bad thing that happens on our planet?" There was bitterness in her tone, but she couldn't help it. Fortunately, Jessa seemed to take it in stride.

"That could be true, but not if someone who isn't from your planet speaks up on your behalf. I'd be willing. We just have to find a way to get word to the right people."

Kylin stared at her, trying to parse out what she was saying. "You'd help us? And you think someone would listen?"

Jessa nodded, her brow furrowed. "I can think of a number of people who would be interested in helping. But we'd need someone from your world to speak up, too. Someone who cares." She rested her hand on Kylin's.

And there it was. More responsibility. More people depending on her, more people to let down. "We'll find someone." She turned back to the nomad couple. "What are you doing to stay safe?"

"We're staying by the water, where we can get away if we need to. We've got boats hidden, and we'll spend the winter here, in the trees."

"You'll freeze." Jessa looked horrified.

Creta gave her a weary smile. "We've faced worse, and things will change, just like the land around us does." She turned to Kylin. "So if you're going back to Quasi, you need to think about your way in."

Kylin sighed and closed her eyes. This part was supposed to be easy. Relatively easy, anyway.

Asol crashed to the ground beside them, three kids wrapped around her, wrestling with her for a toy. "Slavers disguises?"

It was good she'd been listening, even from a distance, so they didn't have to repeat things. "It won't work a second time, not after they caught on to us on the ship. Word will have spread that we're traveling that way." She stared into the fire, thinking. "Is there anyone they're *not* attacking?"

"People who are well armed and will fight back."

"Then that's who we become." Jessa motioned around the camp. "Do you have weapons and outfits?"

"Jessa, this isn't a game." Kylin couldn't imagine walking right toward a slaver's caravan. "If they take us, we're dust."

Asol sent the last child running and smoothed down her hair. "I agree with Jessa. They expect people to run, not to face them down. If there are weapons to be had, I say we do it. Walk right past the prowler shits and shoot any who come at us."

It made sense that Asol would feel that way, and Jessa had no way of truly understanding. But if either of them got caught, she'd never forgive herself.

Jessa stood and looked down at her. "This isn't your decision, Kylin. Asol and I are willing to try it, so you're outvoted. Deal with it." She turned to the couple, who were smiling. "I've got an energy gun in my bag, but that won't be enough. Can you help?"

They stood and Kylin, Jessa, and Asol followed them to a massive white vehicle with enormous tires. They pulled the back doors open, and Asol started laughing.

"They're not going to know what hit them." Asol jumped in and started riffling through the assorted weapons and clothing, and she tossed things down to Kylin as she found them.

"And how do we explain three guards out in the open on their own?" Kylin asked.

Jessa held up one uniform top, then another. "They're different uniforms. So we say we're from the cities working together. We'll be armed, and we'll fire if necessary."

Kylin turned to Jessa. "Do you really think you could shoot someone?"

Jessa took a deep breath and stepped closer. "To save you? And Asol? Yes. And these people have to be stopped." She cupped Kylin's cheek in her hand. "When I decide to do something, there's no stopping me. You might like that about me, one day." She gave her a small smile. "If you're asking if I understand what this means, I do."

Kylin searched Jessa's eyes for any doubt, for a flicker of hesitation, but there wasn't any. Just…no. It wasn't love. It was too early for that. But there was emotion and that alone made Kylin's breath stutter. She turned to Asol. "Get whatever you think we can carry, on our backs and in our bags."

"Creta, there's a boat tied to dock fifteen. It has plenty of food and water in it. It also has a couple things we need. Can you help us get the things out of it? Then the boat is yours."

Creta called out in her own language, and several young people dashed out of sight through the trees. "They'll empty the boat and bring everything back here."

Asol kept handing down items from the truck, and Kylin and Jessa stacked them on the ground. The young people came back lugging the food and water bags, as well as the few items they weren't already carrying in their own bags.

Jessa held out the domicile unit to Creta. "Please take this. It's not big enough for your whole community, but it might help at some point."

Creta took it and turned it over. "What is it?"

While Jessa took Creta aside and showed her how to use it, much to the amazement of the tribe, Asol jumped down next to Kylin. She kicked the stack on the ground.

"I need you to promise me something."

Kylin checked a piece of uniform that looked like it might fit. "Yeah?"

"If they catch us, you shoot me in the head."

Kylin set the clothing down slowly and stood. "What?"

Asol held out her upper arm, showing Kylin the jagged scar running up the inside. "They hurt people for fun. Because it's funny when people bleed and cry and shit themselves from pain and fear." She lowered her arm. "You've seen it, I know you have. You know what it means. And I can't go back to that. If they catch us, and I can't do it myself, I need you to do it."

"Swooper shits, Asol." Kylin shoved her hands in her pockets, ill with the knowledge that she'd do it if she had to. She wouldn't let Asol go back to that life. She wouldn't get out of it twice. "Yeah. You have my word."

"Good." She slapped Kylin on the back and gathered a pile of stuff from the ground. "Let's go get dressed. If we travel by night we might slip by unseen."

Kylin liked that idea and waved Jessa over. She left the group walking around the unit, talking excitedly.

"Want to play dress up?" Kylin asked, holding out a uniform top.

Jessa gave her a sultry smile. "I think that would be fun."

Asol whistled, and Kylin elbowed her in the ribs. They went to a small hut and spent time finding the right uniforms, and then they went through the weapons. Jessa was surprisingly handy and knowledgeable about the various options, something Kylin found exceedingly sexy.

"How long will it take us to get there?" Jessa asked.

"About three hours if we can move fast. We landed at a good spot, and we'll see the light of Quasi as soon as we get out on the sands."

Asol looked up, the excitement clear in her eyes. "Wow, I didn't realize we were so close."

Kylin's stomach was in knots. Now that they were that close, the enormity of what she had to deal with at home really hit her. "Yeah. We'll be there soon."

Once they were repacked and ready to go, they sat with the tribe and had dinner, and they regaled Asol and Jessa with tales of Kylin's wild childhood antics. She laughed along with them, but her mind was far away, trying to make plans, and backup plans, and exit plans. Once she had Jessa and Asol within the walls of Quasi, she could leave them with Auntie Blue and go deal with Orlin. And Maana. And her father. Then, once all that was done, she'd see if she could find Jessa and her crew a way to get to the Heathers. Jessa had credit chips, there was no question there, but finding a flyer to take them to the Heathers would still be difficult, especially if there wasn't a transport due. But Kylin had no doubt that Jess and her crew would be safer and more comfortable in the Heathers than in Quasi.

The thought of Jessa still being on Indemnion but so far out of reach that she might as well not be, hurt. But she'd do what she needed to this time. It would be on her terms.

CHAPTER EIGHTEEN

Kylin's words rang through Jessa's head, over and over again. *You'd shoot someone?* She'd answered without hesitation, but now, as the three of them jogged over the sands, only the first moon and stars to light their way, she felt the gun tremble in her grip. It was true, she'd shoot in self-defense, and if it meant saving Kylin and Asol, she didn't think she'd wait to pull the trigger. But that didn't mean it would be easy, either.

But then again, these slavers were the worst of human kind. Their actions made Jessa ill, and seeing what had happened to Asol made it even worse. And although she hadn't seen Kylin fully naked in the light of day yet, she'd felt the scars on her back. Those might not be from slavers, but they were unquestionably from a society that allowed that kind of violence against its people. The thing was, they wanted change. They just needed someone who could help them, and Jessa knew deep down she could.

Kylin held up her arm and Jessa and Asol crouched low, like she'd told them to. She peered around Asol and saw the bobbing lights in the distance. They watched for several long minutes, and when it became clear the lights were moving away from them, Kylin motioned them forward again. They kept silent, moving quickly, and there was an element of thrill to it that Jessa hadn't expected. It was so far from the life she'd known. Like Kylin said, the lights from Quasi made the sky glow, and Jessa was glad the sands had dunes they could duck behind if they needed to, but that also meant there could be things between themselves and Quasi they couldn't see. It was a chance they had to take.

Voices seemed to come from nowhere, and Kylin motioned them down again, but this time they ducked behind a dune. Kylin shimmied to the top to look over it and then moved back down beside them.

"Small convoy of slavers. Two trucks, empty cages in the first one, two cages with people in the second one," she whispered.

"Can we save the two?" Asol asked.

Kylin tilted her head. "We could, but we risk getting caught ourselves."

The sound of wheels spinning in dirt came over the sands, followed by shouts and angry voices. This time, all three of them crawled up to look over the dune.

Nearby, one of the truck's tires was buried deep in the sand, and it only got worse as the driver tried to gun their way out of it. Jessa studied the setup and leaned over to Kylin.

"If we created a distraction, something up ahead that drew their attention, we could open the cages and set them free. At least if they run they'll have a better chance, right?"

"What kind of distraction did you have in mind?"

Grateful that Kylin didn't resist setting the captives free, Jessa pulled a glowing ball from her bag, one the children of Volare had given her. "We set this going. They'll think it's someone running and follow."

Asol grinned, her teeth gleaming in the darkness. "And we're nowhere near it. Solid idea."

Kylin looked at the trucks. "We'll need a laser cutter to release the cage locks, and we're going to have to move fast. Asol and I can jump into the trucks, cut the locks, and then Jessa can help them down." She took the ball from Jessa and moved back down the dune. "Give me two minutes to get it set and going. The moment you see them leave the trucks, head in. I'll meet you there."

She loped off into the darkness, and Jessa thought her heart might beat out of her chest. If this didn't work, they could end up in cages beside the people they were trying to save. She heard

Asol counting the seconds, and it wasn't long before they heard the excited shouts, and when they looked, the slavers had left their trucks to chase after the "person" running off into sands.

They clambered from their position, ran to the trucks, and found Kylin already working on one of the locks. Asol jumped up, took out her own cutter, and started working on the other one. The cage Kylin was working on held a young woman, and the other cage a child who stared at them wide-eyed. Both seemed to understand that silence was important. The woman watched the laser, and the moment the lock broke, she pushed the door open and went to the other cage.

Jessa motioned to her to get down, and the woman reluctantly accepted her hand down but never looked away from the other cage. When it was open, Asol took the child from inside and handed her down to the woman, who held her tight, tears streaming down her face.

Kylin picked up a long pole from the bed of the truck and wrapped a piece of rope around the end. She handed the rope to Asol, who wrapped a piece around the other end. She motioned to Jessa to lead the way, and Jessa touched the young woman's arm to guide her. They ran, covering enough distance that the voices and sounds of the trucks faded. Sweat dripped down Jessa's back and her hands were slippery on the gun, but the elation of saving someone made her giddy. She looked over her shoulder and saw that Asol and Kylin were running almost shoulder to shoulder, dragging the pole along behind them to wipe away their tracks. Simple, but effective. The slight breeze would be enough to wipe away the edges left by the pole.

They crested another dune and the young woman dropped to her knees, the child still clinging to her.

The three of them dropped beside her, all breathing hard.

Jessa opened her water pouch and handed it to the woman, who gave the child a long drink before taking one herself.

"How much farther?" Jessa whispered. "I don't think they've got much more in them."

Kylin nodded and jogged ahead to the next dune, where she crawled up it to look over before coming back to them. "Maybe another hour and a half. We're nearly there. Can you make it?"

The young woman drank some more and nodded. "If I have to crawl."

It was a good answer, and it gave Jessa hope that they'd make it.

"Let's go. The more distance we put between us and them, the better." Kylin stood, and the others joined her. "Ready?"

They set off again, moving swiftly, and they didn't come across any more noise or voices. The second moon rose, which didn't help. While they could see their way better, it also meant they could be seen.

Jessa's legs and shoulders ached, and her head pounded by the time they made it to the city walls. Kylin walked right up to the guardhouse and demanded entry for herself, two other guards, and two captives. The gatehouse guard looked them over but seemed mostly disinterested. He opened the gate, and they entered Quasi. When the gate slammed shut behind them, Jessa thought she might crumble with relief.

Kylin stopped and took a deep breath. "That was fun." She smiled at the others, her relief clear. She turned to the young woman and child. "Do you have somewhere to go here?"

The young woman nodded, the fatigue and terror of her experience obvious in the lines around her eyes. "Thank you so much. I can't ever repay you for saving our lives."

Asol tousled the child's hair, and Jessa saw the knowledge no one her age should have in her eyes.

"Good luck. Stay behind the walls for a while, eh?"

The woman thanked them again, then turned and disappeared down a narrow walkway between…Jessa wasn't really sure what she was looking at. Rectangular boxes with doors and windows were stacked on top of each other, almost haphazardly. Stairs led to each box, and she couldn't imagine being the person who lived at the top of a stack and had to climb all that way. There were stacks as far as she could see, towers of them sitting along wide streets and then divided by small alleyways.

And there was so much color. The boxes were different hues, some painted with flowers or designs, some with dots or stripes. Plants hung from window boxes, and she wondered what they'd look like in the light of day. Lights were on in many of the boxes, but given how late it was, it wasn't surprising many were dark.

"Welcome to Quasi." Kylin looked around like she was trying to see it as an outsider.

"Cosmos dust and prowler balls," Asol whispered, turning around, trying to take it all in. "It's amazing."

Kylin grinned. "Come on. Let's get out of these uniforms and off the streets."

She led the way down one street, then another, until Jessa was completely turned around and couldn't have gotten back to the gate if she'd wanted to. Kylin stopped in front of a beautifully decorated box on the bottom of a stack, one with a bright red door with blue dots. In script along the front was a sign: Vesta Blue's Inn. Only one light shone in the window.

Kylin knocked, a rapid three-two-one-three knock, and the door was answered almost instantly by a large woman with beautiful pale blue hair and eyes that sparkled. She pulled Kylin into a tight hug. "By all the creators of the cosmos, Kylin Enderson. You've had me worried out of my skull." She held Kylin at arm's length. "I tried to tell them you had only gone to check the wreckage like everyone else. But Orlin wouldn't hear it."

Kylin looked over her shoulder. "And my father?"

Auntie Blue looked at Jessa, then at Asol. "The captain, I'm guessing, and another stray?"

Jessa nearly retorted that she wasn't a "stray," but Kylin nodded. "Friends. It's quite a story. You have room for us?"

Auntie Blue motioned them inside. Jessa tried to ignore the way her heart hurt at being referred to as a friend, after what they'd shared. But then, it wasn't like there was another label that fit better yet, either. She swallowed the emotion and forced herself to focus on the moment. She held out her arm. "Captain Jessa Arabelle."

Auntie Blue studied her for a moment before grasping Jessa's arm with her own. "Your crew has told me a little about you. It's good that you're alive." She looked at Asol. "And you, darling thing?"

That was a far warmer welcome than Jessa had received, and she looked at Kylin, who in turn looked thoughtful.

"Asol. Dock rat looking for a new life, beautiful lady." Asol kissed Auntie Blue's hand, making her laugh.

"She's just like you at that age," she said to Kylin. "Come into the kitchen. Let me tell you what's going on here. In the morning, we'll gather all your people, and you can tell us your story all at once."

They sat at in a homey kitchen with room enough for ten. Various breads and spreads were arrayed on the table, along with pitchers of drinks. She motioned for them to help themselves, so they did. As they ate, she talked.

"Kylin, your dad's cough is worse." She put a clear bag of what looked like thick grass on the table. "He's been drinking his flagweed, but…" She squeezed Kylin's hand. "I'm sorry, but I think that's the most important thing to tell you first. He sleeps a lot, and he's not in pain."

Kylin pushed her plate away, and Jessa wasn't sure what to say. Kylin hadn't mentioned her dad hardly at all and certainly not that he was sick. Now she understood why she was so worried about hurrying back. Her heart ached that Kylin hadn't shared something so important, and she wondered why she kept that to herself.

"Your crew are fine," Auntie Blue said to Jessa. "Well, most of them."

Jessa's stomach turned. "Something happened?"

"The big one. Teckoe, I think his name was. My understanding is that when you left with Kylin, he thought you'd abandoned them. When they arrived here, he refused to stay indoors. He went looking for information and got duped in the Stables. He lost a bet and was sold to the slavers. He's been gone for days."

Jessa ran to the sink and vomited. Tears ran down her face. She'd been impetuous and selfish when she'd decided to go with

Kylin, and the result of that was that her chief crew member, someone she'd worked with for years, had been sent into a horrible fate.

She felt Kylin's hand rubbing soothing circles on her back, and she turned to her, letting Kylin wrap her in her arms.

"It's not your fault, Jess." Kylin rested her cheek against Jessa's head. "He would have done that if you were here, too. He just used it as an excuse." She pulled away slightly to look down into Jessa's eyes. "He told me it was every person for themselves in a situation like this. That you felt too responsible."

Jessa wiped at her face. "He said that?"

Kylin helped wipe away her tears. "He did. And it doesn't surprise me he got into trouble. I'm sorry, though. I know it must hurt."

"The rest of your crew said the same thing, Captain." Auntie Blue remained at the table, watching them. "He was ungrateful and arrogant. We can lament his journey but not our part in it."

She let Kylin lead her back to the table, grateful when she kept her arm around her shoulders. "Thank you for taking care of them in my absence. It helped knowing they were safe."

Auntie Blue nodded, and Jessa didn't miss the way she was looking at Kylin's arm around her. "They've been good guests. And the credit chips they've offered will keep the inn running for some time. It's been good for me too."

"And what other news do you have?" Kylin asked, picking at her food.

"Orlin has doubled the bounty on your head. It seems he has an important—"

Kylin interrupted her with a sharp shake of her head. "I told him I'd be back. My time runs out tomorrow. I don't understand why he's so worked up."

Auntie Blue shrugged and started removing plates from the table, though she glanced at Jessa, her expression thoughtful. "Who knows why Orlin thinks what he does. But you know he thinks you ran?" Kylin nodded, looking tired. "Well, that might be all he needed. He likes his theatrics." She finished clearing the plates and then clapped her hands together and made a shooing motion. "Up the stairs. Take your bags. Sleep. We can discuss everything else tomorrow."

They dutifully followed her up two sets of stairs, past various doors with markings on them, until she stopped. "You can take that one, Kylin." She pointed at another door. "Captain, that's yours." And at a third. "Cute little dock rat, that one should suit you."

Jessa swallowed, unsure what the protocol was in this situation. She didn't want to sleep in a room on her own. Not in a new place, and not without Kylin at her side. But she also didn't want to be rude or presumptuous. Fortunately, Kylin took her hand.

"We'll share a room, Auntie, thank you."

Auntie Blue narrowed her eyes and pursed her lips. "We'll talk about this tomorrow." She turned and made her way gracefully down the steps.

"I don't think she likes me," Jessa said, watching her disappear through the door at the bottom.

"Nope. I don't think she does either. But she already adores me." Asol laughed and opened the door to her room. "See you tomorrow."

Kylin opened the door to their room and tugged Jessa inside.

"Don't you need to tell your father you're back?" Jessa asked.

"He'll be asleep, and I don't like to wake him when he's resting. I'll see him in the morning." Kylin sat on the bed, her shoulders slumped. "I'm sorry I didn't tell you about him."

Jessa sat beside her and took her hand in her own. "May I ask why you didn't?"

Kylin stared at their hands. "I'm a private person. My dad is all I have left, and I do what I can to protect him and take care of him. I feel like the less people who know about him, the less I have to worry about someone coming after him. It's a habit, and if you understood the way my life is here, you'd understand why I live this way."

"Can you tell me more about your life here?" It was intrusive, and yet, she remembered what Kylin had said when they'd first met. If you don't ask, how will you ever know?

Kylin kissed Jessa's hand and stood. "Let's save that for another day, okay? I'm beat."

Jessa understood a deflection when she heard one, but it was Kylin's story to tell, and she wouldn't push her. They stripped off the borrowed uniforms, changed into clothes they could sleep in, and curled up on the fairly comfortable bed together. Kylin turned out the light and wrapped Jessa in her arms.

"Thank you for bringing me in with you," Jessa murmured as sleep claimed her. "Thank you for not leaving me alone."

Kylin's response was just to pull her closer, and for tonight, that was enough.

❖

Noise woke Jessa from a deep sleep, and she lay there listening to it, trying to make sense of it. Voices were raised in rhythmic timing, music played somewhere, and the chatter and clatter of people outside could be easily heard. She thought of the way the city was composed, and the noise made sense. There must be thousands upon thousands of people in this city. The thought made her uncomfortable. Surely it was claustrophobic, living among so many others? On board, she had her private quarters in her own part of the ship, and she could go for days alone in silence if she wanted to. She couldn't imagine that being possible here.

Kylin nibbled at her shoulder. "Want to tell me what you're thinking?"

She wriggled around so she could face her. "I'm processing what life here must be like. I've never heard so much communal sound."

Kylin looked at the ceiling, like she was listening. "Yeah, I guess that's true. Definitely louder than on Volare, right?" She smiled gently and tucked Jessa's hair behind her ear. "Maybe I can show you around later. If you want."

Jessa was torn. She wanted to see it, but she didn't want to look like a voyeur, an outsider looking at exotic animals. But Kylin had offered, which meant it was okay. "I'd like that."

"What else would you like?" Kylin asked, and her hand slid between Jessa's legs. "Would you like to see how much I want you?"

Jessa moaned and opened her legs wider to let Kylin in. With only a few strokes, she was wet and ready, and Kylin pushed into her, making her arch and gasp. Sex with her wasn't just physical. It was about the intensity in her eyes, the way being filled by her made Jessa want to weep with the beauty and rightness of it. And as Kylin took her slow and deep, she pressed into each thrust, wishing they could stay right there, entwined that way, forever. She came hard, and Kylin moaned with her, her eyes closed and her hips pressed hard to Jessa's thigh. They'd come together, a first for Jessa and something else that felt deeply special.

When they'd caught their breath again, Kylin kissed the top of Jessa's head. "We should probably get cleaned up and go downstairs. Blue will have told my dad we're back."

Jessa pushed away the flash of resentment. Not at Kylin's dad, but at the life wanting them back, when all she wanted to do was stay right there in Kylin's arms. She got up, and they had a quick and sexy shower together before they went downstairs, hand in hand.

When they entered the dining room, there were exclamations and hugs all around from Jessa's crew. Asol had already gone out exploring. Over breakfast, Jessa told them about the trip with Kylin, and about the things she'd seen. When she described the Volare, even Auntie Blue looked stunned.

"But why didn't you tell us you were staying behind?" Asanka asked.

Jessa allowed the twinge of guilt. "I didn't know myself until the last second." She took Benika's hand. "I'm so sorry. But if there was a chance other escape pods came down, I needed to see for myself if there were survivors."

"And were there?" Peshta leaned forward.

Jessa thought of the damaged pod and the grim carnage inside. "One pod. No survivors."

Peshta nodded and seemed to sense what Jessa wasn't saying. The room was silent for a moment before Auntie Blue clapped her hands and stood.

"Now that you're all together you can decide what the next step is." She turned to Kylin. "And I believe you have several people to see."

Kylin rolled her eyes and stretched. "Yeah." She turned to Jessa and touched her cheek. "I have to go, but I'll come back and show you around later, okay?"

Jessa sighed with pleasure at the light caress. "I'll hold you to that."

Kylin grinned and left the room, and Jessa felt her absence. But she pushed it aside and focused on her crew, whom she hadn't realized she'd missed quite so much. "Tell me, what have you been doing here in Quasi?"

She listened, but in the back of her mind she wondered if Kylin was safe, if she would be okay given the nature of the people she had to go deal with. She still didn't fully understand the nature of what was going on, but maybe in time Kylin would trust her with that information.

CHAPTER NINETEEN

Kylin held the door handle but couldn't bring herself to turn it. Auntie Blue's suggestion that he didn't have much time left made her tremble inside. When he was gone she'd truly be alone. Although he'd fallen apart after her mother died, he'd done his best to train her and help her through the tough times, but neither of them had ever really recovered from her loss.

Steeling herself, she pushed open the door, but when she saw him lying in the bed her knees went weak. She didn't recognize the frail, yellowed man propped up by pillows, his breathing shallow and whistling. She choked back the emotion and went to his side.

"Hey, Dad."

His eyes slowly fluttered open and he held out his hand to take hers. "Hey, kid. Good scrounge?"

She swallowed the pain and attempted a smile. "You wouldn't believe the insanity of this trip. I got to stay with the Volare again, though."

He started to speak but was quickly overcome by a coughing fit that left him wheezing, his eyes watering. She poured some flagweed and held it to his lips so he could drink. When he motioned for her to take it away she set it down, but some spilled because of her shaking hands.

"Blue didn't want me to know, but I could hear it when people were passing the window. You're in trouble with Orlin?" His voice was hoarse and soft.

"Nothing I can't handle."

He shook his head. "Not good, kid."

Hopefully, he didn't know just how bad it really was. He didn't need that kind of worry. "I'm going to head into the Stables today to talk to him. I'll set it straight."

He squeezed her hand. "Listen to me."

She moved closer and let the tears fall. The finality of the moment ran through her like a setting moon in winter.

"You were meant for more, and if your mom had lived, you would have been more. I did my best, but it wasn't nearly what you needed." He stopped to breathe slowly and take a sip of flagweed. "You fix things with Orlin. And then you do whatever you have to in order to get off Indemnion. Fly. See the universe." He started coughing again, and she wiped the water from his eyes. "Promise me."

"Dad—"

"Promise." He squeezed her hand hard. "No matter how long it takes."

He wasn't asking her to do it tomorrow. Just to make sure she tried to make it happen. It was a loophole, but it meant she could promise without breaking it. "Okay, Dad. I will."

He nodded and his head lolled on the pillows. "Sleep now."

She stayed with him until his breathing had slowed and he was asleep. The tears slid down her cheeks unchecked, making little dark spots on the white sheets. She couldn't bear to leave him, but the sooner she dealt with Orlin, the better.

She slipped from the room, giving her dad one last look, and then headed into the alley behind the stack. She made her way quickly through the maze and into the Stables, always making sure to stay in the shadows and avoid groups of people. She wasn't about to get taken to Orlin and have the bounty added to her debt. A fresh rope of bread was steaming on the baker's lintel, and she couldn't resist picking it up. He poked his head out and looked at her in surprise before glancing around.

"Better get into the shadows, K. And you're going to need more than bread to keep you going." He tossed her a package. "Eat before you get there."

She blew him a kiss and tore into the cheese and meat as she walked, dodging and weaving to keep from being seen. She finally made it to Orlin's section of the Stables. She finished her impromptu meal and made a mental promise to do something nice for the baker. Straightening her shoulders, she sauntered into the market stall and whistled.

Orlin turned around, and she could see his sharp teeth and yellow eyes in the darkness.

"Well. Kylin Enderson. I thought you'd found some little hole to crawl into. I'm glad to see you came to your senses and returned." His long, bony hand shot out and grabbed her arm. "Did you think you could run from what you owe me?"

She didn't try to pull away, instead affecting a bored look that she hoped would put him off. "If you had to pay that bounty, it would have been your own fault. You told me to be back by this time, and look, here I am, just like I said I'd be. You got overexcited, water spider. I just went scrounging. Nothing more."

His oval eyes narrowed and he hissed. "You disrespect me after running?"

Okay, name calling might have been a bad move. "You put a bounty on my head. I would have been here sooner if I wasn't dodging most of the planet. I think we're even. And I didn't run."

He stared at her for a long moment before letting go of her arm and laughing. "You're right. I overreacted. What you do on your own time isn't any of my business."

She frowned. Could it be that easy? Would he back down like that?

"Of course, there's still the matter of your debt." He folded into his chair, his long, spider-like legs cracking as they bent. "And you'll begin paying it off tomorrow."

She'd figured as much, though she'd hoped to have time to show Jessa around before she got into the ring. "Yeah, whatever. Who am I fighting?"

His smile was menacing and sent shivers down her spine, though she made sure not to react.

"You'll see when you get here. Be here at second moon rise."

She waved and gave a mock bow. "You like your drama, don't you?" She looked at the guards arrayed around the room. "Speaking of which, mind sending out the word the bounty is canceled? No point in you paying something you don't have to, right?"

He motioned at two of the nearest guards. "Get the word out that the bounty is null, and that there will be a magical event tomorrow night. No holds linari wagers in effect."

Her heart sped up. "No holds? Isn't that a little risky? I'm good, but that doesn't mean I'm a definite."

He blew a yellow smoke ring at her. "Who says I'm betting on you?"

His laughter followed her out of the market stall and into the Stables. Her pulse pounded in her throat, and she couldn't breathe. No holds betting meant he didn't have any doubt at all that she was going to lose. And that was very, very bad for her.

A tall, beautiful woman stepped in front of her, blocking her path. "Maana would like to have you over for a drink."

Kylin only just managed to keep from groaning out loud. *That* meeting she'd hoped to put off for a little while. She plastered on a smile, hoping she'd get something to drink, rather than be the thing being consumed. "Lead the way, hot stuff."

The woman smiled, and her small, pointed teeth made Kylin wince. She followed her through the Stables to the outer stacks, where many people ran small businesses. They got in the lift and rode it to the top of a stack, where the white house with black trim stood out like a beacon against the dark. If, that is, you didn't know what went on there.

They entered, and it was bitterly cold inside. Maana's kind lived on a snowy planet, but there wasn't any snow in Quasi. If there had been a city she could feed on near the cryo volcano, Kylin figured that's where Maana would have positioned herself.

Maana came out of the back room, wiping blood on a white towel. "Kylin."

The bloody towel brought back memories she'd rather forget. "Always nice to see you. Thanks for the deal to bring the crew back."

Maana took a drink from the woman who had led Kylin there and motioned for Kylin to sit. "I could have made a lot of money if

I'd let the slavers have them. But a deal with you is precious, and I'm interested in what you have to offer."

What Kylin had to offer last time was herself, and Maana had enjoyed toying with her like a prowler playing with its prey before a kill. The sex had been rough and violent, and Maana had enjoyed Kylin giving as good as she got. But after Jessa, that offer didn't feel right, even if she'd been interested in a replay, which she wasn't. And she had a feeling Maana wanted something else, anyway.

"What do you have in mind?" Kylin accepted the drink from Maana's house toy.

Maana leaned forward, her moonless eyes glinting. "You're fighting tomorrow."

She nodded and shrugged. "Nothing new there."

Maana's laugh hissed through the room. "But who you're fighting...and a no holds night. That's new."

Once again, the feeling of something out of control about to happen made her breathing twitch. "You know who I'm fighting?" she asked casually.

She waved her finger back and forth. "Now, now. I wouldn't want to spoil the surprise." She leaned forward and traced a sharp claw down Kylin's leg. "Everyone will be betting against you tomorrow. But not me. I think you'll take them. I know how..." her claw pressed deeper into Kylin's leg, "resilient you can be."

That meant there was a chance she could beat whoever it was tomorrow, and that was something. But what did she mean by "them"?

"But, just in case." She waved her servant over. "I want you to take this. If it looks like you're going to lose, push it into the other fighter. It will give you the edge you need to take them down."

The blue vial was smaller than her pinky nail, and when Maana pressed a tiny button on the side, a needle slid out of it.

"You want me to cheat? If Orlin caught me, I'd be prowler food. That's crazy."

Maana left it on the table between them. "You owe me, and this is what I want. And think. If you win tomorrow, on a no holds night, you could pay off your debt to Orlin once and for all. You wouldn't owe him, and you wouldn't owe me." She sipped her drink. "How long has it been since you've been free?"

Glinting blue temptation winked at her on the table. Her father's demand echoed in her ears. Fix things with Orlin. Leave the planet. But was it worth her life? Because if she got found out, there was no question what would happen.

"I'll have to think about it."

Maana pushed the blue vial toward her. "See that you think the right things."

Kylin pocketed the vial and stood to leave. "And if I don't use it? If I lose?"

Maana licked her lips, her forked tongue flicking over her teeth. "Then you'll pay another way, but you won't like it as much as you did last time, I promise." She tilted her head. "And maybe we'll bring in your cute little woman, the one you asked this favor for in the first place. I'm sure she'd be interested in seeing how we play."

The thought of Jessa anywhere near Maana made the bile rise in her throat. "She stays out of this. Come after her, and you'll see I'm not a plaything."

"Ooh, our little fighter has teeth." Maana laughed. "I'll see you tomorrow."

Kylin left, ignoring the lift and taking out her frustration on the long staircase to the ground instead. This was bad. Really bad. If she won, Orlin would go crazy with the money he would lose, and he'd probably try to take it out on her. But then, if he wanted to keep his reputation, if he wanted to keep fighters in the ring, he'd have to wipe her debt clean without retribution. But if he found out she'd cheated, then her life was as good as over. And if she lost and lived through it, Maana would come after her, and maybe Jessa. She couldn't let that happen, either.

She wandered through the stables, glad she didn't have to look over her shoulder anymore, but barely registering the people around her anyway. If it weren't for her dad, they could run. Go back to Volare, where they wouldn't be found. Live in idyllic seclusion.

But her dad was still battling for every moment, and she wouldn't abandon him. She'd stay beside him to the end. And Jessa wasn't about to live out her time on Indemnion. When Kylin made it back to Auntie Blue's she was no closer to a solution, and all she could come up with was that she'd have to play it by whichever way the wind blew. She opened the door and found Jessa and Auntie Blue in deep conversation. Asol leaned against the counter, a mug of something steaming in her hand. She gave Kylin a sympathetic look.

"Am I interrupting?"

Jessa smiled, but she saw Auntie Blue's look of concern.

"We've been thinking, and we want to pass something by you."

Kylin sat at the table with them, wondering what else was about to fall on her plate.

"You've got a government official here. Someone who knows the ins and outs of this world, someone who sends reports to the Intergalactic Alliance."

Kylin nodded. "He lives in the Heathers. I don't think he's ever set foot in Quasi."

Jessa pulled over a sheet of paper with lists on it. "But it says here that he does business in the Fesi District, that he has a second house there. Isn't that nearby?"

Confused, Kylin nodded. "Only about two hours. We can walk along the wall that connects Quasi to Fesi, so it's safe, too. What are you thinking?"

Auntie Blue stood. "I'm going to check on your father." She squeezed Kylin's shoulder as she walked past, and it felt laden with meaning.

"We could go talk to him. Tell him about us, and maybe once he gets back to the Heathers he can get a message out. But more than that," she tapped on the schedule, "we can talk to him about making changes. About his being an ambassador who calls for help with the slavers."

Kylin couldn't help it. She laughed and shook her head. "Jessa, where do you think the majority of the slaves go? The Heathers. You think he wants to clean his own house? And if he wanted to help change things, don't you think he would have done it by now?"

Jessa sat back, her expression downcast. "I hadn't thought of that." She traced circles on the map. "Have you met him? What if he's not that bad?"

Ragweed shit. "Why not? I don't have to be anywhere until tomorrow night, and the bounty has been lifted. If you think it's worth asking, let's go."

Jessa jumped up from the table and wrapped Kylin in a tight hug. "I do think it's worth trying. People can surprise you."

The phrase felt like a bad omen. Whatever happened tomorrow night, Jessa was bound to not like the outcome. If Kylin didn't die, she'd probably take a damn good beating. And if she lost... She couldn't stomach the thought of Jessa in danger.

"Maybe you should take your crew, too. All of you could stay at the official's house, where it's safe. He might even have a transport big enough to take you to the Heathers."

The hurt in Jessa's eyes was unmistakable. "You want me to go?"

Kylin sighed and took her hands. "Of course I don't want you to go. But we both know you'll be going as soon as a transport comes, and if you can get on one sooner, I know you want to get back." It was a swooper shit move, deflecting the question by making it sound like it was Jessa's choice. There was truth to it, but still.

Jessa slowly pulled her hands away, looking confused. "Sure. I'll tell the others."

She left the room, and Kylin sat back down. She put her head in her hands and tried to breathe through the emotions swamping her. She sensed someone else and looked up.

"That's the right thing to do." Auntie Blue looked sympathetic as she and Asol sat down at the table with her. "News is already going around about tomorrow night."

"It's worse than that, and you know how bad that could be."

Auntie Blue's skin paled to eggshell. "How could it be worse?"

"Maana. I owe her for bringing the crew here. And she wants a piece of the action."

Blue shook her head and clicked her tongue. "Oh, darlin'. Then there's no question it's best to get these visitors to a safe place."

She put her hand over Kylin's. "But you've found someone, haven't you?"

Kylin groaned. "You'd think I'd learn not to fall for women I can't have."

Blue stood. "If you want something, you find a way, Kylin. Your parents taught you that. If you want to be with this woman, the universe will step in and help. I believe that."

She left the room, her blue scarf fluttering behind her.

Asol whistled softly. "Your life is way more exciting than anything I want. What can I do?"

"Just stay out of the shadows. Keep to the light, okay? In fact, maybe you should go to Fesi with the others."

"No way!" Asol splashed some of her drink on the table. "I love this place. It's wild, but the people are crazy friendly. And thanks, but I don't want to go talk to some guy who would look at us like we're...well, us." She stretched and looked at Kylin seriously. "I've heard what they're saying in the maze out there. You're in deep, aren't you?"

Kylin's stomach sank. Of course Asol would have heard. She was good at being invisible and she'd been wandering, looking at the place she wanted to live. "Yeah. But I don't think it's anything I can't handle."

"That's what a lot of the people are saying, too. It sounds like the odds are in your favor." She got up and washed out her mug. "I'm going to keep my ear to the ground, and if I hear anything you might find useful, I'll let you know." She rolled her eyes when Kylin started to speak. "I know, stay in the light. I'll keep out of the way, I promise." She punched Kylin's shoulder lightly as she left. "You've got this, scruff."

Kylin wished she had her optimism, but from where she was standing, there was no way out. She was trapped.

CHAPTER TWENTY

Fesi felt like a different world from Quasi. No stacks, no mazes. Simple, one-story houses lined clean, open streets. Kylin only vaguely remembered her childhood here, before her mom had died, and she wondered if she would have liked growing up here, or if she would have gotten bored. She'd never know. Right now, it felt alien and more daunting than the Stables on fight night.

Jessa and her crew had carried on the conversation on the walk to Fesi, discussing how different this world was from others they'd been to, and though Kylin mostly just listened, it was good to hear Jessa asking questions and really delving into the things she didn't know. They hadn't been here very long, but she was a different woman than the one Kylin had met running through the trees. She was more open, her hair was down, and she looked at home in the soft clothes from Thalla. She was heart-achingly beautiful, and Kylin wanted to remember her just this way.

She pointed to the top of the hill, where a two-story house sat looking over Fesi. "That's where we're headed."

Jessa took her hand, and she held it tightly. There was every chance she'd be going back to Quasi alone. If Jessa was having the same thoughts, it didn't show.

They made their way to the big house, and though several people on the street stopped to watch them pass, there wasn't any ill feeling in the air. Just curiosity, which was understandable.

At the house, a guard asked their business. Jessa stepped forward.

"I'm Captain Jessa Arabelle. My ship crashed recently, and I'm here to discuss the options to get off planet."

She said it so easily. But the words were like needles in Kylin's heart.

He turned away and spoke into a comm before turning back to open the door. "Wait here. Someone will come get you."

As a group they entered and stood looking around. White-washed walls blended into white furniture and a white stone staircase. It was like looking at a canvas begging for paint.

A young woman entered and bowed. "If you'll follow me."

They followed her down a corridor that led to an outside seating area. A lithe man with thinning hair sat at a large table beneath an umbrella. He motioned to the seats. "Please."

They arranged themselves around the table and Kylin raised her eyebrow. This was Jessa's idea, so it was her show.

Jessa smiled at the administrator. "Thank you for seeing us."

He looked at her contemplatively. "I'm intrigued, Captain. I was under the impression there weren't any survivors from the few escape pods that landed here. It's amazing you've survived long enough to seek me out."

Jessa tilted her head toward Kylin. "We were lucky that our pod didn't sustain more damage. We lost one of the crew, but we made it out. If it hadn't been for Kylin, we would have been caught and sold to the slavers by the end of the first day."

The others echoed the sentiment, and Kylin gave a half smile, embarrassed by the attention.

"And you managed to keep them alive. That's impressive, scrounger." He made a show of looking at the mark on her hand.

"All in a moon's work, right?" She couldn't get a handle on him. He was less flashy than she'd expected, and more direct. He actually seemed interested in them being there, and that was strange too.

"How can I help?" he asked Jessa.

"We wanted to talk to you about several things." She held up one finger. "First of all, we sent out a help call when the pod was hit, but I doubt it went through. Our life-sign scanners are all operational, so we can be tracked if they sent a rescue vessel, but that's highly unlikely, as you know. We understand that transports off planet are rare, but they do happen. We wanted to know if there's a scheduled transport, and if you could get word out that we're here."

He nodded and wrote something down on the pad in front of him. "And second?"

Jessa looked at Kylin. "I think this one is yours."

She hadn't planned on saying much, if anything, and struggled to find where to start. "The slavers are out of control. They need to be stopped. If you give a prowler's shit."

He grinned and sat back in his seat, his hands folded. "You don't know me, so I won't take exception to that, given that I do know how my contemporaries act. Believe it or not, I do give a prowler's shit. Explain, please."

Kylin decided she liked him. There was nothing shifty in his eyes, nothing in his body language that suggested he wasn't being honest. "We've just come across the sands, by way of Thalla and Volare. The slavers have decided that the old codes no longer suit them, and that anyone outside city walls is fair game. They've extended open market territory to mean anything not walled in. Soon you'll have people from Fesi, or Thalla, or even the Forest, enslaved. Imagine the price for someone from the Heathers. No one is safe. They've even taken one of Jessa's remaining crew, and the universe only knows what they've done with him. We've turned a blind eye to it for too long, and it has to stop. The rest of the universe sees us as lawless animals, and if we let this continue, that's exactly what we are."

Jessa squeezed her leg under the table, which she took to mean she'd said things right.

He tapped his stylus on the pad, staring at her hard. "Before I get to the main issue, what do you mean you stopped at Volare?"

Kylin winced internally. Flagweed and prowler tits. She hadn't meant to mention it. But then, maybe this was the right time. "We stopped and stayed with the last of the flying people. They saved me once before, and they gave us shelter. They've been in hiding because they were hunted almost to extinction, and now they're afraid of the slavers, too. But they're dying out, and unless they're allowed to roam free again, they'll become the myth people think they are."

It felt strange talking about people she cared about, like she was divulging their secret. But she knew people, and she'd have bet tomorrow's linari that this one could be trusted.

He sat back, looking stunned. "Is this true?" he asked Jessa. "No offense meant, scrounger, but I'd like to know someone else saw this."

Jessa nodded. "They're remarkable people. Peaceful and kind."

He shook his head. "We miss so much, staying in our bubble."

He thanked the woman who set drinks on the table, and Kylin noticed there was no slave collar on her.

As though he knew what Kylin was thinking, he said, "I don't have slaves, myself. I think it's an abhorrent practice. And if it's out of control, then you're right, we need to do something." He tapped on his pad again. "The problem is, we don't have the kind of army, or guards, that can take them on. I've sent messages before, but I'm the only government administrator on this planet, and you can imagine the response I've gotten."

"Call for help again." Jessa leaned forward and tapped on his pad. "Let them know we're here, and while you've got them on the comm, tell them you need help dealing with a rebel force trying to enslave the population. Tell them to contact the Arabelle fleet commander on Othrys, and tell her that her daughter is on Indemnion and sends this message. It's our cosmic duty to assist a planet in dire need. Code 369A of the Intergalactic Policies. I can assure you that she'll listen."

The daughter of a fleet commander. It made Jessa's lack of emotion and desire to be captain of her own ship much clearer, that was certain. And the reminder of their differences was like a wet slap in the face with a scupper fish.

He nodded slowly. "That's quite the connection, and likely the one we need. Thank you. I'm willing to try." He looked at Kylin. "You were raised a scrounger?"

She nodded, not bothering to go into detail.

"But you're well spoken. And you've traveled more of the planet than most people, I'm willing to bet. You kept the Volare's secret, even when you could have benefitted from it. And you helped these people when it would have been in your best interest to hand them over to the slavers."

Again, she nodded, not sure where he was going.

"If we get help, we're going to need someone who speaks for the people. Someone who truly understands our planet and what we need. That's not going to be someone from the Heathers, although they'll shout from the tops of their globes that they should be the ones listened to. It won't be me, because even I haven't been to large parts of our planet. The people wouldn't trust me, even if the others in the Alliance did. But you..."

Her heart sped up at what he was suggesting. "No one would listen to a scrounger."

He sighed, his expression sympathetic. "If you weren't marked, and you dressed in the clothes of Thalla, like our captain here, you'd see that who you are isn't defined by the role you play. You're not a tree. You're not rooted in one place and destined only to be a tree."

Peshta laughed, and it made the others laugh too, breaking the tension.

"You're the *only* people to come tell me about this. Outsiders and a scrounger from Quasi. Everyone else is hiding, or pretending it won't affect them, or waiting for someone else to do something." He pointed the stylus at Kylin. "But you're here." He stood, indicating the meeting was over. "I'm going to put you forward for the liaison position, and you can decide whether or not you want it when the time comes. If, of course, anyone comes to help us."

Kylin swallowed the flare of hope and excitement. There was far more to deal with before something like that fell in her lap. "I think there are people way more qualified than me, but we can talk about that if the time ever comes. One more thing. These people don't belong in Quasi. They'd be better off here, with you. If you can take them back to the Heathers with you, that would be even better."

"They're welcome to stay here. I can leave some of my staff behind. But I'm afraid I've only got a two-seater flyer, so I can't take everyone back."

"Do you know when the next interplanetary transport is scheduled?" Kylin asked. They couldn't go to the Heathers, but they could stay in Fesi, and that was a good second choice. It also kept Jessa just a little closer.

"It's not for another five months, as far as I'm aware. But I'll double-check, and I'll try to find out if the distress call went out." He looked at the position of the sun. "I'm sorry, but I have another meeting to go to." He held out his arm and Kylin grasped it. "I hope I see you again soon. Even if we don't get help from outside, maybe you and I can work together on another solution. Make sure you leave your name and contact details with my staff before you leave." He turned to Jessa and her crew. "Please make use of my home, if you decide to stay. I'll get word to you about a transport as soon as possible, and if you truly want to come to the Heathers, we can always bring you over one by one." He stopped and smiled. "But if I'm honest, I'd rather stay somewhere interesting, where every nuance of life can be experienced. And that's not in the Heathers, where you would be welcome as a curiosity and would quickly grow bored with our shallow and lackluster ways." He waved over his shoulder. "I'll be in touch."

And then he was gone, leaving a strange vacuum behind him, like all the energy had been sucked away.

Kylin blew out a noisy breath. "Wow. He wasn't at all what I expected."

Jessa shook her head. "I wasn't sure what to expect, and what a pleasant surprise." She turned to her crew. "Do you want to stay here?"

Benika bit her lip. "If I can be candid, Captain? This feels very exposed. I know it isn't, and there are walls. But it feels so open, and we don't know anybody here."

Asanka nodded, her gills opening and closing rapidly. "I agree with Beni. We've gotten to know people in Quasi, and we like Auntie Blue. At least there we know who to go to for help. And the baker has the most amazing bread."

Peshta pretended to pout. "I thought mine was the best?"

They laughed, and Kylin laughed along with them, but she was a mess of nerves inside. It was Jessa she was truly worried about, and Jessa being back in Quasi put her in danger. But then, at least there she'd know where Jessa was, and could keep an eye on her.

She yelped when Jessa pinched the underside of her arm. "Hey!"

"I can see you making decisions, planning out contingencies. But this isn't your decision to make. It's ours, and we're going to back to Quasi." Jessa folded her arms, clearly ready for a fight.

Kylin sighed. "Okay. You're right, it's not my decision. I'm sure Blue would love to have you there for as long as your credit chips hold out."

They left their contact details with the nice lady who had served them drinks, and then made their way along the top of the wall that led back to Quasi. First sun was setting and the sky was painted with strips of oranges and purples that made Kylin think of her life. Bright oranges, like the light Jessa had brought with her, and the deep purples of her nights, where violence and darkness pushed against her.

"We'll still have to figure out our next move, though," Peshta said. "We can't stay at Blue's for another five months. Or however long it will take to get an interplanetary transport."

Five months. That was a gift wrapped in inevitable heartache. She could have another five months with Jessa by her side, in her bed. She was pretty sure Jessa wanted that too. But then she'd be so fully invested, so desperate to stay with her...and maybe Jessa wanted her now, here on Quasi, but it wasn't like she was going to take her home to meet her fleet commander mother, was it?

She'd stay behind, losing love yet again. But at least this time she'd know it was coming and could brace herself, right?

"Kylin?" Jessa's voice was soft.

"Sorry. I was somewhere else. What's the question?" She looked around to find them all staring at her.

"About where we should go that isn't Blue's." Asanka's expression suggested she had an idea what Kylin had been thinking about. Her kind were incredibly perceptive.

"There are always places for rent in the stacks. Finding you a large enough one that you can stay in together wouldn't be a problem, but then, you could probably find plenty of separate ones, too. I'll help you start looking tomorrow, if you want."

They started walking again and Kylin and Jessa walked together at the back. Jessa took her hand.

"Could I stay with you?"

Kylin winced, torn. "Blue's is much nicer."

Jessa started to pull her hand away. "I see."

Kylin kept hold of her hand. "I don't mean anything else by that, Jess. I mean Blue's is nicer, and you might be more comfortable there. My place…" How to describe it? "Dad and I have lived there alone since Mom died. It's a singles place, rough and ready and functional. We never bothered to decorate, and we rarely bothered to clean. It's mid-stack, so there are people above and below us—"

"Will you be there?" Jessa asked.

"Well, yeah."

"Then that's where I'd like to be." She frowned slightly. "But only if you want me there."

Kylin stopped walking and turned to face her. "I think you know how I feel, Jess. If you want to stay with me, I'd love to have you there. I was thinking I'd offer the couch to Asol, though. Until she's on her feet." She kissed her softly, letting her lips linger until Jessa gave a contented sigh.

"That's settled then."

The rest of the way back was filled with questions about the stacks, which Kylin tried her best to answer. It was good to see them so excited, so interested in making the rest of their stay here comfortable. It was also interesting to know they never even asked about the cost of things, yet another reminder that they weren't from around here. She had no idea what ship crew made, but apparently it was enough to live on for another five months without blinking an eye.

They got back to Blue's and everyone said good night, tired out from four hours of walking. She and Jess went to their room after Kylin looked in on her dad, who was still sleeping.

Kylin took her time undressing Jess, reveling in every curve, in the sweet scent of her, in the way she moaned and the way she held on to Kylin like she'd never let go. Whatever happened tomorrow night, this could be the end of what they shared, and she wanted to take the memory of Jessa's beautiful body with her into the ring, just in case she didn't make it out.

CHAPTER TWENTY-ONE

Jessa woke and listened to the communal noise. She wasn't sure if she'd ever get used to it, but it was a fascinating aspect of life here. On her ship she'd had utter silence in her quarters, and the foredeck was always quiet too, as crew were busy making sure everything ran smoothly. Until that last flight, of course, when life had turned inside out.

She turned onto her side and studied Kylin, who was still sound asleep. Her short blue-black hair framed her pale skin, and her strong features were softened in sleep. She was handsome and hard, but soft and sweet, too. She was a gorgeous mix of strength and vulnerability, a heady mixture Jessa was finding she didn't want to be without. Since the moment Kylin had pulled her onto the forest perch she'd been intrigued, and now...well. She wasn't sure what she was feeling, except that it was deeper and more engulfing than anything she'd felt before. Five months. That's what the government official had said. And that should have upset her, made her rail at the injustice of having landed on a planet so out of the way.

Instead, her heart raced at the amount of time she'd get to spend with Kylin, learning new things and asking questions. She'd found that she really liked asking questions, and she was taking Fina's advice to heart. She didn't have to stay removed and lonely. She could be spontaneous. She could get to know people and not feel like she was intruding, or that they weren't worth her time because they had nothing to offer. She didn't have to be her parents, and she had a feeling she'd be an even better captain with this newfound knowledge.

Kylin opened one eye. "You're staring."

"I'm wondering if that third eye is just an Indemnion thing, and if it will go away. It's slightly disconcerting."

Kylin closed her eye again, not falling for it. "Wait till the fourth one pops up, in a place you'll never expect it. That will really weird you out."

Jessa burst out laughing and kissed Kylin hard. "I'm starving."

Kylin smirked, her eyes still closed. "You worked me hard last night, but I'm sure I can get going again."

Jessa pushed her and jumped out of bed. "I'll have more of that later, thank you. For now, I'm heading to the kitchen."

Kylin groaned and grumbled but pulled herself from the bed. She slipped her top on and said, "I'm going to check on my dad first. I'll meet you there."

Jessa hesitated by the door. "Can I…" She swallowed the old fear of being intrusive. "I'd love to meet him."

Kylin winced. "I'm sure he'd love you. But he's not exactly the man he was. Are you sure?"

Jessa hadn't been around anyone ill. Ever. Sick people on ship went to the medical bay, and people on Othrys didn't get sick. Ever. So she wasn't sure what she'd see, but she knew she wanted to meet the man so important to Kylin. She nodded.

"Okay." After quickly getting dressed, Kylin took her hand and led her downstairs, to a room at the back. She knocked softly and then opened the door. "Dad? You decent? Not knocking boots with the beauty of the Falls?"

He chuckled tiredly and waved them in. "She left early this morning. Didn't want to do the walk of shame." He raised his head to look at Jessa. "Actually, it looks like you may have found her."

Kylin pulled Jessa forward. "This is Jessa, the ship's captain Blue told you about. You've probably heard her crew around."

He held out his arm and Jessa took it. He was so frail, and the yellow in his eyes, which had once probably been bright like Kylin's, was tinged with a sickly green. His breathing was shallow, and it was easy to see he struggled with every breath. She wanted to cry for him, for Kylin. For anyone who had to watch their parent languish this way.

He smiled at her. "I hear you've been taking her on quite a ride, Captain." He started coughing, and Kylin quickly got him a drink of something.

"She's impossible, Dad. Stubborn, intelligent, and always hungry."

Jessa felt the heat rush to her face, and she elbowed Kylin in the ribs, who made a show of doubling over and gasping.

"Don't mind her." Kylin's dad closed his eyes. "She only picks on the girls she really likes."

They turned to leave him to rest when he didn't say anything else, but before they got to the door he said, "Kylin, a quick word?"

Jessa nodded and made her way to the kitchen. Poor Kylin. She couldn't imagine how hard that was for her. When Jessa thought of her own parents, there was a detachment she couldn't deny, but that was true of most family relationships on Othrys. Once again, she wondered if they were upset by her disappearance, or if they chalked it up to a disappointing end and simply moved on.

Everyone was at the table, talking excitedly about looking for a place in the stacks. They'd decided to stay together for support and so they'd be easy to find when the time came to head to a transport.

Kylin came in looking subdued, the lines around her eyes deep.

"Everything okay?" Jessa asked.

Kylin gave her a small, tight smile. "Yeah, no problem."

Jessa watched as she clearly put on a mask when she turned to the others. "All ready to go looking for a place?"

There was a chorus of excited replies, and Kylin listened as they talked about what they'd like to find. Jessa was excited for them, but her concern was for Kylin. She just seemed off somehow, and she wondered if it had to do with whatever her father had needed to say. To ask felt like prying, and it was a step that felt out of bounds. So she took her hand and squeezed it, just to let her know she was there.

Kylin winked at her. "Well, then let's get going, shall we?"

They got up to leave, and Jessa didn't miss the look between Blue and Kylin. Was there something else going on? A shiver went down her back. Something wasn't right.

There was no question something was going on, but when Jessa tried to ask Kylin what it was, she got deflected with a kiss or some tidbit of information about the area they were in.

They made their way to the larger stacks at the back, nearer the city walls. Kylin stared at one at the top, a large white one, before she turned them in a different direction.

As they made their way through the maze of streets, people stared and whispered. Several wished Kylin good luck, but she just nodded politely and kept walking. Everywhere they went there were people who wanted to stop and talk to her. It was a little unnerving, because the atmosphere suggested it wasn't just because they wanted to chat. Something big was happening, and Kylin was at the center of it.

They took a lift to a mid-stack house with a simple wood door and trimmed windows. It wasn't flashy, but the inside was spacious. It had four rooms, even though they only needed three, along with a big living room and a nice view over the wall. Peshta, Benika, and Asanka were all delighted with it, and Kylin put in a call to the owner, who was happy to rent for a short-term lease that could be broken if necessary. For a fee, of course, but they weren't bothered by that.

"It's not like you have a lot of stuff to move in, but we can hire a local kid to bring your packs from Blue's."

"We're happy to carry our own," Benika said.

"And that's great. But a local kid will know how to get your packs here without anyone stealing anything along the way, and it will put food on someone's table. So, it's a win for everyone." Kylin whistled and a young man came running over.

"Hey, K. Tonight is going to be better than a cryo storm. I can't wait—"

"Can you bring three packs from Blue's for me? These fine ladies will pay you to get everything here safe and accounted for." Kylin gave him a brief grin.

He looked flustered but recovered quickly. "Yeah, of course. Will Blue know what I need?"

Peshta glanced at the others before speaking for all of them. "We haven't packed everything, but if she just throws whatever is out into the pack, that will be fine."

He loped off into the maze without another word. "So, that part is taken care of. Now we need to get you the basics. Away we go." Kylin led them into another maze, this one full of shops and people hawking their wares.

Jessa laughed and smiled with the others as they picked up various treasures as well as necessities, and Kylin hired another young person to carry the goods as they went. The stares and shouts continued, but Kylin continued to politely ignore them.

When they stopped for food in the late afternoon, Jessa pulled her aside. "Kylin, what's going on tonight? What are they talking about?"

Kylin lifted Jessa's hand to her mouth and kissed her palm, but didn't make eye contact. "Just a thing I have to do. I probably won't be back until really late, so you should stay at Blue's tonight."

Jessa pulled her hand away. "Are you in trouble?"

Kylin flinched and gave a deep sigh. "Nothing that you need to worry about."

The others joined them, cutting the conversation short. They went back to the new house, and then Kylin and Jessa left them there to get settled.

Kylin looked deep in thought when she said, "Would you like to go to my place?"

Jessa took her hand. Whatever was going on, it was clearly affecting her. "Yes, I'd like that."

They walked quietly through the maze and took the stairs to Kylin's house, which didn't have a lift. There was laughter from the houses around it, and music, and some divine cooking smells. People shouted and greeted Kylin, and this felt more authentic, more like a community. Jessa liked it and could see young Kylin growing up here, among people who cared for her.

Kylin took a deep breath, her hand on the door handle. "Remember, it's basic, okay?"

Jessa tugged on her shirt. "Just show me."

Kylin slowly pushed the door open and waved Jessa ahead of her.

The house was comfortable. Lived in. Handwoven blankets covered well used chairs, the pictures were slightly yellowed with age, and the kitchen was small but workable. It felt like Kylin and her dad. Solid, comfortable, and without pretense.

She turned to look at Kylin, who was looking at the floor, her hands shoved deep in her pockets. Her expression made Jessa ache for her.

"I think it's lovely. It's warm and comfortable, the way a home should be."

Kylin shrugged. "It's not the captain's quarters on a ship, or a house in Othrys. But it's ours."

The defensive tone, the way her shoulders hunched, the hardness in her eyes…it was all about keeping the sense of shame, of not being enough, at bay. Even though she wasn't great at reading people, Jessa could see that clearly.

"Show me your room?" She held out her hand.

Kylin took it and led the way down a dim hallway. Her bedroom was brighter than the other rooms thanks to a large window. The corner was cluttered with parts of things partially put together and other metal things waiting to be used. The rest of the room was fairly sparse, with little in the way of personal effects. Beside Kylin's bed was a photo box with a picture of her, her dad, and a woman Jessa assumed was her mother.

"Wow. She was stunning." She picked up the unit and studied her. "You look so much like her. Like both of them."

Kylin nodded. "Yeah. I got lucky there. I may not have a lot going for me, but at least I'm outstandingly sexy." She grinned, but it didn't reach her eyes.

"Please tell me what's going on?" Jessa cupped Kylin's cheek in her hand. "Can I help?"

Kylin held Jessa's hand to her cheek. "The best possible thing you could do to help me tonight is stay at Blue's, where I know you're safe. If I can, I'll explain everything after."

Jessa searched Kylin's expression for anything more, something that might hint at what was going on, but there was nothing. "Does this have to do with the bounty? Or the woman you made the deal with to get us to Quasi?"

Kylin let go of her hand and took the family photo. She studied it like she was trying to memorize it. "Both. It's complicated. And hopefully it will be all sorted out by tomorrow, and I won't have to worry about either one ever again."

"Kylin—"

"Jessa, please. Let it go, at least for now." Kylin opened the front door. "Let's head back to Blue's. I have somewhere I need to be."

Startled by Kylin's harsh tone and stiff posture, Jessa walked past her and down the stairs. They were silent on the way back to Blue's, and once they were there, Kylin didn't go inside.

"I'll see you tomorrow, okay?" Kylin kissed her softly.

"Sure." Just as Kylin was about to walk away, Jessa grabbed her arm. "Whatever it is, please be careful."

Kylin's laugh was utterly without humor. "I'll do my best."

She walked away and was quickly swallowed up by the maze. Jessa went inside, dread pushing into her like a monster waiting to pounce.

Blue sat at the table, sewing something, and Jessa sat opposite her.

"Do you know, Kylin once stole bread from the baker. When she was just a young thing." Blue's fingers were nimble as they flew over the cloth. "He chased her through the maze, determined to teach her a lesson. She thought she'd lost him, and she slowed down. He couldn't figure out why she wasn't eating the bread, so he followed her at a distance." She smiled and tugged the material straight. "She went to one of the poorest areas of Quasi and left the bread on the doorstep of a family that was truly struggling. She wasn't a lot better off, but that family was going to starve to death."

"And did the baker come after her?" Jessa could easily picture that side of her.

"He felt so bad for thinking she was a common thief, and he was so impressed by her desire to help someone, that he started making midnight deliveries to them himself. Good food meant the mother was able to recover from her illness and get back on her feet. She found work at this bakery that was suddenly hiring..."

One good deed. Kylin did something simple and showed someone else the way. The government official was right. She'd make an amazing ambassador, if she'd just trust herself enough to walk through that door.

"Do you know what's going on tonight?" she asked.

Blue tugged at the material, maybe a little too hard. "I do."

"Will you tell me?"

"Did you ask Kylin?"

Jessa fingered the material. "She wouldn't tell me anything, except that it has to do with her debt and the woman she made a deal with."

Blue tilted her head and considered her material. "And perhaps it's best that that's all you know."

"I don't understand why. It's not like she's going out to murder people, is it? What could be so bad that I can't know?"

Blue put down her sewing and looked at Jessa. "You're good for her. I can see that you make her happy, and the universe knows she could use some of that in her life."

Jessa waited for the caveat.

"But you also come from a very different place, Captain Jessa. A clean, civilized world where people work things out. You've seen some of the horrors of Indemnion, but you can't ever really understand what it's like to live here. How you have to fight for every inch of space, every scrap of food. Life here is hard, and it can breed hard people."

"Kylin doesn't seem hard. She's kind, and gentle."

Blue's eyebrows raised. "She is those things. But she's more, because she's had to be more. And after a few weeks of traveling with her, you haven't really gotten to know her." She touched Jessa's hand gently. "When you leave, it will break her heart. I've seen it happen once before. But she's expecting it this time, which makes it a little better. Maybe." She gathered up her sewing. "Enjoy the parts of her you already like, and let the others remain in the shadows. It will make whatever time you have left together here better." She went to leave but stopped. "We're all allowed our secrets."

When she was alone in the room, Jessa rested her head on her arms. Was it true? Was she so far removed, so used to the pristine environment she'd lived and worked in, that she wouldn't ever be truly a part of Kylin's world? It felt false, like it didn't have to be one or the other, but when she thought of the people who were shouting to Kylin, there was an undercurrent that made her skin crawl.

CHAPTER TWENTY-TWO

Asol carefully wrapped Kylin's hands, paying attention to how the wrapping went on and making sure there were no awkward overlays. Kylin had been on her way to the Stables to get ready in the room set aside for fighters, and she'd never felt so alone in all her life. Even with the crowd pressing around her, wishing her luck, she hardly knew a single face. When Asol had bumped against her and raised Kylin's arm in the air, the resulting cheer had made Kylin shake her head, but the relief of having a friendly face who actually cared about her at some level was almost dizzying.

The crowd had thinned out by the time they got to the Stables, with just the usual lowlife bet takers hanging around. Kylin had stopped at the entrance and told Asol she should head back to Blue's, but Asol had laughed her off, saying she wasn't about to miss this.

Kylin flexed her hands. The wrapping was perfect. Not too tight but not loose enough to come unwrapped. Her knuckles were perfectly protected. "Where'd you learn to do this?"

Asol played with a piece of tape, sticking it to her nose and eyes and making funny faces. "Dock rat, remember? We used to set up fights at night just for something to do." She stuck her tongue out, doing a good impression of a tree waftler. "And my bio dad. He was a fighter, like you."

"In debt and about to get his ass handed to him?"

Asol laughed. "All the damn time."

Kylin rolled her shoulders, trying to work out the tension. "Hey, before I get in there. I know Blue's is nice, but I thought you might want a space where you can settle in a bit. If you want it, my couch is free."

Asol dropped the tape. "You mean it?"

"Yeah." She pressed along her collarbone. All the color was gone, and it was only a little tender. Thank the universe she was a quick healer. "And if things go flying prowler shit wrong tonight, that offer stands, even if I don't make it home."

Asol frowned. "You think there's really a chance of that?"

It was more than a chance. And if she did walk out of there, she might not be around long anyway. "It's always a possibility when you get in the ring. You know that. And I think the stacks might be weighed against me this time."

Orlin pushed open the creaky door and scuttled slowly inside. Even upright he looked like something that should be spinning a web somewhere. His ugly, foul-smelling guards were behind him. "I see you've finally got someone in your corner. How adorable."

Kylin smacked her fists together and started bouncing lightly on her toes. Oftentimes her opponent had been bigger, but she'd been faster. She moved and turned until Asol was effectively hidden behind her. "Your pep talk could use some work."

"Oh, no pep giving here. Of course, it would be best if you lasted long enough to give the audience a show, but no matter when you go down, I'll be happy."

She shadow punched a shot near his head and then squared up to him. "And if I win?"

He laughed that slick, oily sound of his. "You won't."

"But if I do?"

Instead of looking pissed off, he looked like he was having fun. "If you do, your debt with me is cleared, and we never do business again."

That told Kylin what she needed to know. If there was any chance at all that she could beat her opponent, he wouldn't make that kind of wager. Her stomach churned, but she wasn't about to let him see any fear. The fact was, she wanted to win on every level. Winning would get her clear of Orlin, even though it would make him an enemy she'd probably have to watch for throughout the rest of her life. Winning would also get her clear of Maana, which meant she was free, and Jessa would be safe. Winning would mean everything. Too bad there wasn't a flagweed's chance it would happen.

"Deal." She held out her arm and had to work not to pull away in disgust when he clasped it with his own skeletal one.

Orlin kept talking to his guards about how wonderful the evening was going to be as he pushed back out the doors, though they never responded.

"That sounds like a good deal, right?" Asol asked. "And what possessed you to make a deal with that crawler?"

"It's a good deal if I had any chance of winning, which I don't. And you do what you have to when someone you love needs help." She slumped onto the bench. "Asol, if I don't walk out of here, you need to get Jessa out of Quasi. Take her to Fesi, to the administrator's house. Promise me."

Asol nodded, pale. "I promise."

Kylin pulled the little blue vial from her pocket and watched it sparkle in the sickly light of the dressing room.

Asol glanced at the closed door and moved to block Kylin from anyone who could look in, then she put her hand out and Kylin handed it over. She pushed the little button on the side and grunted softly when the needle popped out. She pushed the button again, and it retracted. She reached for Kylin's hand and studied it, turning it over and over. Then she pushed the vial below the fabric between her thumb and forefinger, and it looked like it was just a bubble of wrapping. She nodded at it, and Kylin pressed her thumb against the side of her hand. The needle popped out through the wrapping and disappeared again when she pressed her thumb against the side of her hand again.

Their eyes met and Asol said, "Whatever it takes to get out of that ring and back to Jessa." She grinned. There was no telling who was listening. "How can I be like you when I grow up if you're not around?"

They spent the next hour getting ready. Kylin moved around, got the blood flowing, warmed all her muscles. Without knowing who she was fighting she couldn't picture any specific moves she might make, so she practiced all the ones that had worked in the past. Asol commented and teased, and she had to admit it kept her shoulders relaxed. She'd never had someone there before a fight before.

The blue light flashed on over the door, and she took off her robe. She wore only a tight tank top and knee length shorts. Her feet, also wrapped up, were otherwise bare. Other fighters liked to have on all kinds of crap, but she wanted to be able to move freely and as lightly as possible.

The blue light turned green, and she took a deep breath.

Asol went and pulled the door open. "Come on, prowler scruff. Go kick his ass so you can get out and teach me how to build shit."

Kylin bounced at the entrance to the door. The crowd was chanting her name, a solid reminder of how long she'd been doing this. "You'll remember your promise?"

Asol punched her shoulder. "I'm not senile. Yeah, I'll remember." She lifted Kylin's right hand and tapped the hidden vial. "But make sure I don't have to, okay?"

And then the announcer was yelling her name, and she half-ran out the door. Time was up.

CHAPTER TWENTY-THREE

Cosmos shit and prowler tits. Kylin stared at her opponent and tried to make out what she was seeing. One creature, two ugly, massive heads. A long, snake-like body covered in flashing, buzzing orange scales turned into a human torso, complete with four arms that looked made of stone. Three eyes on each face made it hard to know where to look, though it seemed to be able to look everywhere at once.

She looked down at Asol, who waited by her corner with a towel and water pouch. She shook her head, her eyes wide. She'd probably never heard of a creature like this, either. Imagine a planet full of those, Kylin thought and shuddered. She needed to get her head in the game. She studied it, scanning it for any potential weak spots. The scales covered it from the neck down, and aside from flashing, which she took to mean some kind of electricity, they also looked like metal. The bulbous heads were knobbed and hairy, and the eyes mean and dark.

If she hit the scales, she'd likely get a shock. If she took a hit with those massive hands, it would probably knock her out. Avoiding its sight would be next to impossible. And there was nowhere to slide the vial in, even if she got the chance.

No, it didn't look like she'd be going home after all. All she could do was hope Asol could get Jessa to safety, and that the government official would come through and get them off planet. Surely once she was dead, Maana wouldn't bother with Jessa. It wouldn't get her anywhere. And Orlin would have his money, so her dad would be safe.

The problem was, she didn't want to die.

The bell rang and she moved forward, moving cautiously. It was easily three times her size and when someone threw liquid at it, the liquid hit its scales and sizzled, sending steam into the air and making the orange flickers burst into suns along its body. Heat surged off it, making Kylin jump back. Its black eyes followed her every move, and when its tail lashed out, swinging around to knock her feet from under her, she barely escaped being sent flying. She leapt, landed lightly, and spun to face it. The crowd roared its approval.

The tail came back and slammed into her stomach, knocking the wind from her and pushing her into the corner ropes, but there was no electrical shock. She threw herself into a roll to avoid another hard hit and managed to dodge it a second time. Back on her feet, she thought quickly. It liked to stun with its tail, which meant she needed to keep avoiding that. She bet that once she was down it would use those enormous fists to finish the job.

She ducked, dodged, jumped. There wasn't anything to hit, though she did manage a good solid kick to its side. The metal edges cut her foot, but she saw its eyes widen at the impact, so it must have felt something. She couldn't understand why it hadn't shocked her yet. Maybe it had been told to make the match last long enough to please the crowd.

The bell rang, and she retreated to her corner. Asol handed her a water pouch.

"I don't see how this ends," Asol said close to Kylin's ear. "Why isn't it attacking?"

Kylin shook her head, equally puzzled. "No idea. See any openings?"

"I think I saw one under the tail, and another right up in its sweaty armpit. That's it so far."

The bell rang again, and Kylin moved forward. Under the tail might be an option, but it meant getting hit and holding on. Not optimal.

She jumped over its lashing tail and missed the fist coming at her until it connected to her side. It missed her ribs, but the impact on her kidneys made the sick rise in the back of her throat. She hit the mat hard, gasping for air, and couldn't help the cry that escaped when the tip of the tail, glowing orange, touched her hip, sending a shock through her that made her body arc.

Faces melded into each other as she looked at the crowd, sound far, far away, mouths contorted in screams and grisly laughter. The world slowed into a blur and water blurred her vision. There wasn't another strike, and slowly, sound returned, deafening. They didn't care if she died, they just didn't want it to happen too soon. She blinked against the slowly receding pain and saw Asol yelling at her to get up, to move.

She struggled to her knees, then to her feet. She swayed, the section of her side pulsing. Turning, she looked at the creature who waited in his corner, one head tilted as it looked at her, the other gazing at the crowd.

And that's when she saw it.

The intelligence in the creature's expression. The emotion. It grimaced and snapped its tail as someone in the crowd hit it with a stick. The eyes looking at her were sad, the expression contemplative. It didn't want to fight any more than she did, and she wondered just how a creature like this had been forced into one of Orlin's fights. Had it been captured? Could it speak the common tongue?

In the moments that they stared at each other, Kylin knew they were the same. Captives, forced to do what was necessary to survive. With that kind of electric power, it could have killed her quickly. What would happen to it if it lost?

She moved toward it, circling it, and they went back to their dance of ducking and dodging. It let her get in a few kicks before it swiped at her, knocking her across the ring. The crowd was growing restless, drinks and food being thrown at the fighters as they circled one another, and Kylin kept looking for a moment, a way out that wasn't immediately obvious.

The creature roared with both mouths as someone stabbed his tail. It jerked forward, swinging his mammoth fists, and there was no way for Kylin to get out of the way. One fist connected to her temple, another to her opposite side, and she thought she might actually break in half as her body moved in horribly opposite directions. She put her hands up to ward off another blow...

And slid her hand against the creature's exposed skin under its arm. She managed to activate the needle and plunge it in before her body slammed into the mat and nothing but a rush of red filled her vision. She rolled to her side, gasping, wrapping her arms around herself and trying to figure out if she was still in one piece. The crowd came into view once more, and she wished she'd kept her eyes closed.

Jessa stood with her hands over her mouth, tears streaming down her cheeks. As Kylin watched, she backed into the crowd and disappeared.

The bell rang and Asol was instantly beside her, half-lifting, half-dragging Kylin to her corner. She emptied a water pouch over Kylin's face before giving her one to drink while Asol dabbed at the blood coursing down her face and dripping from her chin. But all Kylin could see was Jessa's look of horror as she'd run the other way, just the way Kylin had known she would.

Asol shook her, forcing her to focus. "C'mon, Kylin. Look at me."

Kylin blinked and wiped the blood from the corner of her eye. "I did it."

Asol frowned slightly and then her expression cleared as she understood. "Well, thank the prowler tits for that. Let's hope it works."

"Jessa was in the crowd. She saw." The words burned.

Asol flinched and shrugged slightly. "She was bound to find out, and now you don't have to explain why you look like you've been used as a flyer runway." She squirted more water on Kylin's face. "Right now, you've got to worry about not dying, okay? Stay out of its way until you've got a shot. You've hung in and taken a good enough beating. Time to end it."

Kylin nodded and managed to stand when the bell rang. Her legs shook and her hands trembled as she held them in front of her.

The creature moved toward her, but three of its six eyes were glazed. If she could take it down, they wouldn't have to kill each other. Maana would get off her back, and Orlin wouldn't have a spider leg to stand on.

It moved toward her in a kind of falling, graceless movement, swinging wildly. She got ready, bracing herself. One swing swept passed her, and she kicked with all she had, connecting to its side, throwing it off balance. But where her foot hit she met pure, horrifying electricity that shot up her leg and slammed into her spine, sending her crashing against the ropes. She hung on, barely holding back the scream that needed to erupt, and watched as the creature fell and stopped moving altogether.

The final bell rang and the crowd went silent. Asol jumped into the ring and caught her as darkness swallowed the last of the light.

CHAPTER TWENTY-FOUR

The tea spilled as Jessa tried to pour it for Kylin's father. He hadn't woken, but when she'd fled back to the house, unable to watch the brutality Kylin was involved in, she hadn't known what else to do, and being next to the person closest to Kylin seemed like the only place she could be. He coughed occasionally, his breathing shallow. Did he know where Kylin was? He'd asked to speak to her alone. Did he actually approve of what she did? Was this how she earned money?

Jessa covered her face with her hands and cried. Seeing Kylin fall to the floor, her body wracked with pain, while the horrid creature loomed over her had been too much. The agony in Kylin's eyes, the shame in her expression as she'd met Jessa's gaze...was this why she knew they could never be together? Jessa had learned so much in the time she'd been here, but she'd never thought for a second that Kylin would be in the midst of that kind of violence.

What if she didn't come home? What if that thing killed her? Sobs shook her as despair swamped her. She should have stayed. She should have been beside Asol, taking care of Kylin and making sure she had whatever support she needed. But the roar of the crowd desperate for blood, the creature's flashing scales, the knowledge that Kylin had walked willingly into that ring...it had all been too much. The market stalls had blurred as she'd shoved past people, desperate to get back to a place of safety. Did she know Kylin at all? How was the woman she'd grown to care about willing to use her fists against another being? Even one as disturbing as that one. The horrors of this planet were never ending, and now she saw what Blue had tried to say. There were things you should never find out about the woman you cared about.

Kylin's father coughed, and she wiped away her tears as he opened his eyes. When he focused on her, he sighed softly. He accepted the cup of tea she offered, then handed it back after only a small sip.

"She didn't want you to know." His voice was hoarse.

"I wish she'd told me. At least I would have been prepared."

He took her hand in his own. "Can anything prepare you for that?"

She took a shuddery breath. "No. Perhaps not. It was so awful." She stared at the paper-thin skin of his hand covering hers. "How can you allow it?"

He was quiet for a long moment, and she looked up to see if he'd fallen back asleep. Instead, he was looking at her thoughtfully. "I imagine she's told you that life here isn't what you're used to?"

She nodded but didn't want to interrupt his train of thought.

"When you're raised in the gutter, you learn how to live there. Thrive there, even. She's done what she has to, and you may not like it, but she's good at it." He frowned. "Did you see who she was fighting?"

Jessa described the creature as best she could, and he began coughing so hard he turned crimson. After sipping some tea and taking deep breaths, he settled back against his pillows.

"That bastard Orlin. He knew there was no one he could say for certain she'd lose to. So he had to find something she had no chance against." Tears began to slide down his face. "She did it for me, you know."

She picked at a loose thread in the blanket. "What do you mean?"

"Flagweed helps my cough, but it's expensive. It's hard to scrounge enough to get food on the table, let alone medication." He tapped at the cup on the table. "When I got sick, she got a loan. And to pay it off, she had to get in the ring. Plenty of people here have to do it, or things similar to it, in order to survive. She just happened to have a talent for it, and it meant Orlin started paying her in flagweed instead of linari. That way she never got out of debt, and he had a fighter he could count on."

Jessa's hands still trembled and she didn't check the tears still falling. "Does she like it?"

He coughed and glared at her. "What if she does? What if part of her likes the fight and uses it to get out her frustrations? Does that destroy your civilized sensibilities, Captain?"

She didn't miss the irritation in his voice, and she didn't blame him for standing up for Kylin. But she couldn't understand wanting to hit someone. She couldn't understand the desire to hurt another creature, and she didn't think she could be with someone who could.

When she didn't respond, he sighed and closed his eyes. "Let me know when she gets home, will you?"

Jessa squeezed his hand. The tension of unsaid words stretched between them, and it was best they remain unsaid. He didn't have the strength to argue, and she didn't have the words. She went back to the room she'd been sharing with Kylin and sat on the bed with her knees pulled to her chest. When Blue knocked and came in, she could tell that Blue would say the same thing Kylin's dad had said.

She came over and wrapped her arm around Jessa's shoulders. "I warned you that some things should remain in the shadows."

"I had to know."

Blue sighed heavily. "And now you do. The question is, what are you going to do with that information?"

Confused, Jessa leaned into Blue's embrace. "I don't know. Kylin told me, you told me, even her father told me, about how hard this place is. And of course I saw plenty of it while we were looking for pieces of my ship. I just didn't think…"

"You can't handle seeing it in person." Blue gave her a squeeze and then got up to go. "When you love someone, Jessa, you love all of them. You don't get to pick and choose, or ask them to be something they're not."

She left Jessa alone, and Jessa cried silently until she was drained of all the tears she had to cry. She kept seeing Kylin's body, the blood, the screaming crowd. Did she love her? Was this what love was? Watching the person you cared about getting beat to death? Whatever the reasons she did it, did the ends justify the bloody demands? Could she live, even temporarily, with that kind of violence? Othrys was a non-violent world, where they used debate and political institutions to settle disputes. Not only was violence intolerable, it was considered something only lower life forms succumbed to. Kylin's reasons were noble, she understood that. And maybe, somehow, she could come to terms with it in the long run. But after what she'd seen tonight, it was possible there wouldn't be a long run. It didn't look like there would even be a tomorrow.

With shaking hands, she packed her bag and quietly left the house. She couldn't imagine being there when they brought Kylin's broken body home. She wanted to remember her as she was, the handsome, roguish woman who made her laugh and protected her. Not the broken, beaten, woman they'd bring home. If they even brought her home. She stopped outside the door. Maybe she should stay. Maybe she could simply accept her, as Blue had said. But… what if Kylin didn't come back at all? Jessa couldn't face being there when they brought that news. With a choked sob, she left the house and headed into the maze.

The streets of the stacks were eerily empty, but she knew just where everyone was. She made her way to the new place her crew had rented. It had an extra bedroom, and she'd make use of it until it was time to get a transport. As much as it hurt, she couldn't allow herself to fall in love with someone who handled violence so casually. Tonight had shown her just how different their worlds were; Kylin had been trying to tell her, but they'd foolishly abandoned that logic and moved ahead as though this were a children's fairy tale.

Before she made it to the stack where her crew was, a group of people laughing loudly walked past.

"Did you see the way her body went rigid? I can't believe she didn't scream. That prowler bitch was hard as stone. Too bad we won't see her fight again. She put up a hell of a fight for her last one."

Jessa sank to her knees on the cold ground. Her last one. So she wasn't coming back. She'd left Jessa with a beautiful memory tarnished by the image of her in the ring. There was no question of going back to Blue's now. She couldn't be there when they told Kylin's dad. The pain of it would surely take him too. Perhaps that was a blessing. He wouldn't have to live with this pain, this anguish eating through her like her soul was on fire. Something she knew she'd live with for the rest of her life.

She wasn't sure how long she knelt there on the cold ground, sobbing until there were no more tears. People filtered past but thankfully no one stopped to help. She couldn't have expressed herself and didn't want to. She just wanted to get off this cosmos forsaken planet. Eventually, she forced herself to her feet, emptied and exhausted.

When Asanka opened the door, Jessa fell into her open arms and began a fresh bout of crying. She was back with her crew, and soon she'd be back on a ship. That was her world and where she belonged. She had to shut out the emotions, regain control. But as she sobbed at the loss of something she'd never known she wanted being lost to her forever, she knew she'd never be the same.

Kylin groaned as awareness slowly filtered back in, bringing with it a tidal wave of pain. Every bone in her body hurt, and she was immediately aware that more than one was probably broken. Something cool touched her face, and she murmured her thanks. Opening her eyes felt like too much work.

"Glad you've come back around. We lost you for a little while there."

Asol's voice lacked its usual lighthearted tone. Where was she? She shifted slightly and moaned. She was lying on something hard, but her head was cushioned. The smell of flagweed and oster flowers assailed her, and then she heard the slow, steady beep of a med machine. She forced her eyes open and groaned again as the light sent shards of pain into her head.

She was in a med unit room. Bare walls and a single open window weren't overly welcoming, and a comm screen was showing images from her fight. "Turn it off," she whispered.

Asol flipped the switch then gave her a drink of water.

"How long?"

"Three days, if you mean how long have I been sitting faithfully by your side in this stunningly beautiful room with the amazing view of that brick wall."

Kylin grinned slightly and tried to sit up. Her bound ribs protested, but she managed with Asol's help. "Jessa?"

Asol grimaced. "Safe, like you wanted her to be."

"But?" The fact that she wasn't in the room couldn't be good.

"But...she thinks you're dead. Most everyone does."

Kylin's eyes snapped open. "What? Why?"

"Because you were. Dead, I mean." Asol moved the side of Kylin's hospital tunic aside. "The electricity of the thing went in here and killed you. You died on the mat."

Kylin went cold and started to shake. "And then?"

"And then a medic in the crowd jumped in. He started working on you, and someone else joined him. But most of the crowd had already filtered out by then, going off to get their money or whatever, so the word went out that both you and your opponent died. Fight of the century and all that prowler shit."

Kylin motioned for another drink of water, and Asol gave her some before continuing.

"So no one really saw them take you out on a med bed, and even if they did, they assumed you were dead. You've been here since, and I have to admit, I wasn't sure you were coming back to us."

Asol brushed tears away and looked out the window.

"My dad?" Kylin couldn't imagine the pain he'd be in.

"I got a med student to go tell him what was going on. So he knows you're not dead but not exactly alive, either."

Kylin reached out and grabbed Asol's arm. "Thank you. For staying."

Asol gave a half-shrug, her eyes still glassy. "Like I said, you've got shit you need to teach me. I had to make sure you pulled through."

Kylin rested her head against the thin pillow. "Can you get word to my dad that I'll be home as soon as I can?"

Asol stood and moved toward the door. "And Jessa?"

Kylin hesitated. "I need to think about that. Just don't tell anyone else yet, okay?"

Asol nodded. "Yeah. Good call." She scuffed at the floor with her boot. "Like I said. She's one of the shiny people, and I don't think shiny people would understand what you did in that ring." She smiled, and this time it reached her eyes. "Even though it was epic."

She left, and Kylin imagined Jessa's face once again. The horror in her expression, the fear and confusion evident as Kylin tried to get back up. Maybe she was better off thinking Kylin was gone. She wouldn't feel any obligation to look after her, to pretend like it was all okay. Because Kylin knew it wouldn't be okay. She'd tried to warn her that this world was hard, but she'd allowed Jessa in, let her see the soft, beautiful side of Indemnion. Now she'd seen what terrors played in the shadows and how those games were won.

If they cut ties now, would it be better? Would it keep her heart from feeling like it had been stomped on by that creature? She let the tears fall, and part of her wished she hadn't woken up at all. This was what love got her. A woman who couldn't deal with all the baggage she came with. A woman who was better off believing she was dead than she would be trying to fit into Kylin's world. She was safe, and that was what really mattered.

It felt like hours later when she heard the door to her room open, but it might have only been minutes. She was still groggy and the room wasn't completely steady. But when Orlin came in, she forced herself to focus.

He sat in the chair Asol had been using, his long legs looking uncomfortable in the small space. "Did you cheat?"

She half-laughed and held her ribs. "I died. Does that sound like cheating to you? If I was going to cheat, I would have been sure to stay alive."

He grunted, clearly more irritated than a prowler with a tick. "You cost me a fortune. I should take it out of your skin."

She glared at him. "You said I was free if I won. And I won. You renege on that and people will do business with prowlers before they come to you for anything. And believe me when I say I'll make sure everyone outside the Heathers knows if you back out." She closed her eyes again, tired of the game. "It's not my fault you bet against me. You should know by now that I'm a survivor."

Surprisingly, he laughed. "That's true. And fortunately, the people here like death in their entertainment. They're clamoring for more fights like yours, with crazy odds and unbeatable underdogs." He stood and dusted himself off like the med ward would stick to him. "We're done."

The door closed softly behind him, and Kylin took a long, deep breath. Aside from people thinking she was dead, which she could deal with later, this was the outcome she'd needed. She was out from under Orlin's spiny hand for the first time in years. In the scheme of things it wasn't a huge thing, but it was a step in the right direction. The door opened again, and this time it was Asol.

"What's wrong?" Kylin's heart stuttered at the look on Asol's face.

"I told him you were okay, and that you'd be home soon." She swallowed and stared at the floor. "But he doesn't look good, buddy. I'm not even sure he heard me."

Kylin's body went cold and the room started to spin. But she got herself under control and started to move. "Help me." She pulled the tube from her arm, and Asol pulled the wires from the monitors on her chest and back. The alarm bells on the machine started going off and a med-lead ran in.

Kylin held up her hand to stop the barrage. "Don't. It's an emergency, and I'm leaving. If I have to, I'll come back. But right now, I have to go."

The med-lead shrugged and moved aside without a word. Asol wrapped a jacket around Kylin. "I could help you walk, but it would be a lot faster if we put you in a chair."

"Do it." The thought of having to use a chair to get through the maze bothered her, but whatever got her to her father fastest.

Asol left and came back with a chair. She was also wearing a hat, and she'd brought one with a wide brim for Kylin. "If you're not ready for news of your rebirth to get out, we should try to do this with a little bit of subtlety."

Kylin got in the chair and put the hat on, pulling it low over her face. She pulled the jacket closed around her and focused on the ground as Asol pushed her efficiently through the maze toward Blue's place. Once they were there, Asol gently wrapped her arm around Kylin's waist and helped her up the stairs. Blue came out and took the other side without a word, and they went straight to Kylin's dad's room.

Her knees gave out and she would have slumped to the floor had Asol and Blue not been supporting her. One look told her that he was nearly gone. They lowered her into the chair beside his bed and she took his hand, not bothering to wipe away the tears falling down her cheeks.

"Hey, Dad. I'm here." She held his hand to her cheek. "I'm here."

She didn't know how much time had passed before she felt his hand twitch in hers. She raised her head from the edge of the bed and searched his face.

His eyes fluttered open and he smiled when he saw her. "I knew you'd make it."

"You raised me to be a fighter."

He shook his head when she offered him some tea. "Damn right I did." He squeezed her hand. "It's time for you to start a different fight."

She frowned. "What do you mean?"

"It's time for you to leave, Kylin." He took a shuddering breath, his dry lips barely moving. "You make something of yourself. Be more than a scrounger. Chase a dream. Make things better." Tears slid down his papery cheeks. "It's time for me to go, and you have to be strong. Let someone love you, but make sure they love all of you. You deserve that."

"I don't want you to go," Kylin whispered, barely holding back the sobs building in her chest.

"Your mom and I were so lucky to have you." He closed his eyes and his grip loosened on her hand. "I did my best…you made…me…proud."

His breathing slowed, and his hand fell open. Kylin sobbed, holding his limp hand against her face. "Please don't leave. Please." Over and over, she said it, until her voice was hoarse and the room went dark.

A hand squeezed her shoulder and she turned toward the person, not caring who it was.

"Let me take care of him." Auntie Blue sounded like she'd been crying too.

Kylin got up and stumbled from the room.

Jessa was there waiting, and Kylin fell into her arms. She helped her to their room and into bed, and wrapped her arms around her as she sobbed, as grief threatened to drown her. She held on to Jessa like a log in a raging river. If she let go, she'd never resurface.

CHAPTER TWENTY-FIVE

Jessa sat at the kitchen table, a long forgotten mug of tea in her hands. The last week was a blur. When Asol had shown up in the dead of night and asked her to come to Blue's because Kylin needed her, she'd thought it was a dream. But when she'd arrived and heard Kylin pleading with her father not to go, it had broken her heart, and any anger, fear, or confusion she had about the way she felt about Kylin melted away like the night before dawn. When she'd stumbled from the room, reeling with pain, she'd let go of the fury that she'd been grieving Kylin's death for the last three days, only to find out she'd been lying in a hospital bed within sight of the stack she was living in. She'd let go of everything but the desire to hold Kylin, to cherish each moment, to help her get through what would probably be the blackest moment of her life.

And although she wasn't entirely sure Kylin knew she was there, she made sure to be at her side as often as possible. Kylin's eyes were blank, and she moved listlessly through the house, letting Jessa help her shower and rebind her ribs without so much as a blink of recognition.

Now, as she watched Kylin grieve, she once again tried to understand why people would want to feel anything when this was always going to be the end result. Devastation and despair were love's ultimate price.

But then, the times leading up to that wreckage were something truly special, weren't they? At Kylin's father's funeral, it seemed like all the residents of Quasi had turned up to say something about him. Anecdotes of times he'd made people laugh, or helped them put food on the table by giving them items he'd scrounged himself, or how he'd been a wonderful friend in other ways. Kylin's voice had broken when she'd thanked them for coming, for being part of her father's life.

"She sleeping?" Asol flopped into a chair opposite her.

Jessa nodded. "I feel so helpless."

"Yeah. Death is so damn final."

They sat in silence for a while before Jessa needed conversation to stop the whirl of circular thoughts in her mind. "Have you decided what to do in Quasi yet?"

Asol laughed. "It's not like I've had a lot of time to think about it. Kylin could teach me to be a scrounger, and she can teach me to build things. There's always work down by the river, getting stuff off the barges, but that feels a little too much like what I left behind." She shrugged and stretched. "I'll figure it out."

"I know you will." It had been four days since the funeral, and Jessa wasn't sure if it was time to suggest to Kylin that they return to her home. Would being surrounded by her father's things be too much? She couldn't help but feel that Kylin should be in her own space, grieving her way. Asol had been staying at the house and said there was all kinds of food and such being dropped off daily. Auntie Blue looked like the wind had whipped through her, too, leaving her deflated.

They both looked up when Kylin shuffled into the kitchen, her eyes red and swollen, but less glazed than they had been. She gave Asol a friendly shove and kissed the top of Jessa's head as she walked past. As she poured herself a drink, Jessa watched for signs that she was coming back to them a little bit.

She joined them at the table. "What are two of my favorite people talking about?"

Asol leaned forward. "I was about to go ask out a girl who lives two stacks over. She's a server at the Quasi Arms."

Kylin gave her a small grin. "That sounds like a good thing to be doing."

Asol spread her arms. "If I've got the master's blessing, I'm out of here." She blew Jessa a kiss as she headed for the door. "Don't wait up, Mom."

Jessa spluttered into her cold tea. "I'm not nearly old enough to be her mother."

Kylin actually laughed. "No, you're not. But it's funny."

Jessa took Kylin's hand in hers. "It's good to see you with us, a little."

Kylin sighed. "I'm sorry I've been gone. I just can't imagine my world without him. But he wouldn't want me to sit around moping. He'd want me to move forward. I'm not sure what that means yet, but I'll get there."

There was a knock at the door, and then a woman strode in. At least, Jessa thought it was a woman. But the spiky little teeth and strangely shaped eyes, as well as the claws, made her reevaluate.

Kylin shifted so that she was in front of Jessa. "Maana. This is a surprise."

The woman looked around Kylin and smiled at Jessa. "Yes, I imagine it is."

Kylin moved to block her again. "This isn't a great time. And I thought our business was over."

Maana's eyes twitched, and she tapped a black claw against the table. "I'm actually here to be nice."

Kylin crossed her arms but didn't say anything.

"Thanks to our business, I came into a substantial amount of money. And because I believed in you so fully, I placed a bet on your behalf." She tossed a thick envelope on the table. "I didn't think you'd mind." She took a step back, the expression on her face inscrutable. "And I'm sorry about your father. He was a good man."

She left without another word, and Kylin picked up the envelope. She dumped it on the table and a hefty amount of linari fell out. She moved quickly to the door and Jessa heard her say, "Hey, Maana. Thanks."

She couldn't hear a response, but Kylin looked confused when she came back to the table.

"Isn't that the person you had to deal with to get us to Quasi after the crash?" Jessa asked.

"It is. And she's not known for her generosity. She must feel bad that she nearly got me killed. Although, in a way, she kind of saved my ass." She shook her head and stuffed the linari back in the bag. "This is more than I make in two years scrounging."

Jessa wanted to say she'd nearly died for that money, but it didn't need to be said. "That means you don't have to fight again, right?"

Kylin rubbed at her face. "Yeah. No fights."

Something in the way she said it made Jessa wonder if she'd miss it, but now wasn't the time to ask. She thought of Kylin's father's words, about loving all of someone, even the parts you weren't sure about. And there was no question she did love her. That didn't mean she wasn't glad she wouldn't be fighting again while Jessa remained on the planet.

"Are you ready to go back to your house?" she asked.

Kylin took their mugs to the sink. "I think so. It won't be easy, but it's probably time." She looked over her shoulder at Jessa. "Will you come?"

Jessa got up and wrapped her arms around her from behind. "If you'll have me there, yes. I'm sorry I didn't stay at the fight. I was a coward, and I never should have left."

Kylin turned around in her embrace and wrapped her arms around her. "I don't think asking the woman you love to watch you get your ass handed to you in the ring is a fair expectation." She rested her head against Jessa's. "I thought you'd be better off if you thought I'd died there. So you wouldn't have to deal with my crazy life. With…us."

Jessa closed her eyes against the onslaught of images of Kylin in the ring. "Part of me died when I heard that you didn't make it out. I've never felt such crushing despair. I knew what all these emotion words meant, but I'd never experienced them before you."

Kylin smiled and kissed her softly. "I think that's the nicest thing anyone has ever said to me."

Jessa shook her head. "I don't want to feel that particular emotion ever again. You're going to have to find a way to become immortal."

Kylin laughed, a sound that Jessa had sorely missed.

"Let's get our things and go home."

Jessa followed her upstairs and pondered that word. Home. Something she'd never had in a truly meaningful way. That it was here on Indemnion, with a woman who fought like a demon and cared deeply for everyone around her, was both surprising and gratifying. The future would come at them with whatever it would. For now, she could simply be in the moment.

❖

Kylin steadied herself on the doorframe when she stepped inside. The house smelled of her father's scent, his old smokes, his flagweed. The walls echoed with the laughter and tears they'd shed throughout the years. And the laughter they'd never share again. Jessa's arms went around her, holding her up.

"We can go back to Blue's if it's too much."

Kylin pushed herself into the room. "No. He wouldn't want me to be the star of my own pity party."

Asol walked in after them, lugging food from the marketplace. She popped the bags on the kitchen counter. "I'll make dinner while you two…do other stuff."

Kylin made her way slowly through their little house. She touched her dad's bedroom door but left it closed. That she definitely wasn't ready for yet. They went into Kylin's room and she looked around. "It feels like someone else's house."

Jessa sat beside her on the bed. "I can't imagine how strange it must feel. Is there anything I can do?"

So often lately there simply hadn't been words. She was drained, exhausted from walking through days knowing she had no one left, that she was truly alone in the world now. Even surrounded by people who told her to reach out if she needed anything, the sense of isolation was suffocating. And yet, Jessa had been there the whole time. She'd held her hand, steadied her, and let her cry. She'd never pushed or demanded attention Kylin didn't have the wherewithal to give. Now that everything was over and she was supposed to get on with her own life, she had no idea where to start. Doing what she'd done every day—eating, scrounging, eating, going to bed—sounded so lacking, so dull. Her dad had made her promise to do something bigger, but right now, just breathing felt like an accomplishment.

"Kylin?"

"Sorry." She took Jessa's hand in hers. "You've been amazing. Thank you for standing with me through all this." She could still see Jessa's expression in the crowd during the fight. "We haven't had a chance to talk about that night."

"I don't know if we need to."

Jessa's tone was cautious, hedging. Which suggested they definitely needed to talk about it.

"What makes you say that?"

Jessa shifted to face her but kept looking at their clasped hands. "Something Blue told me. That we should enjoy each other in the light, and leave the shadows where they belong."

Kylin could imagine Blue saying that, but she also remembered her dad's final words, that she needed to be with someone who could accept all of who she was. But then, this was temporary, wasn't it? At some point, she'd lose Jessa too. Why bother with deep conversations about struggle and violence? Maybe Blue was right, especially now that Kylin didn't have to scrounge or fight for a while. They could travel, she could teach Asol some of the building stuff she wanted to know, and they could pretend like life was a fluffy adventure.

She slid her hand from Jessa's. "I'm not someone to pretend, Jess. People are complicated; they're not plants in pots. I'm a good person, and I've done some things that are probably tough for you to understand. Yeah, I got myself into a bad situation, but Orlin put me in the ring because I'd already been fighting in one. I did it for fun, and for money, and to test myself against other people." She swallowed hard against a fresh flood of tears. "I'm not ashamed of who I am and who I've been. I don't know who I'm going to be."

Jessa had that look in her eyes that Kylin knew meant she was truly pondering what she'd said. One thing about Jessa was that Kylin never had any doubt she was listening.

"I love you."

Kylin's breath caught at the simple, clear words.

"I love you, and walking away from the fight that night was a huge mistake. I don't know what the future holds, and there's not much point in worrying about something you can't do anything about. All I can do is tell you that I love you, and that although I may not understand your desire to be in the ring, I'll never judge you for it. I've had a lot of time to think over the last week, and I realize how narrow my view of existence is. I don't always know how to react or respond, but I'm learning. I love you. All of you."

Kylin's legs shook as she sat on the bed, pulling Jessa to her. She buried her face in Jessa's hair and held her as close as she could. "I love you too. Whatever the future brings, or how little time we might have together, I love you. I think I fell for you the moment you climbed off that cliff to save your crew."

They stayed that way for a long time, and the moment was bittersweet. She'd found someone to love, who loved her back. But she had no doubt that Jessa would leave Indemnion at some point. She'd go back to being a ship's captain, and Kylin would stay behind, wandering through her days trying to forget the woman with the green eyes, gentle smile, and passion that could put a goddess of love to shame.

Asol knocked on the door. "Food's ready."

They pulled apart, and Jessa wiped away the tears on Kylin's cheeks. "That's what I meant about not living in the shadows. We live for now, for the people we are today. The future will take care of itself. For now, you can enjoy being in the light with nothing hanging over you."

Kylin followed her out of the room. It was a nice sentiment, but knowing Jessa would one day leave wasn't something she could simply forget. It would be worth it, but that didn't mean it wouldn't hurt.

CHAPTER TWENTY-SIX

The weeks went by and they settled into a relaxed rhythm. Jessa spent time wandering the maze with her crew and learning about the many people from different planets. She'd go home and tell Kylin and Asol all she'd found out, as excited to be learning as she'd been when she was training to be captain.

Kylin started teaching Asol what she knew about engineering and mechanics, and together they started building a new flyer. News about the slaver raids outside the walls of the cities came in every day, and the people of Quasi, in an unusual public consensus, made it clear the slave trade wasn't welcome there. As much as Kylin wanted to get back to Thalla to retrieve her flyer and all the parts of Jessa's ship she'd scrounged, she wasn't willing to take the risk of going beyond the walls.

Jessa wished they could go back and see Sherta and Liselle. In another world, she thought they could have been close friends. And she couldn't imagine never seeing the Volare again. She enjoyed her trips out with her crew mates, who were also becoming friends, something Jessa had never had and a fact that sometimes made her almost giddy, another emotion she'd never experienced before. Kylin was slowly returning to herself, and her smile came more often. She and Asol teased one another like siblings, often resorting to wrestling with one another in the living room.

Kylin had taken to running the walls between Quasi and Fesi every morning, usually stopping to watch the nomads and slavers beyond the walls before she headed back. Sometimes Asol went with her, and they both always returned subdued.

Jessa was trying to cook a new dish while they were out running one morning, and what she'd made was smelling worse than it looked, which was an accomplishment since it looked pretty foul. With a sigh, she dumped it in the bin and started opening windows to air out the house. A shadow passed in front of the window just before a knock sounded on the door. People here often announced themselves when they arrived, so a silent visitor made Jessa nervous.

She opened the door a crack to see who it was, and when she did her stomach rolled. She opened the door all the way.

"Captain Arabelle?" The fleet soldier reached out and lifted her arm to run the life-scanner over her reading. "Your presence is requested by Fleet Commander Arabelle, and the administrator of Indemnion requests that Kylin Enderson accompany you."

Jessa stared at him, the words lacking any meaning. When Kylin and Asol appeared behind him, she managed to focus. "The fleet commander is here? On Indemnion?"

He nodded and his eyes flicked toward Kylin, who was standing within striking distance, her arms crossed over her sweaty chest, her body turned slightly. Jessa recognized the combat stance, and it made her heart race. There was something incredibly sexy about Kylin in protective mode.

"Thank you, Officer. If you'll tell me where to go, we'll get ready and then meet you there."

He looked surprised that she wasn't going to come right away. "I was told to return with you, Captain."

Jessa raised her eyebrow. "And I'm telling you I'll be along shortly, Officer."

He nodded and looked at Kylin. "We've landed at the open space just beyond the South wall. The fleet commander is waiting at a place called the Quasi Arms." His expression suggested exactly what he thought of the place.

Kylin moved to the side to let him pass. "We'll be there within the quarter sun."

He saluted Jessa and set off down the stairs.

Kylin and Asol came in, and Jessa closed the door behind them. She leaned against it, the surprise of the officer's visit turning into a strange sense of panic.

"Did I hear right? Your mom is here?" Asol asked, her eyes wide.

"She is." She leaned into Kylin's embrace, grateful for the closeness even though she was sweaty. "And the administrator wants to talk to you."

Kylin took a deep breath. "I guess we'd better get ready then."

Asol stood by the door, biting her lip. Jessa knew this would be just as worrying for her. "Why don't you come with us? That way we won't have to try to remember all the details to tell you later."

She darted past them. "I'll shower first!""

"Well, that took some convincing." Kylin's grin was strained. "I think I'll wear my clothes from Thalla. Seems like the best idea."

Jessa wondered if she should wear her uniform, but somehow that didn't feel right. She too put on her Thalla clothing, and once they were all ready they headed to the South gate. Jessa couldn't imagine why her mother had felt the need to come herself. There were plenty of envoys she could have sent in her place. She took Kylin's hand and drew strength from it.

When they arrived at the Quasi Arms, several soldiers saluted her as she entered the community space. The smell of roughweed beer and fried crispin made her wince, and it took a moment for her eyes to adjust to the dim lighting.

Her mother was studying a picture on the wall, her hands clasped behind her back, her posture ramrod straight, her hair pulled into a bun so tight it looked painful. In that moment, Jessa saw herself, and the woman she'd been when she'd crash-landed here. Dressed in the loose, soft clothing of Thalla, with her hair down, and holding tightly to Kylin's hand, that world felt incredibly far away.

"Fleet Commander." Jessa spoke softly, the gravity of the moment overwhelming.

Her mother turned around and her gaze swept over Jessa. When she met Jessa's eyes, Jessa was stunned at the tears in them. She came forward and clasped Jessa in a tight, brief hug. But in her touch Jessa felt her mother trembling.

She pulled back. "Daughter. You look well. Your family has been extremely concerned with your well-being since the news of your ship's destruction." Her hand fluttered as she reached out and almost touched her, then she put her hands behind her once again. "We were glad to get the message from Indemnion's administrator regarding your distress signal. Only part of it got out, and we weren't certain where to begin our search. Once we received his message we were able to pinpoint your life-scan, and we moved with haste to begin your retrieval."

Jessa looked at the administrator, who tilted his head and gave her a knowing smile.

"Mother. As you can imagine, losing the ship was difficult, and I've felt great responsibility for the loss." Slipping back into the language she'd been raised with was both easy and foreign. "I'm sorry it caused any emotional hardship on the family."

Kylin whistled, drawing both their attention. "Wow. Forgive me, but I have to interrupt. I can't handle all the crazy emotions whirling around in here." She held out her arm. "Kylin Enderson, Fleet Commander. Nice to meet you."

Jessa's mother looked bemused and accepted Kylin's arm. "I understand you're responsible for the initial retrieval and safekeeping of our captain and her crew."

Kylin looked like she wanted to laugh. "I pulled her into a tree after she drew the scavengers away from her crew. And then she duped me into taking her with me to see if there were other survivors." She grinned at Jessa. "I didn't really have to do any safekeeping. Your daughter is tough as prowler hide."

There was no mistaking the pride in her mother's expression, something Jessa had never seen before.

"Shall we sit? Or would you prefer to go back to the ship?"

Jessa gave Kylin a questioning look. She'd be fine talking here, but she wondered if Kylin wanted to see the inside of the ship. Kylin winked at her and motioned to the table where the administrator sat. "Why don't we stay here for a bit?" She turned and pulled Asol forward. "This is Asol. She got us out of a particularly difficult situation and has been with us since. We wanted her to join us, if you don't mind?"

Jessa's mother frowned, clearly unsure what to say. Asol's presence was based on emotion, on their connection to her, and not on something concrete. It would be lost on her, and Jessa was incredibly grateful she'd learned that being connected to people was about more than their usefulness.

Kylin didn't wait for an answer. She gave Asol a little push toward the table, and then took the seat next to her. Jessa sat beside her mother, and once again noticed that she reached out to touch her but pulled back.

"Nice to see you again," the administrator said with a smile.

"You kept your word." Kylin motioned for drinks and got him another.

"I try." He took a sip of his drink and nodded at Jessa's mother. "The fleet commander had been searching for the captain, but her life-scan didn't show up on their readings. Indemnion is too far outside the connective comm system for a personal scan to show up without a definite location." He grinned at Jessa. "There were some very happy people when I reported you were here."

Jessa's mother cleared her throat. "Yes, well. Continuing on." She took a sip of beer and winced. "The Indemnion administrator has informed us that there's an extreme situation involving the trafficking of people, and he has requested intergalactic assistance with the issue. Have you found the problem to be as reported, Captain?"

Jessa nodded. "I have, Commander. The situation has devolved greatly just in my short time here, and free people are now afraid to leave the walled cities. Anyone outside them is in grave danger."

"As you cited the intergalactic policy 369A, we have been required to begin the deployment of security officers to Indemnion. However, as you know, there's a requirement that there be intermediaries in place for such an operation." She looked at Kylin, her expression appraising. "Though the administrator is in place, he assures me that you would be better qualified to act in that position, Kylin Enderson. Do you feel that to be the case?"

Kylin's lips twitched, and Jessa knew she was trying hard not to laugh. Had she sounded so stilted and formal when she'd landed here? She knew the answer.

"I believe I could act in that capacity, yes. I don't have any training, but I understand the politics and problems here, and I'd be acting for the people with no agenda of my own. I think the administrator and I would make a good team." She nudged Asol. "And I think it would be good to train the youth here in new tech, because that will be one of the ways we move forward."

Asol's eyes were wide and she looked from person to person. "Yeah. What she said."

Jessa's mother took a deep breath as if to avoid saying something sharp before she turned back to Jessa. "Then that's settled. We'll accept Kylin Enderson as the ambassador for change on Indemnion. What is your intention, Captain? Will you be returning to take a new position on a new ship? Or will you be returning ho—to your planet of origin?"

Home. There was that word. She studied her mother and saw beyond the distant facade. She'd been worried. She'd come to Indemnion when she could have sent any number of other people, because she'd needed to see Jessa for herself. It was a revelation, and it made her want to grab her mother and embrace her. Instead, she reached out and touched her mother's hand, which made her mother smile slightly.

"I admit I've been living in the moment, and I haven't given much thought to what would happen if I could leave. I'd like a little time to think about it, if I may?"

A flash of disappointment was quickly followed by an implacable nod. "You may. We'll need to spend a few days understanding the full scope of issues involving this planet, and Kylin Enderson will need to begin working with the security forces as soon as they arrive. You may take the time you need to decide on your next position." She swallowed and looked at the table. "And perhaps we may find some time to have a discussion of a personal nature."

"I'd like that." Jessa had never had that kind of discussion with her mother, and she found that she very much wanted to. She wanted to tell her about Kylin, and the Volare, and her friends Sherta and Liselle, and how she'd learned to ask questions and let people in.

Kylin pushed back her chair and stood. "Unless you need us now, it might be a good time to take a break. Maybe we can meet for dinner?"

The administrator stood and held out his arm. "Good idea. I've got some calls to make. But let's meet on the ship. I've always wanted to see what the inside of one of those beasts looks like."

Jessa took Kylin's hand and noticed the way her mother looked at their hands, as though trying to work out a puzzle. "Thank you for coming for me. We'll see you soon, and I'll bring my remaining crew with us when we come tonight."

Her mother gave her a quick nod but didn't say anything else.

They made their way back to Kylin's house, and Asol, who hadn't said more than a few words while they were there, couldn't stop talking. She thanked Kylin repeatedly for including her in the new plans, and though Kylin laughed and smiled, Jessa could tell her thoughts were a million miles away, as were Jessa's.

She thought they'd have months together, but the time had come when decisions had to be made. And what she'd told her mother was true. She'd always thought she'd go back to being a ship's captain, but was that what she wanted now? Where did that leave her and Kylin?

When they reached the house, Asol went inside, still chattering away, but Kylin stopped Jessa at the door.

"You're thinking so loudly you might as well be saying it out loud." She kissed Jessa's hand. "Let's work it out."

Jessa's heart broke with relief at the simple statement. It was that simple. They just had to work it out.

When Kylin had seen the fleet officer at their door, her heart had nearly shattered before she made it up the stairs. She knew it meant Jess would be leaving her, far sooner than she was prepared for. But when she'd looked into Jessa's eyes, she'd seen what she needed to.

Jess wasn't about to just up and leave. It wasn't like last time. Jessa looked as stunned as Kylin felt, and that made it bearable. When Jessa had taken her hand and hardly let go throughout the meeting, she'd known they'd work it out. Somehow.

"Let's talk out our options." Kylin poured them all a cup of tea, and they sat around the table.

"You're going to be the ambassador for Indemnion. That's decided. Right?" Jessa smiled. "Congratulations."

Kylin shrugged. "It sounds like a hell of a job, if it means helping security decide how to deal with what's going on. But I think it's worth it."

"It's more than just helping the security forces here, though." Jessa motioned toward the window. "It's acting as the go-between for Indemnion and the Intergalactic Alliance. You'll be able to tell them about the beauty of the lands here. You can help shape Indemnion's image on a massive scale."

"Tourism." Asol spoke around a mouthful of fruit. "People should see what we've got."

Kylin nodded slowly. "I like that idea. But we'll take it slow, and there's a lot of work to do before that's an option." She took Jessa's hand. "What about you, love? What is it you want?"

Jessa stroked the top of Kylin's hand as she thought out loud. "I love what I do. What I was trained to do. And now that I know what I've been missing by being, well, my mother," she grinned when Kylin and Asol laughed, "I think I'd be an even better captain than I've ever been before." She didn't miss the way Kylin's eyes tightened slightly. "But that means leaving you, and that's not an option. So how do I keep doing what I do and keep us together?"

There was silence as they considered the question. The fact that Jessa didn't want to leave her made her heart soar, and if there was a way, she'd find it.

"I'm going to have to leave the planet to talk to people, right? People in high places." Kylin tapped on the table as she thought. "And I probably have to do that sooner than later. So I can leave with you, and we can go do that together."

Jessa nodded, her gaze glued to Kylin. "Go on."

"There's no question I need to be here, helping get things underway and watching out for people. But while I'm doing that, maybe you can help elsewhere."

Jessa frowned. "You want me to go?"

Asol stood up and backed toward the door. "I think I'll go to my room. Or go find an underground crime ring. Whatever. You probably need to have this conversation without me."

Kylin laughed and threw a wad of paper at her. "Coward. Why don't you go tell Jessa's crew what's happened and bring them to the ship at dinner time?"

Asol nodded happily. "Perfect way out. Thanks." She slipped out of the house, closing the door softly behind her.

Kylin turned back to Jessa, shaking her head. "Back to what I was saying. No, I don't want you to leave. Obviously, I want you by my side. But things are likely to get unstable before they get better, and you know how I feel about keeping you safe."

Jessa folded her arms and glared at her. "You know how much I love you making decisions for me."

"Oh, sweet lady, I wouldn't dream of it. Just hear me out." She poured them more tea and sat down, thinking. "You've got connections. You can tell people about Indemnion. About what we can offer, and Asol's right, the tourist thing would be great. It would bring in money and help the people here prosper. And…" The idea flashed up and she grabbed it. "You could be the person who runs the tourist ship that brings people here. You'd still be captaining your own ship, but this time you'd have intimate knowledge of the place you were taking people to. You'd still be flying, but this would be your home base, so we could still be together. And when things have settled down here, I could fly with you occasionally." She waited, carried away by the perfect idea.

Jessa stayed quiet, thinking, and Kylin let her process. Finally, she nodded.

"I think it would work. And because it would be part of a regeneration project, we'd get the funding to do it well, and maybe even put environmental protections in place from the start."

Kylin slid from her chair and knelt in front of Jessa. "It will be hard for a while, but you know I'm in love with you, and I want this to work. But being with someone shouldn't take away their dreams, it should just mean you help them achieve those dreams in a different way." She held Jessa's hands between her own and kissed her fingertips. "Your dream was to fly, and I won't take that away from you. And if I know you're coming back, I'll always be able to wait."

"Your dad wanted you to leave Indemnion," Jessa said gently.

"He did." Kylin blinked back the sudden tears. "But he also said to make a difference, to help people. And if I can help the people here, and then get away to fly with you sometimes, I think I'll have kept my promise to him."

Jessa leaned down to rest her head against Kylin's. "Thank you for loving me so much. Crashing onto this planet was the best thing that could have happened to me. You're my home, and if you're here, then that's where I'll always be."

Kylin kissed her, slowly, deeply. "You changed the course of my life, and together we can make the stars jealous." She stood and led Jessa to the bedroom, where they took their time making love, and Kylin caressed every inch of Jessa's beautiful skin. She wanted to remember this moment, the one that would give them a future together, the moment they decided to try for forever. Life was about to change in every way, and she was ready.

EPILOGUE

Eighteen months later

Jessa stepped off the luxury passenger ship and smiled at the few stragglers still pulling their bags behind them. She scanned the landing dock, which had been moved to the grasslands on the other side of Quasi, much to the dismay of the people who were used to having the privilege in the Heathers. Kylin leaned against a post, her arms crossed over her black uniform with deep blue trim. She was looking at Jessa with that grin she loved, the one that promised she wouldn't be sleeping at all tonight. She ran down the dock and threw herself into Kylin's arms.

"Mmm." Kylin nuzzled her hair. "There's my sweet-smelling mate."

Jessa pulled back and smiled at her. "I never get tired of hearing that."

"And I never get tired of saying it. Good trip?" Kylin put her arm around her waist and led her toward a small flyer.

"Really good. Great passengers who are excited to see the cryo volcano and visit the Falls." She got into the flyer and belted in. "How are things here? And why are we getting into a flyer?"

Kylin smiled and got the flyer off the ground. "I have a surprise for you."

No matter what questions Jessa asked, Kylin wouldn't tell her where they were going. But once she saw the red sand below them, she laughed. "Thalla?"

Kylin set the flyer down just outside the walls, where several other flyers were parked under protective shields to keep the storms from damaging them. "It's been way too long."

They made their way into the city easily. The giant gates were no longer shut, as the threat from the outside was no longer an issue. When the door opened, Sherta pulled them both in for a hug.

"It's about time." Liselle came to the door as well and gave Kylin a solid punch to the shoulder before giving Jessa a hug.

Asol peeked around the corner, and Jessa laughed when she jumped forward and swung Jessa around in the air. She looked older, wiser. But she still had the infectious laugh and enthusiasm she'd had when they'd met her on the docks. That felt like ages ago.

They settled down for dinner around the table and talked about life.

"Did you know Kylin gave me the flyer she built?" Asol still talked with her mouth full. "I made modifications, thanks to all the new tech flooding in. But she'll always be the best girl in the air because she was built by Kylin."

Kylin nodded her approval. "And Asol has been teaching as many people who want to learn about the tech brought in by the IA. We're not behind the rest of the universe anymore."

"And the slavers?" Jessa asked. She was glad to have this time with their friends, but she couldn't wait to get Kylin alone.

"Eradicated, for the most part. All slaves have been freed and helped to start new lives, either here or on a planet of their choosing. Most of the slavers have been taken off planet to a Claxon colony, where they'll serve out their lives making things of use to other planets. The nomads are free to roam, and the general fear of them seems to have dissipated massively."

It was like a different planet. Jessa and Kylin had gone with her mother to Intergalactic Fleet headquarters, where they'd given a full report, and Kylin had been able to detail what she saw as the primary issues facing the planet. They'd been taken seriously, and plans had been put in place almost at once.

The best part about it had been Kylin's reaction to the ship. She'd caressed it like a lover, taking in the curves, the controls, the facts, and options. She'd been truly amazed, and Jessa was so glad she'd been able to share it with her. When they'd left the docking station in the Heathers and moved into space, Kylin had kept her face and hands pressed to the window, watching as Indemnion fell away. As they'd traveled, Jessa had pointed out various areas they were passing. The name of that nebula or star, this moon or that nearby planet. Kylin had been in her element. But when they returned to Indemnion to meet with the security forces, she'd been in her element there, too.

Jessa loved that she simply adapted to the moment, to being the person she needed to be. It was sexier than anything on any other planet, and she was so incredibly proud of Kylin for taking her place, for being the person she wanted to be.

"And the Volare?" Jessa asked. "I mention them on the ship."

"They're doing great. They're taking it slow and only letting a certain number of people on their island per year, but some of them have gone out into the world. There's still a lot of mystique around them, but they're doing well. They're going to survive." Kylin's face lit up, and it was clear how much that meant to her.

"And how is it going with your family?" Sherta asked. "I understand you had some changes there?"

Jessa laughed. "That's an understatement. When I disappeared, my father wrote me off, as is expected on our world. But my mother and siblings refused to give up hope, and were all caught off guard at how much they cared about my welfare. After I told my mother about my time here, and all I'd learned, she decided it would be good for her and my siblings to learn some of what I did. They traveled to various planets in order to learn more about the inhabitants and cultures from a closer perspective." She smiled and shook her head. "We're closer than any family on Othrys, and I think others are starting to develop emotional ties as well."

Liselle smacked Asol's hand with a spoon when she went to dip her fingers into the stew to pluck a piece of meat out. Asol shook her hand and stuck her tongue out.

"Thanks to the tourism trade, the clothing we make in Thalla is really helping the city move forward. We're even taking in apprentices to learn the trade, but we ask that they stay here to work. Trade secrets and all that." Liselle grinned and sat back with her hands over her stomach. "Who knew that saving your asses would make our lives so much better?"

Kylin sipped her drink and winked. "I could have told you that anything to do with me would have made your life better."

They all laughed, and the chatter continued long into the night. Asol stayed behind, since she was working with some young people on new methods to help speed up the dye production in Thalla the next day.

Jessa and Kylin took the flyer back to Fesi. Kylin had moved into the old administrator's house. She had to take so many meetings and work with so many people it simply hadn't been possible to stay in her place in Quasi. Asol lived there on her own now, though she didn't spend a lot of time there, thanks to all the traveling she was doing.

Kylin held Jessa's hand as they made their way to their bedroom. She pulled Jessa close and kissed her, long and deeply, until Jessa was out of breath. "I've missed you."

Jessa shivered as Kylin slowly unzipped Jessa's uniform, kissing the exposed skin all the way down. "I've missed you too."

They fell into bed, and as she gave herself to the beauty of what they had, she knew there was no other place she'd ever call home.

About the Author

Brey Willows is a longtime editor and writer. When she's not running a social enterprise working with marginalized communities on writing projects, she's editing other people's writing or doing her own. She lives in the middle of England with her partner and fellow author and spends entirely too much time exploring castles and ancient ruins while bemoaning the rain.

Books Available from Bold Strokes Books

A Moment in Time by Lisa Moreau. A longstanding family feud separates two women who unexpectedly fall in love at an antique clock shop in a small Louisiana town. (978-1-63555-419-9)

Aspen in Moonlight by Kelly Wacker. When art historian Melissa Warren meets Sula Johansen, director of a local bear conservancy, she discovers that love can come in unexpected and unusual forms. (978-1-63555-470-0)

Back to September by Melissa Brayden. Small bookshop owner Hannah Shepard and famous romance novelist Parker Bristow maneuver the landscape of their two very different worlds to find out if love can win out in the end. (978-1-63555-576-9)

Changing Course by Brey Willows. When the woman of your dreams falls from the sky, you'd better be ready to catch her. (978-1-63555-335-2)

Cost of Honor by Radclyffe. First Daughter Blair Powell and Homeland Security Director Cameron Roberts face adversity when their enemies stop at nothing to prevent President Andrew Powell's reelection. (978-1-63555-582-0)

Fearless by Tina Michele. Determined to overcome her debilitating fear through exposure therapy, Laura Carter all but fails before she's even begun until dolphin trainer Jillian Marshall dedicates herself to helping Laura defeat the nightmares of her past. (978-1-63555-495-3)

Not Dead Enough by J.M. Redmann. A woman who may or may not be dead drags Micky Knight into a messy con game. (978-1-63555-543-1)

Not Since You by Fiona Riley. When Charlotte boards her honeymoon cruise single and comes face-to-face with Lexi, the high school love she left behind, she questions every decision she has ever made. (978-1-63555-474-8)

Not Your Average Love Spell by Barbara Ann Wright. Four women struggle with who to love and who to hate while fighting to rid a kingdom of an evil invading force. (978-1-63555-327-7)

Tennessee Whiskey by Donna K. Ford. Dane Foster wants to put her life on pause and ask for a redo, a chance for something that matters. Emma Reynolds is that chance. (978-1-63555-556-1)

30 Dates in 30 Days by Elle Spencer. A busy lawyer tries to find love the fast way—thirty dates in thirty days. (978-1-63555-498-4)

Finding Sky by Cass Sellars. Skylar Addison's search for a career intersects with her new boss's search for butterflies, but Skylar can't forgive Jess's intrusion into her life. (978-1-63555-521-9)

Hammers, Strings, and Beautiful Things by Morgan Lee Miller. While on tour with the biggest pop star in the world, rising musician Blair Bennett falls in love for the first time while coping with loss and depression. (978-1-63555-538-7)

Heart of a Killer by Yolanda Wallace. Contract killer Santana Masters's only interest is her next assignment—until a chance meeting with a beautiful stranger tempts her to change her ways. (978-1-63555-547-9)

Leading the Witness by Carsen Taite. When defense attorney Catherine Landauer reluctantly becomes the key witness in prosecutor Starr Rio's latest criminal trial, their hearts, careers, and lives may be at risk. (978-1-63555-512-7)

No Experience Required by Kimberly Cooper Griffin. Izzy Treadway has resigned herself to a life without romance because of her bipolar illness but wonders what she's gotten herself into when she agrees to write a book about love. (978-1-63555-561-5)

One Walk in Winter by Georgia Beers. Olivia Santini and Hayley Boyd Markham might be rivals at work, but they discover that lonely hearts often find company in the most unexpected of places. (978-1-63555-541-7)

The Inn at Netherfield Green by Aurora Rey. Advertising executive Lauren Montgomery and gin distiller Camden Crawley don't agree on anything except saving the Rose & Crown, the old English pub that's brought them together. (978-1-63555-445-8)

Top of Her Game by M. Ullrich. When it comes to life on the field and matters of the heart, losing isn't an option for pro athletes Kenzie Shaw and Sutton Flores. (978-1-63555-500-4)

Vanished by Eden Darry. A storm is coming, and Ellery and Loveday must find the chosen one or humanity won't survive it. (978-1-63555-437-3)

All She Wants by Larkin Rose. Marci Jones and Tessa Dalton get more than they bargained for when their plans for a one-night stand turn into an opportunity for love. (978-1-63555-476-2)

Beautiful Accidents by Erin Zak. Stevie Adams and Bernadette Thompson discover that sometimes the best things in life happen purely by accident. (978-1-63555-497-7)

Before Now by Joy Argento. Can Delany and Jade overcome the betrayal that spans the centuries to reignite a love that can't be broken? (978-1-63555-525-7)

Breathe by Cari Hunter. Paramedic Jemima Pardon's chronic bad luck seems to be improving when she meets police officer Rosie Jones. But they face a battle to survive before they can find love. (978-1-63555-523-3)

Double-Crossed by Ali Vali. Hired thief and killer Reed Gable finds something in her scope that will change her life forever when she gets a contract to end casino accountant Brinley Myers's life. (978-1-63555-302-4)

False Horizons by CJ Birch. Jordan and Ash struggle with different views on the alien agenda and must find their way back to each other before they're swallowed up by a centuries-old war. (978-1-63555-519-6)

Legacy by Charlotte Greene. When five women hike to a remote cabin deep inside a national park, unsettling events suggest that they should have stayed home. (978-1-63555-490-8)

Royal Street Reveillon by Greg Herren. Someone is killing the stars of a reality show, and it's up to Scotty Bradley and the boys to find out who. (978-1-63555-545-5)

Somewhere Along the Way by Kathleen Knowles. When Maxine Cooper moves to San Francisco during the summer of 1981, she learns that wherever you run, you cannot escape yourself. (978-1-63555-383-3)

Blood of the Pack by Jenny Frame. When Alpha of the Scottish pack Kenrick Wulver visits the Wolfgangs, she falls for Zaria Lupa, a wolf on the run. (978-1-63555-431-1)

Cause of Death by Sheri Lewis Wohl. Medical student Vi Akiak and K9 Search and Rescue officer Kate Renard must work together to find a killer before they end up the next targets. In the race for survival, they discover that love may be the biggest risk of all. (978-1-63555-441-0)

Chasing Sunset by Missouri Vaun. Hijinks and mishaps ensue as Iris and Finn set off on a road trip adventure, chasing the sunset, and falling in love along the way. (978-1-63555-454-0)

Double Down by MB Austin. When an unlikely friendship with Spanish pop star Erlea turns deeper, Celeste, in-house physician for the hotel hosting Erlea's show, has a choice to make—run or double down on love. (978-1-63555-423-6)

Party of Three by Sandy Lowe. Three friends are in for a wild night at billionaire heiress Eleanor McGregor's twenty-fifth birthday party. Love, lust, and doing the right thing, even when it hurts, turn the evening into one that will change their lives forever. (978-1-63555-246-1)

Sit. Stay. Love. by Karis Walsh. City girl Alana Brendt and country vet Tegan Evans both know they don't belong together. Only problem is, they're falling in love. (978-1-63555-439-7)

Where the Lies Hide by Renee Roman. As P.I. Camdyn Stark gets closer to solving the case, will her dark secrets and the lies she's buried jeopardize her future with the quietly beautiful Sarah Peters? (978-1-63555-371-0)

Beautiful Dreamer by Melissa Brayden. With love on the line, can Devyn Winters find it in her heart to stay in the small town of Dreamer's Bay, the one place she swore she'd never remain? (978-1-63555-305-5)

Create a Life to Love by Erin Zak. When sixteen-year-old Beth shows up at her birth mother's door, three lives will change forever. (978-1-63555-425-0)

Deadeye by Meredith Doench. Stranded while hunting the serial predator Deadeye, Special Agent Luce Hansen fights for survival while her lover, forensic pathologist Harper Bennett, hunts for clues to Hansen's disappearance along the killer's trail. (978-1-63555-253-9)

Death Takes a Bow by David S. Pederson. Alan Keys takes part in a local stage production, but when the leading man is murdered, his partner Detective Heath Barrington is thrust into the limelight to find the killer. (978-1-63555-472-4)

Endangered by Michelle Larkin. Shapeshifters Officer Aspen Wolfe and Dr. Tora Madigan fight their growing attraction as they work together to destroy a secret government agency that exterminates their kind. (978-1-63555-377-2)

Incognito by VK Powell. The only thing Evan Spears is focused on is capturing a fleeing murder suspect until wild card Frankie Strong is added to her team and causes chaos on and off the job. (978-1-63555-389-5)

Insult to Injury by Gun Brooke. After losing everything, Gail Owen withdraws to her old farmhouse and finds a destitute young woman, Romi Shepherd, living in a secret room. (978-1-63555-323-9)

Just One Moment by Dena Blake. If you were given the chance to have the love of your life back, could you ignore everything that went wrong and start over again? (978-1-63555-387-1)

Scene of the Crime by MJ Williamz. Cullen Matthews finds herself caught between the woman she thinks she loves but can no longer trust and a beautiful detective she can't stop thinking about who will stop at nothing to find the truth. (978-1-63555-405-2)